Violet

Violet

A Gritty Story of Endurance and Love

Tina Bruce

ISBN 978-1-952194-20-7

Design by River Sanctuary Graphic Arts

Cover image wtercolor painting by Karen Haughey
proart99@aol.com

Printed in the United States of America

Additional copies available from:

www.riversanctuarypublishing.com
amazon.com

River Sanctuary Publishing
P.O Box 1561
Felton, CA 95018
www.riversanctuarypublishing.com
Dedicated to the awakening of the New Earth

CHAPTER ONE

1992

It was more than that Violet wasn't there for him. In the beginning she never left him. Not one moment since he fell out of her. He stunk. He cried with big wailing screams. She couldn't look at him. He laid next to her in the filthy bed where she had given birth to him hours before. The bed was beginning to reek with a stench that filled her nostrils each time she drew a breath.

He was suddenly quiet. She looked down. She had hated him since she had first learned he was there. Since before she knew he was a he. She hated everything about him. Now that she could see him, smell him, hear him she hated him more than she had ever hated anything. And she had hated a lot. She hated her mom. Her dad. She hated her brothers. Now this stinking thing was making noise again. It was burrowing towards her warmth, toward her fat belly to her huge, aching tits.

Maybe *this* was why she was hating him so much, she thought, *because every time he screams my tits rage with pain*! Her breasts had gotten hard and dark red. Her nipples started dripping hot, clear fluid. *Gross!* she thought, *I can't even make milk!* She didn't know what to do.

He found her nipple then with his hot little mouth. It felt good at first, the heat and the wetness. But it hurt so fucking bad when he finally latched on to suck on her sore, swollen nipple that she screamed. She tried to get up. She felt dull pain in her belly. He was still latched on, so she sank back onto the bed. She tried to let him suckle. She lasted about 30 seconds. When he unlatched for a breath she covered her nipple. She stood up slowly. She took from him his life-sustaining nourishment. She never truly came back.

She called 911. She had tried to take care of him, tried to shush him, feed him. She told herself she didn't want anyone else to do it. He was hers. She knew they would take him when they figured out she was a junkie. She had her first two babies in the hospital. They took the first one. Then they made sure she was not using drugs for the last one (she wasn't, she was on methadone then). They, being the county social services. She made the call to 911 anyway. The stench of giving birth was too much. She didn't have energy to clean up. The baby's father Cade was nowhere to be seen, he wasn't in their bed. He hadn't been around to hear her grunts or moans. Their son Chase was probably with him. She guessed their daughter Arianna was asleep. *Fuck it!* thought Violet *they can take her, too, maybe give me a break.*

Arianna didn't wake up before Violet and her new baby were loaded onto an ambulance. Violet never got to explain to her what was happening. By then, Violet's thoughts were dominated by a need to get high. She started to wail. She told the medics that she was in terrible pain. *Couldn't they give her something for the fucking pain?* She begged.

"Who is home with you, ma'am? Is anyone else home?" said a man's voice.

"My four year old. She's sleeping," sobbed Violet, "upstairs."

She sobbed into the oxygen mask they were fitting onto her face. *It wasn't supposed to go down like this!* She was going to quit dope and get onto methadone. She was going to get cleaned up before the baby came so she could keep it. She had been clean on methadone for a long time in the past. She had only started using heroin again when she found out she was pregnant. She could get methadone, legal dope everyone called it, from the county. But she had known throughout the pregnancy that if she got on methadone when she was pregnant she would have all kinds of restrictions put on her. Violet didn't like restrictions.

She had wanted to abort the thing but here it was. She couldn't think. Her hatred welled up inside her as her craving for junk ripped into her very being. She begged for pain relief as they rode toward the hospital.

"We'll be at the emergency room soon," is all the attendants would say.

Violet remembered getting to the emergency room. But she didn't remember when they finally gave her some dope. She woke up feeling no pain. She was glad to see she was alone. No baby. Her tits didn't ache anymore. She tried to sit up a little, she had to pee. She swung her legs over the side of the bed. She stood up slowly to make her way toward the bathroom door that was open across the room. She sat on the toilet with a thud and started to pee.

"Wait!" she heard, "I need a sample!"

She tried to stop peeing just as a hand holding a plastic urine sample cup thrust through the door. She managed to get some of her pee into the cup before totally losing her composure.

"Can I get my meds?" asked Violet without hesitation as she handed her urine to the nurse. She didn't even know what her meds were but she fully expected to be getting sick soon. She braced for the way her spine would stiffen just as her bowels would loosen.

"Your nurse will bring your medicines on schedule. Let's see," said the woman who Violet had thought was the nurse, "looks like it will be in about two hours. I'm Louisa, your nurses assistant. Do you have any other questions for me? Are you hungry? Do you want to see your baby?"

"Why?" asked Violet, "I can't take it home, can I?"

"It's a he, you will have to talk to the doctor about the details. I know you can see the baby if you want to," said Louisa gently, "What is his name?"

Violet was unable to answer. She didn't know his name. But they would make her name him before they would let her leave the hospital. She wrote his name down for them. She swore she would never speak it. She had signed acknowledgement that she had used dangerous illegal drugs while pregnant. Her baby was going into Child Protective Services/CPS custody after recovering from heroin dependency. Violet was glad to leave the baby to the county. She knew how hard it was to wean a baby off heroin because she had been on methadone when Arianna was born. She had to give her morphine liquid drops every three hours for weeks. So she signed an agreement with the county to get into the methadone clinic to work toward getting the baby back. She left the hospital alone after they gave her a bus pass to get home. Violet was tired and dirty when she got off the bus. She walked into the house.

Cade was out cold when she came home with news of his son. His second son. His third child. Not that he even acknowledged his second one. The second one was a girl. Violet was sure he would notice her when she had tits. He always noticed tits. But the girl didn't have tits yet. The kid was hungry and mad when Violet got home. The county must have found Cade to come home for Arianna. He didn't question her about not having the baby with her when she came in. He knew Violet was smoking dope again. He knew the county would keep it.

She sat down on the couch next to Cade. She lit the pipe that was on the table. She took a long pull, held it in, then let it out of her body as slowly as she could. *Fuck! That feels good …* she thought as she took another drag just before Cade woke up. He snatched the pipe from her. "Get your own, Vee," he said, "I've been waiting to hear from Sandi." *Damn.* The methadone she was on at the hospital was wearing off. The methadone clinic, where she had agreed with the county to go, didn't open until tomorrow morning.

Violet

"I need a hit, Cade! I'm going to be sick and I can't go to Sandi's! I'm bleeding, too, and my tits hurt!" wailed Violet, "let me have a drag! Just a little!" She reached for the pipe. She tried to scrape a chunk out of the pipe but it was too late, all she got was ashes under her fingernail. Cade got up and left. He didn't say when he would be back or where he was going. Violet knew he was going to wait at Sandi's house until he could get his shit. And she knew he wouldn't be bringing any back for her. She tried to get up but fell back onto the couch. She managed to open a pack of pop tarts for Arianna before falling into a disturbed sleep. She told herself she would get up and go to the clinic at five in the morning to be there when they opened at five-thirty. *Fucking Cade what a selfish jack-off* she thought as she drifted off.

This was the third baby they had made together, Violet and Cade. She had a boy and a girl and now this third one that she didn't want. Violet hated all of them. She hated the boys more but she usually felt nothing but hatred for her girl, too. Sometimes she would feel flashes of what felt like sadness when she looked at her girl. She thought *maybe that is love*. She had been on methadone when Arianna was born. After that, she then managed to stay away from heroin for almost four years before she started fooling herself again. Methadone could only replace heroin for so long for Violet. This time, she started smoking heroin again as soon as she found out she was pregnant for the third time. She lost all love for everyone in her life, especially herself. Since then when she looked at her girl she felt hatred. She would scream an order at her with a sneer on her face, "Arianna! Shut up! Get down! Go outside!" or "Shut the fuck up you stupid little cunt! You're too loud!"

Sometimes, when Violet had just had her medicine, her dose of methadone, her *doe-say-doe* as she like to think of it, she could be nice, at least in voice. "Ari, bring me a blanket honey" was more likely after she had her medicine. Violet hated her medicine. But she hated being sick even more than she hated her medicine. So she took her medicine so she wouldn't get sick. Violet couldn't remember a time when she wasn't trying to not be sick. Over time her face took on a pinched look. She had a constant grimace from a young age. In the moment, her stomach revolted yet again. She just couldn't win in life and nobody seemed to care. Especially Cade. She wished she'd never met the fucker.

CHAPTER TWO

1980

Cade Ramsey was in Florida. He was running out of options for staying high. He had started a relationship with the fifteen year old daughter of his drug dealer and now everyone he thought he knew wanted to kill him. So he left. He headed for Alabama. He knew his dad was from Alabama. He had a grandma or some uncles up there somewhere, so he split.

It turned out his Alabama family didn't want anything to do with drug user Cade. He ended up hustling in Andalusia on George Street. He hustled anything that he could … stolen goods, drugs, sex, anything. Except work. No one ever saw Cade hanging out in front of the hardware store trying to get in on a labor gig.

The biggest events for young people in small town Andalusia were parties in the woods. Huge fires were built. Kegs of beer were tapped. And teenagers were hallmark to these parties. Twenty-six year old Cade was irresistibly attracted. He put a camper top on the back of his truck. He kept his truck stocked with beer and blankets. He was always ready to help anyone who had too much to drink. He met an especially pretty teen one night. Her name was Violet. She was thirteen and so drunk she sloshed beer all over his truck. That pissed him off but she was so pretty. She didn't resist him even a little so he forgot she was sloppy. She was scared when she woke up before sunrise, probably because she didn't remember getting into the truck. She didn't remember meeting anyone. She scrambled to get out the open back flap of the truck.

"Hey, pretty flower, where ya going?" said Cade gently from behind Violet. She froze. She couldn't find her jacket. She knew she had left home with her denim jacket, it had everything she owned in its pockets including her money and cigarettes. "Looking for this?" he asked. She looked back. He pulled her wadded up jacket from behind his head. He said, "thanks, I forgot to bring a pillow, I didn't mean to stay all night out here but you asked me to keep you safe. I didn't know where to drive you. So we slept here. I kept you safe. I'm Cade. And you're Violet, right? You told me last night before you passed out."

He drove her home then, to her mom's boyfriend's house. She started crying thinking of how she would likely be caught sneaking into the house. She would get badly punished for it. Her mom would probably be passed out but her mom's boyfriend wouldn't. He would be up waiting for Violet. He was so creepy to her. It was as if he could smell Violet when she was in the house. He hovered around her like a bee around a flower. Violet sensed it was only a matter of time before he got ahold of her when no one else was home. She started staying out more. She was only coming home now because she had a headache. She felt gross. She felt grimy and used; she could tell she had sex, she could feel it. It wasn't her first time. It didn't occur to her that she had just been raped by, was riding with, a pedophile. She wiped her face with her jacket sleeve as he pulled up to where she pointed. They were half a block from her house but she didn't want anyone to see her get out of a man's truck. Everyone in her family thought she was slut. This would give them reason for her brothers to tell her again how slutty she was. *They made me slut,* she thought, *with their ugly dicks.*

"I hang out at the pond in the woods a lot if you want to find me, pretty Violet. You can stay with me anytime, I have a place where no one can find me, it's cool," said Cade as Violet opened the door. He didn't mention that people wanted to find him to hurt him for what he had done to Nathan's daughter back in Florida. His dick stirred in his pants thinking of this young this pretty flower here, much younger than his friend's kid. He licked his lips, squeezed his hard dick through his jeans, and drove away. But he didn't go far. He rolled slowly along watching Violet, seeing where she was headed. He drove past her place then turned around. He parked across the street from where he'd seen her go in; he waited. *God damn she had been so fucking delicious last night* he thought as he pushed on his dick again through his jeans. He knew better than to take it out. He couldn't risk getting arrested for jacking off in his car. He figured sooner or later she would come out.

Violet hadn't noticed Cade following her. She went into the screened porch of her house as quietly as she could after stopping to take off her shoes. She heard someone walking inside. She knew it was Rick, her mother's creepy boyfriend. She stayed still trying to will him away with her weary brain. She heard him grab the door handle, she expected it to turn. Just then she heard her mom's voice yelling out to Rick, "what the fuck are you doing? I fucking passed out! Why didn't you wake me up?" He started yelling back, defending himself as he moved away from the door. Their voices faded as they retreated into the house.

I am so tired, thought Violet, *maybe I'll skip a shower ... not risk getting caught ...* But she felt disgusting. She locked herself into the bathroom. She got into the shower as fast as she could. She peed while the hot water ran over her head. *I feel so sick,* she thought, *no more beer ... beer makes me sick, next time only wine coolers.* She was aching all over but washed herself quickly anyway. She barely managed not to puke.

She heard a knock on the door. "Vee-bee, open up!" she heard Rick say through the door, "I gotta pee!" She hated when he called her that. It was his way of calling her baby he said. He knew she hated it. He did it anyway. "Come on, Vee-bee, I'm going to mess myself," he pleaded in a sickening, mocking supposed-to-be childlike voice. She shivered. Then she got out of the shower to dress into the same filthy clothes she had been wearing for hours. She could smell puke on her t-shirt when she slipped it over her head. She almost threw up again. But there was nothing to throw up. Her stomach was empty. She wretched. Then she opened the door.

She tried to walk past Rick but he blocked her path. He put his hands on her forearms, folding her back against the doorway so she couldn't move or use her hands. She squirmed until she realized that's what he wanted. She could feel his hard penis against her body. His hot breath stung her nose. She put her knee in his crotch as hard as she could. He let go of her arms. She twisted herself around to run past him as he bent. He yelled, "you little cunt!" She ran out of the house without looking back.

Outside, Cade almost missed the pretty flower he'd found when she ran past his truck. But not quite. He got out of the truck. He called out, "hey, pretty Violet, where ya going so fast?" She slowed. He jogged a few yards toward her. He said, "my truck was running funny so I pulled over here to figure it out. It's Cady from last night, remember me?"

Violet stopped. She turned around. She didn't see Rick like she had expected but instead saw the man who she had woken up next to a little while ago. *Fucking slut* she thought. "Oh! Ok, I remember," Violet said breathlessly, then, "can you give me a ride? My parents are fucking pissed. I don't want to go near them!" She glanced behind Cade to see if Rick was coming after her even as she knew Rick wouldn't want her mother to find out what he had done. He likely wouldn't chase her. Violet climbed into Cade's beat up truck. She never did come back to her mom's house. She started sleeping with Cade in his truck or in a tent he would pitch somewhere.

Cade taught Violet to lay low. He also taught her to smoke heroin. Dope, he called it. She came to crave the vinegary taste and sweet release from life that dope brought her. She could lay low for hours after smoking. Soon days and nights ran together for Violet. She lost track of time and place. The only thing she wanted to do was use dope. On some level she knew she couldn't live this way forever but in her teenage mind she didn't think much about time. She lived in the moment.

What she didn't know was that she had become pregnant. By the time she started to notice she wasn't getting her period she was smoking heroin daily while Cade injected. Sometimes they would burn a chunk of heroin on a piece of foil to inhale the smoke as the dope burned. Cade called this type of smoking 'chasing the dragon' and Violet loved it. Cade told her it was better for her than injecting. She believed him.

Time went by fast for Violet in the short months of her pregnancy. She didn't go to a doctor or see anyone about it. Violet was still fourteen when one day while sitting in the truck with Cade her water broke. Cade thought she had pissed her pants. He told her, "get the fuck out of my truck." Violet had started crying. She didn't know what was happening. Her body locked up in pain. She screamed. Labor pains gripped her. Cade realized what was happening then and, after wrapping Violet in a sleeping bag, he put her in the truck. He drove her to the hospital to leave her standing outside the front entrance. Then he drove off into the night.

The hospital staff were not strangers to children having babies by adults. When a nurse entering the hospital saw Violet standing outside bent over holding her knees while trying not to cry, she knew not to ask questions. She approached Violet. She quietly put an arm around her waist to gently lead her into the hospital.

Violet gave birth quickly. She had little memory of the event. She had known she was pregnant but never had thought about having an actual baby. Maybe that's why she didn't think of her baby first when she woke up. She thought of Cade. She did remember him leaving

11

her at the hospital. The memory of his truck rolling away from her seemed burned into her mind. She looked around the room. She was laying in a hospital bed. Curtains hung on both sides of her but not at the end of the bed. She could see a tall counter across a hall and the top of someone's head moving behind the counter. She heard a cough from one side of her beyond the curtain. Someone called out to a nurse from behind the curtain on the other side. She thought of her baby and started to cry. *Where is my baby?* she asked herself.

People kept walking past where Violet lay alone and scared. No one had known she was pregnant. Not her mom or her step dad. She hadn't told any of her brothers even when she approached them to buy dope. She had hidden her belly from them. They just never looked twice at Violet. *What do I do? Maybe I should just get up and leave. I have to pee. I want a cigarette ...* her mind raced. She tried to get off the bed. A woman sitting behind the counter noticed Violet trying to stand, she came quickly to assist.

"Let me help you, miss," said the woman, "you had some meds that may keep you feeling tired for a while." She seemed to know what Violet needed. She led her to an open bathroom door at the end of the hallway. "You take your time, sweetie. Just yell or push that red button there if you need me for anything," the nurse explained as she closed the door behind Violet.

Violet started crying anew when she lifted her gown. She had on a large diaper! She pulled it off. She sat heavily on the toilet. *A fucking diaper! I thought they were only for babies! Of fuck* her mind kept circling. She could tell she wasn't pregnant anymore. A light knock came on the door then it opened a crack. Violet covered her lap. A hand slipped inside the crack to hold out another diaper, a pair of panties, and a huge period pad. "Here," said a voice, "you choose, it's up to you but you will be bleeding heavy for a while." The hand slid down to leave the items on the floor at Violet's feet. Violet cried for a while in the bathroom until a second light knock came on the door. "Honey, we need the bathroom, now, ok?" said the same voice through the door. Violet put on the panties and pad. She opened the door. She wasn't sure where she had been laying. The same woman that led her to the bathroom helped her back to her bed. She explained that someone would come talk to her soon about everything.

Everything turned out to be a whole lot more than Violet had expected. Violet learned more about how life rolls by outside her family in the first day of motherhood than she had learned in her entire childhood. She learned about how laws can influence if your baby's father is around. She learned that she could press charges against Cade for having sex with her because he was twenty-six, she was fourteen. She learned the state could press charges against her for smoking heroin because her new baby tested positive for heroin. She learned her baby boy had to be given drugs every three hours or he would scream.

Doctors put the new baby on morphine as soon as he was born with a plan to taper off as he learned to cope with withdrawal. The plan was the baby's morphine dose went down incrementally over weeks. Violet was put on methadone. The nurse came with tablets for Violet to swallow. Staff explained to her that because she was fourteen they had to tell her parents about the baby. They wanted the father's name. Violet only knew Cade's first name. She was left on her own with her new baby while they called her mom. She gave her mother's address as her own then waited to be let go. She wanted a cigarette. She wanted to get stoned, to chase the dragon. She didn't want to think about all the shit they were telling her about keeping the baby. About methadone. She didn't care what happened to the baby. She just wanted to be with Cade. She didn't realize it was methadone that kept her from being dope sick.

When they brought the baby to her she didn't want to look at it or hold it. She didn't refer to it as him. She didn't have a name for him. She asked if she could go have a cigarette. "No," said the nurse, "no smoking." Soon Violet was surprised by the arrival of her step father. She bristled at his approach. Her mother was not with him.

"Violetta! We have been looking everywhere for you!" he said with false kindness. The woman who had led him to Violet left the room. Rick's face turned into a sneer. He stepped close to Violet then said, "you fucking slut! Who did you fuck to get this bastard? The state wants your mom to come get him but I say fuck that! Let his stupid asshole father come get him. Whose bastard is it?" Violet was stunned. She sat silently as Rick leaned in closer. He said, "I know you were fucking that Ramsey fuck-wad. I bet he is long gone. Ha! He could go to prison for having a bastard with you. Your mom wants the fucking baby for the morphine. If you don't let her have the bastard then I will tell them who the baby's daddy is! You are such a stupid cunt, Violetta!" He didn't wait for her to respond or stay to hear her cry. He left her bedside.

Soon a woman visited Violet. She introduced herself as a social worker for the state. "The state wants to keep your family together, Violet. I think your mom is the best choice for keeping custody of your son since you are too young. Your age plus the fact that he was born positive for heroin makes things difficult but if you can show us you want to take care of him with your mom's help we can let him go home. Home with your mom, I mean, later this week if things work out." She paused and smiled kindly at Violet. "Can I get you anything?" She asked.

"I really bad want a smoke," said Violet, "just one, I swear." She really had only been thinking about taking a drag of a cigarette. The moment she saw Rick she went numb. All her drive had drained out of her. She no longer cared what happened to her baby or to her. Her body was demanding a cigarette though. She asked,"can I go outside? Smoke a cigarette?"

The social worker sighed. "I'll see what I can do. Maybe we can take a walk," she answered. "Can you tell me the father's whole name? Is Cade a nickname? You don't know his last name? We don't want to hurt him. Just see if he can be responsible enough to help you with this baby. Think about it. I'll be right back." She left Violet alone.

Violet spotted her jacket in a wad on a chair by the wall near her head. She picked it up. Her belongings spilled out of the twisted wad of clothes. Her jeans had dried, they were stuck in a crumple from her birth-water breaking. *They won't fit me now anyway* she thought. She tied her hospital gown around her waist. She put on her bra and t-shirt then slipped into her jacket. She ignored her aching chest and belly. She looked at her stuff. Her pink lighter and ball of foil were just as she had left them buttoned into a pocket. She was relieved. No cigarettes though. *What the fuck! Where's my smokes?* she thought and almost said aloud.

Violet was pacing at the end of the bed, three steps in one direction, turn, three steps back. Her stomach was starting to get queasy, she felt like throwing up. A nurse arrived and gave Violet three tablets to swallow. "This is your methadone. Thirty milligrams. You need it three times a day but you can wean down. We will send some home with you but it will be up to your mom to get you an ongoing prescription if she can," said the nurse as if Violet understood. Violet had vague memories of her mom talking about methadone but she didn't remember those times as being good times. Not that there were ever good times.

Fuck she thought *I don't want to see my mom! I haven't talked to her in forever!* But she had seen her mom though. She made Cade drive to where she could watch her mom walking to the liquor store. Part of her always wanted her mom to miss her. She never stopped expecting her mom to see her as she ambled along but she only looked at the ground in front of her. When Violet got fat with the baby Cade stopped taking her to watch her mother, he refused, saying it made her cry and he was sick of it. She sat on the edge of the bed as a wave of tiredness hit her. She looked at the thin plastic pillow next to her. She wanted so bad to lay down. She had never felt to tired.

"Looks like the methadone is hitting you hard. It should pass quickly," said the nurse as she helped Violet to lay down. "You will be able to wean off it, honey." She raised the bed a little so Violet could be upright while laying back on the pillow. Violet's stomach settled as it made a growl. "I'll be right back with some dinner for you," she said.

A male voice called out from the curtain next to Violet, "can I have some dinner, too?" Violet stared wide eyed at the curtain expecting it to open. She tried to get up to pace again but sank back into the pillow instead. She heard the nurse reply sharply to the man, "you just ate Carl, you won't be here much longer you better make the best of it! Don't rush me or you'll be out right now without your meds!"

The social worker came back to Violet's bedside just as the exchange between the nurse and the man ended. "Don't worry about them," she said to Violet, "they do this a lot." She smiled. Then she said carefully, "I heard the nurse explaining about your medicines, I hope it was helpful. Everybody hears everything in this place I'm afraid. I talked to your mom. She will be here soon. Your step dad has been here. He signed consent forms already which you don't need to worry about. We have to talk about your baby now, Violet, have you named him? How do you feel about your mom wanting him?"

Violet wanted to say something but she just couldn't get the words out. *I don't give a fuck! I don't care what happens to the fucking thing* was the only thing she could think of to say. She held her words and started to cry hot, silent tears. She cried tears of anger not sadness. *I want a cigarette so fucking bad* she thought.

The social worker then seemed to remember her promise. She said, "come on, let's go out front for a few minutes. We can be back before your food gets here so Carl doesn't eat it." She stepped to

Violet's bedside and held out her arm. They went outside to sit on a bench. She pulled a pack of cigarettes out and shook two of them out. She lit one and put it on the ground next to the bench. She said, "dang someone left a lit cigarette burning. Some kid might get it." She lit another cigarette and took a drag. She winked at Violet. "That one is for you," she said to Violet and gestured to the ground, "I can't give a kid a cigarette. You will have to take it." She smiled as Violet understood and reached for the burning cigarette. The two women smoked for a few minutes.

"Have you thought of a name?" asked the social worker, breaking the silence.

"Chase," said Violet. It was the only word she could think of, it popped out of her mouth before she knew it. He was named. *Chase* she thought *the dragon, that's what I want, to chase the dragon ... where the fuck is Cade?* "I don't care what happens to him. My mom can have him. She wants him. I don't. No big deal okay? Can I go home soon?" she asked as she took the last drag of her cigarette. She felt like her teenage self again, ready to move on to the next thing. She tossed the still smoking butt onto the ground.

Violet stood. The social worker stood with Violet. She touched Violet's shoulder lightly and said, "are you sure you don't want to spend some time with Chase before your mom comes to get you guys?" Violet shrugged and said nothing. She tugged at the gown tied around her waist. Together they walked back into the hospital. Violet ate her dinner while she signed anything that was put in front of her. She wanted out. She didn't care about the baby, custody, methadone, or the state. She didn't want to see her mother. Or Rick. But she ended up leaving the hospital with the three of them- her mother, Rick, and the baby. The hospital gave her mother thirty methadone pills to administer to Violet with instructions for contacting the methadone clinic. They gave Violet a vial of liquid morphine with instructions for administering to Chase every three hours.

CHAPTER THREE

Exhaustion had set in for Violet during the twenty minute ride home. She tried to stay awake to watch for Cade on the way home but the methadone and her fatigue demanded she sleep. Chase's cries woke her as they parked in the street. She hadn't expected to be back here. She felt a heavy dread. *How could he leave me?* Her mind cried out for answers but there were none. Cade was nowhere to be seen. Her mom took the baby into the house. Violet was left to sit outside, no one even asked her to come in. She felt completely unwanted. She started walking toward the trail that would lead her to the woods where she had met Cade. She knew he would be there. She wanted to be with him so bad. She started to run and didn't stop until she saw Cade's truck parked under a tree. She could see the tent set up in the back and she blew a whistle to warn him. She called out, "Cady, it's me" toward the truck. She whistled again.

"What the fuck?" A female's voice came from the tent, "who's out there? Fuck off!" Violet heard rustling sounds then Cade's voice, "Vee is that you? You are supposed to be in the hospital. You didn't give them my name did you? Are you alone?"

Violet took off running. She heard Cade's voice behind her but she didn't look back. She stopped only when she felt Cade grab her shoulder. "Fucking slow down!" Cade yelled, "what the fuck, Vee!" He was shirtless, his jeans unzipped. Violet could tell he had been having sex. *He was fucking someone while I was popping out his bastard* she thought. She flinched away from his hold but stopped running. Her gut was starting to hurt. The rag she had tied around her chest to stop the aching had come loose. She had wet marks where her milk had leaked through.

"Who's in there? I thought you loved me, Cady! I had your baby. Your son," Violet wailed at Cade. She bent and put her hands on her knees. She thought she was going to puke.

"Look Vee, come back to the truck. Chase the dragon with me, ok? You look sick. You have to forgive me about Jenny, Vee. She was selling dope. We got drunk, I don't even remember it, Vee, come on baby, you know I love you!" Cade pleaded.

Jenny came crashing down the trail. "Violet! Vee, honey! I was so drunk, it was nothing!" Jenny called out to Violet. "How are you honey? Come smoke with me momma! You're a momma now!"

Cade looked relieved as he saw Violet relax and smile at Jenny. Violet walked with Jenny to the truck. She climbed to the center seat. Cade and Jenny climbed into the truck on either side of Violet. Wordlessly, Violet unfolded a piece of foil, she held it out to be loaded. Cade loaded the foil with a piece of black tar heroin then lit a lighter beneath the foil. Violet used an old straw to suck up the acrid, powerful smoke. She chased the burning heroin around the foil with the straw. She chased the dragon until it was no longer smoking. She dismissed the thought of Cade and Jenny fucking as she tried to feel the oblivion she had come to love. She was surprised she wasn't feeling it more. *I want to nod so bad* she thought *why can't I get high?*

It was then that Jenny thought to ask what medications Violet had been given at the hospital. Cade had only thought he would be caught for having a kid with a teenager. He hadn't thought about Vee or the baby being positive for heroin. And he didn't know they would be given meds. "What did they give you, Vee, norcos?" Cade asked excitedly.

"Metha-something. Methalin? Giant pills that tasted terrible and were hard to swallow," answered Violet. She started to cry. *How come*

I feel like this? she asked herself. "You guys gave me shit to smoke! I didn't even get high," she cried.

"Methadone!" said Jenny, "shit, Violet, you can't feel the dope much if you are on methadone. It can be dangerous, too, you should wait!" Jenny packed up the foil and dope. She put the lighter in her pocket and tossed the straw out the truck window into the bushes. "It might take you three days or a whole month for it to wear off if you go cold turkey off methadone I heard. I heard, too, that it's hard to get on methadone. If the state will pay for it you can either get straight with it or sell it! It might be different for kids. I forget you're a kid, Vee."

"I heard they give methadone to anyone who wants it in California," said Cade. He hadn't spoken since they had climbed into the truck.

"Probably not to kids!" said Jenny without thinking. Besides, they weren't in California. "Look. I think you should try to get your meds from your mom. If you can't, then wait a couple days. You can chip a little to avoid overdosing." She opened the truck door. "I'll hike back to town no worries."

"Why get the methadone?" cried Violet, "and what do you mean by chip a little?"

"Get the methadone from your mom to help you wean off it. You take less every time until you don't get sick anymore. Then you can feel dope again. Break the tablets into fours. When you use dope, use a little chip of dope so you don't do too much," explained Jenny, "and you only chip once every few days, not for days in a row."

"I heard they give morphine to babies in California," said Cade, interrupting the women. "Did our baby get morphine, Vee?" he asked.

"I have to go," said Jenny. She climbed out of the truck and shut the door behind her. "Come by my house with that baby if your mom will let you, Vee, I want to see it! Him, right? I want to see him! What's his name?" she asked through the open window.

"Chase," said Violet.

"No shit," said Jenny, "you are a trip, Vee! Chase?" She laughed and walked away.

"Chase?" Cade asked. Then he said with emphasis and volume, "Chase Ramsey. I like it. A son. I like having a son. I want to meet my son, Chase!" He started the truck and headed toward town. "Let's get our baby and head for California, Vee, let's get the fuck out of here!"

Violet was stunned by Cade's excitement. She said nothing. She sat next to him as he wheeled the truck toward town. He had never talked about the baby or sons or wanting kids when she was pregnant. She had never before considered leaving Alabama. But she hated living here. She hated the way she was expected to keep her mouth shut and her legs open even as she didn't realize that was the way that Cade liked her to be, too.

No one appeared to be at her moms house when they pulled up but when they opened the truck door they could hear a baby screaming. *That's him* thought Violet *he sounds really mad.* The sound didn't make her want to go to him though. She wanted to run away. She almost did run away if it hadn't been for Cade bringing her back to this shit hole. Her breasts tingled and dripped as her body responded to the baby's cries. Violet stayed in her seat.

"Get the fuck out, Vee! Go get him! And get your medicine, too!" ordered Cade. "The faster you get back the faster we roll. More dope when you get back. Go!" He pushed the door open wide. She had no choice but to slide out as Cade slid his body into the passenger seat effectively ejecting Violet from the truck. She landed on the curb almost twisting her ankle, she fell hard. "You fucking oaf! Get up!" he hissed.

Violet got up and moved toward the sound of the crying baby. Now she was crying again, too. *Fucking asshole* thought Violet *what a fucking asshole!* She went in the place through the front door. Her mother and Rick were both on the couch sprawled out and unconscious. Rick had a needle hanging out of his arm. The baby screamed louder. Violet found the near empty vial of the baby's morphine on the floor and picked it up. She went to the crying baby as it laid on the floor in the bedroom. She tipped the vial into his mouth so a thin dribble coated his tiny tongue. He sucked in his breath and smacked his lips. His cries subsided in big heaving sobs. She picked him up and looked at him. *God he stinks* she thought *he smells like shit!*

Cade grew tired of waiting. He went in to see what Violet was doing. He saw two people nodded out in the living room. He began searching for drugs, including in their pockets. He stepped into the bedroom just as Violet was tipping the vial into the baby's mouth. "Wait!" he shouted, "morphine! Don't give it to him!" He snatched the vial out of Violet's hand but it was too late, the vial was empty. "How much did he get? It could kill him," said Cade. He spotted a prescription bottle nearby and picked it up. He shook it. "Full!" he exclaimed as he read the label, "methadone!" He stuffed the vial into his backpack and looked around for more drugs. He ordered Violet to gather the baby. He gave Violet three methadone pills as they left the place. They did not stop to check to see if her mom and Rick were alive or dead.

The methadone was gone by the time they got to California. The baby was still screaming most of the time. Violet had started riding in the back of the truck with it because the screams drove Cade so crazy. Cade's face would turn deep red, then he would scream, too, huge loud scary screams that made the baby scream even harder. Violet almost gave the baby a little piece of her methadone but she was selfish in the end. She trained herself to ignore the baby's screams as she had to deal with her own body. The withdrawal that she was going through seemed to get worse every day. Cade stretched out her methadone doses. He kept breaking the pills into smaller pieces. He had started taking it, too. Thats why it was gone now. They were rolling into cities along the way to find dope. Cade even tried to find a methadone clinic for Violet but was turned away when he wouldn't tell their names or ages. It was the first time Violet had to kick off opiates. She suffered a lot. She suffered enough so that she swore she would avoid kicking dope for the rest of her life.

Chapter Four

1992

Violet woke suddenly at ten after twelve, *oh shit*, she thought and jumped up. She had been dreaming of that first time she had to go off methadone. *Fucking weird* she thought *that I would be worried about methadone when I went to sleep, then I dreamed about it!* She looked around. There was no sign of Cade. Strict hours of operation at the methadone clinic meant she had to hurry. It was almost closing time. She hustled out the door and started jogging down the street. It was a few blocks to the clinic from her place on Button Street. It was a place, really, and not a home. Violet never thought of it or referred to it as home or even the house. It was the place, that's all. Not much happened at her place that Violet wanted to remember. Thoughts of the birth intruded into her mind. Her tits were still aching but not as much, she had tied them down with a sarong. She was still bleeding heavy and was getting tired, jogging on the road.

She made it to the clinic just before they closed. She bent over in the lobby panting while trying to catch her breath. She hadn't been to the clinic in months. She was doing her best to stick to the agreement she made with the county. As much as she hated getting back onto methadone it was better than being strung out on heroin. Or booze.

Violet was required to be tested for booze before they would give her methadone. Mixing booze with methadone could kill her. So she inhaled a deep breath to blow into the breathalyzer the dosing nurse held out to her. She handed the device back to the nurse and said, "no booze for me today!"

24

Just then David, one of the methadone clinic counselors, came around the corner. "My dear Violet! I heard you blossomed last night! Now for an hour with me, I know you are looking forward to it,'" said David loudly.

"I'm not a fucking flower," said Violet flatly, "I can't stay an hour because I have to go see child services about Arianna and the baby." She had not thought of Arianna since she gave her a pop tart hours ago. And she only thought about the baby if she had to change her pad or she bumped into something with her tits. Now she tried to use them as an excuse to get out of spending an hour listening to this counselor who liked to talk about how meditation will change her life.

I don't even want my fucking kid thought Violet. She wanted to ask David if meditation could change that. She was almost too tired to keep her thoughts together. She followed David to his office and listened to him talk about family bonding for an hour.

Something inside Violet propped her up that day. In the following weeks she gained a different attitude. Probably because she wanted to be out of the clinic as fast as she could. She managed to get off heroin long enough to get the kid back after ninety days. Ninety days being piss-tested weekly or more, seeing David weekly, and reporting weekly to county social workers. She got the baby back when it was three months old, after it was weaned off methadone. She never did hold or snuggle or feed it and, in fact, practically gave it away to Arianna like it was a doll to play with that didn't have actual needs. She weaned herself down off methadone mostly by missing doses or showing up for her dose drunk and thus getting less methadone. By the time a year rolled by Violet was shooting up again, injecting heroin into her body … only talking to her kids if they could somehow help her get into a dope fix or out of a jam. Many times she sent Arianna to the door by hissing at her, saying "don't let them in, tell them I'm gone and you don't know where but that your big brother is here sleeping. They will go away. Shhh. Do it!"

Violet practically couldn't remember the first six years of her third baby's life. She remembered that giving birth to him had been fucking hard. In her warped sense of pride, she felt proud of the fact that child services had kept him in custody for only three months. She never said his name to anyone, not even to him after she got him back. Cade didn't refer to the kid at all until it could talk and walk. Even then Ben was treated as if he had already grown up.

Chapter Five

2016

Ben climbed down from the truck and wiped the sweat from his eyes. He had been trying to unload before it got to be daylight. He just made it. The sun was beginning to lighten up the world even as darkness clouded his heart. He couldn't seem to shake the feeling that he was being watched. He wasn't used to that. No one ever noticed anything he did. He liked it like that. He learned from the past that attention from others often was not solid. Attention could not be counted on as genuine interest.

Even his own mother had ignored him for most of his life. He didn't think about her much these days now that he was living in a different part of the state from her. He tried to ignore her and all thoughts of her but her voice often popped into his mind, "I should have let you cry yourself to death!" Or "I wish you had never been born" replayed in his head in his mother's voice when he felt stress. He tried to hate her.

He walked around the side of the truck, bent over, and threw up the sausage and biscuits he had eaten for breakfast. *I can't do this much longer*, he thought. *I am only twenty-four but I am too old for this*. But this was all he had left. This task. This task the left him bereft and thinking of his mother … maybe she would be glad he had kept the night runs going even if only once a month. Maybe she would even be proud of him. Maybe he will get the chance to tell her, even to show her if she ever came back. He missed her. He hated her. He hated that she got him started on these runs. He knew they were dangerous. *I'm doing it for the other people involved* he thought as he got back in his truck.

He went home. He tried to go about his day as if he weren't wrecked. That's how he felt … wrecked. His head hurt. His stomach ached with hunger but flexed with revulsion at the thought of food. He took a swallow of water. He tried to clear his mind. He thought of the plans he had to swim at the beach later. He hoped it would be a hot day. He went to the clinic to get his methadone dose so he would stop feeling sick. He had been trying to go to the clinic daily but something kept getting in the way. He overslept. He was distracted by other tasks until it was too late and the clinic was closed. *Sucks that they close so early,* he thought. He got in his truck and drove off.

He felt throbbing pain as he drove. The festering wound on his leg was hurting. Every time he had to wrench the steering wheel to turn, pain shot out from the wound. The pain seemed to slice through his thoughts with tangible hotness. He pulled over and shut off the truck. He risked taking a drag from his pipe, smoking leftover dope. He thought back to before he had to deal with this throbbing pain … He imagined he was up in the forest, hiking in the redwood trees, his only purpose to get to his favorite tree. The tree was so old and burned on the inside that he could go inside the tree. He would crawl into the darkness through a three foot high opening at the base of the tree but once he was inside he could stand to his full six foot four.

A passing truck's noise broke through his daydream and he startled to the present. Everything seemed to flash by so fast. The traffic. His thoughts and emotions. The pain, always the pain these days. He started the truck and began to roll. The methadone began to work, his stomach settled. He tried to relax his muscles and let the drug work on his pain.

Maybe I'll go see that old tree he thought *I can drive up to Santa*

Cruz and slip into the woods without anyone even knowing I'm there. Maybe I'll even sleep in the tree. He began to plan and to think of the possibilities of going up to Santa Cruz to see the place. *Just the place … he thought … not the people.*

Ben had been born in Santa Cruz. He lived there most of his life but had not been there since before he went to lockup. His mother had never talked about Santa Cruz much. They, he and his mother and sister, had lived in Beach Flats next to the famous Santa Cruz Boardwalk. He had been born in a motel converted to low income housing. Being labeled low income had set him apart from most kids in Santa Cruz. When he was in school he had felt deeply that he was different. That his dad and brother had died during a drug buy also set him apart. He was seven and in the first grade when that happened. Afterward people either felt sorry for him or they were disgusted that his family were into drugs. He understood none of it, only that he had become the so-called man of the family … a role which he did not want. He could never meet his mother's expectations or needs. Especially at age seven.

He had dreaded going to school. He had hated his classmates and his teachers. Especially the teachers who tried to help him by giving him things that he took home. He never saw those things again because his mother would be jealous. She would take anything that was his. One time she snatched the popsicle right out of his hand that a neighbor had given him before he could even lick it, she took it and ate it as fast as she could. That was before. Before everything. Before they died. Before the stabbing. Before lockup. Before San Diego. Before the smuggling runs.

He started to think again about planning to go to Santa Cruz. He knew his mother might be there. He was both glad and sad about the possibility of seeing her. *Maybe she wouldn't be there after all* he thought. The last place he knew her to be was in San Diego. Five hundred miles from Santa Cruz. But his sister, Arianna, had said during a phone call that their mom was in Santa Cruz. He had stopped looking at what their mom was doing. Partly because he couldn't stand to see what was happening to Violet. Partly because he couldn't see anything while he was nodded out on heroin all the time like he increasingly was. Now, he couldn't nod out because he couldn't fucking get the shit into his body. And he had almost died when he tried to stick his femoral vein, instead hitting his femoral artery. He had gotten a blood infection. Now his leg was infected. He knew he was facing some serious shit so he stayed on the methadone the hospital had started him on to stop him from using more heroin. He tried not to use heroin. But every night at some point he would get the itch to go looking for it. He only smoked it now. He didn't mind if it was laced with fentanyl.

As he planned his trip, it occurred to him he would have to get methadone in Santa Cruz. That idea was almost enough to stop him from planning. The only memories he had of methadone in Santa Cruz involved going to the clinic with his mother when she was in a trying-to-get-my-shit-together mood. His resentment welled up like bile in his throat. His thoughts constantly cycled through memory and resentment- he tried to focus on planning. *Tomorrow* he thought *when I come to the clinic I'll find out how to get methadone in Santa Cruz.* He drove home. He parked on the street around the corner from his place. He went in to crash for a solid six hours before waking to the pain of his seeping wound.

He had forgotten all about Santa Cruz when he woke at three the next morning to screaming pain in his leg. He was burning with fever. He then left his place intending to go to the emergency room but along the way his mind got in his way … *I can make this easier if I get a hit … they will just treat me like crap and call me a junkie* … he had spent twenty bucks on some black tar heroin he planned to save until morning. He pulled over to smoke it.

Chapter Six

B en was alone when he woke the next day. And before he realized where he was, he realized he felt no pain. The wound on his leg was not throbbing or dominating his every thought. He opened his eyes. *Where the fuck am I* he thought. He looked around to see he was in a hospital room. He had a needle taped into one arm and a blood pressure cuff on the other. He was warm. He felt so very comfortable, so pain free, he drifted back to sleep only to wake suddenly when he felt cold fingers press gently into his wrist. He opened his eyes as a nurse took her fingers away. She turned to record the data. He opened his mouth to speak but it was too dry, he couldn't swallow or even clear his throat. He grunted. The nurse looked at him. He could see the concern in her eyes. Until that moment he hadn't realized he was waiting for her disdain, her judgement and hatred … the labels of junkie, drug addict. He was surprised to find kindness in her gaze.

"Hey, are you awake?" he heard her ask, "I'm Angie, your nurse of the moment. I'm going to pour you some water, you've been asleep for a while."

He felt the bed rise slowly. Somehow he extended his hand. He was able to get the cup by his face but not quite to his mouth before trying to drink. Angie carefully helped him bring the cup to his lips. He studied her face as she leaned toward him. She was older. There were some wrinkles and signs of life lived with a lot of laughter. She smiled at him when she noticed him studying her. And because of her overall compassion for every patient she worked for, she started to give him something she knew he would want. Information.

"You're in the hospital because you ingested fentanyl. The drug stopped your breathing and your heart. Paramedics brought you back and then we treated your wound. Now you're on antibiotics and a saline drip. Can you hear me ok?" She forgot to mention pain medicine.

Ben gave a slight nod. He could hear her. Worse, he understood. He remembered his dealer saying the chunk of black she sold him had fentanyl in it but he didn't care, he loved to nod out on fentanyl. But this was too far out. He didn't want to die, not consciously anyway. His sister used to always say he had a death wish but he really never thought beyond the journey and had never considered any destination except out, not dead. He was always about making the journey better. *It was Arianna who had a death wish*, thought Ben, *she's been locked up for trying to kill herself!* He opened his mouth and asked for more water with his eyes and hands. He drank and licked his lips. The last thing he remembered was sitting in his truck thinking about Santa Cruz and trying to get to the emergency room as he lit up that black he had bought. He didn't think twice about the fentanyl because in the past he shot the shit into his veins. He considered smoking to be safe. He was wrong.

He wondered who had called the paramedics ... *stupid fucking junkie* he thought ... he tried to talk but instead grunted again. Angie smiled warmly at Ben, she touched his arm and said, "I'm going to let the team know you are awake and get some food together for you. Your sister has been here since yesterday and will be super happy to see you awake."

Ben laid there awake thinking about this feeling he had, this warmth that was growing in his belly and chest. He felt glad to be alive and glad to be pain free! *They must have him on some good shit*, he thought, *if I'm not hurting for anything.* He tried to find his jones, his craving for black, but it was gone. He wasn't thinking about fixing or smoking or nodding out like he usually did as soon as he woke up. He also didn't see any medicines attached to his IV. He sat up straight and stretched his arms up, cracking his back. Then he felt it. A patch. He could feel it on his upper back shoulder like a sticky bandaid. He tried to reach it but couldn't. He hoped it was fentanyl. He knew it wasn't.

Angie came back into the room with another woman. "Ben, this is Joanna, she is taking over for me and will be your nurse of the moment for the next twelve hours. She will take better care of you than me because she is two years younger!" said Angie.

"Stop giving up my age!" said Joanna to Angie, "you are gracious but you tell too much! What should I know before you go?"

"Ben here needs some rest and a lot of compassion. He seems to have had a hard time trying to manage that wound on his leg and has been in pain for a long time, I think. How do you feel now, Ben?" She didn't mention track marks or heroin or junkies.

Ben struggled to talk but managed to say, "I'm tired. No aches. My leg feels fine. Can I get up?" He had to piss. "Can I go to the bathroom?"

"Yes! We can help you get there, ok. Here, hold on," Joanna said as she stepped to his bedside, "swing your legs over the side if you can."

Ben swung his legs off the bed as Angie stepped to his other side. The two women carefully helped Ben get up and get started toward the bathroom. Angie rolled the IV along and stationed it outside the bathroom. "Goodnight, Ben, it was nice to see you awake and to talk to you. I'm betting you won't be here when I come back to work in a few days so you remember to be kind to yourself, you deserve it!" Angie kept walking out into the hall, "See you, Joanna, have a good evening!" She called as she left work for home.

The bathroom light was so bright Ben could hardly open his eyes to see. He fumbled for the rail by the toilet and swung himself around to sit. He pissed long and hard. He could only think about the fucking patch, he had forgotten to ask what it was. He still felt no pain. No craving. He pulled himself up and went back into the hospital room. He must've stayed in the bathroom longer than he thought. The nurse was gone when he came out. A plate of food and his sister were sitting next to his bed.

"Well you look like shit," said Arianna from her spot standing in front of the window, "you know they won't let you out now without a mental evaluation. Did you mean to do it? What the fuck, Ben, what happened? Are you sure you are done with your shitty life? You almost died! If some person walking by hadn't seen you passed out in your truck and called 911 you would be fucking dead! Your truck was running, Ben, you could have killed not only yourself but someone else, too!"

Now there was the disdain he expected to find in the world. *Just a junkie* he thought. But Arianna was a junkie, too. She just hadn't used any junk in a long time. But she was a junkie nonetheless.

"Why did you come here, Ari? I didn't ask you to" said Ben flatly. He pulled the rolling cart to himself and lifted the cover off the food tray. His stomach turned when the smell of turkey and stuffing wafted up to his nose. He took a bite of a roll and tried to chew. He sipped at the warmish tomato soup and could not come up with a single thing to say to his sister. He had resented her for so long he was surprised to not find the usual dislike of seeing her. But at this moment he felt nothing but gladness.

"Mom's still in Santa Cruz, you know," said Arianna dryly, "I see her rolling along Ocean Street cussing at people. She looks seventy."

Ben stared wide eyed at Arianna. He was stunned to hear such lack of caring and disgust from her. "I thought that step seven or step eight or whatever is about forgiveness in your program? It sounds like you failed that part. Have you actually talked to her? She lost it when Marta died and there was nothing I could do. I tried. Mom might have been ok if Marta hadn't died."

"Well she seems ok now and knows where to get help if she wants to. She goes to the methadone clinic every day I am sure," Arianna sat down next to Ben on the bed.

"Get away from me, Arianna, I know you don't care. I know how you feel about junkies who shoot dope. Did the nurse tell you about my leg? They have me on something now or be sure I would be fixing right now," said Ben without thinking.

Ari stood up next to Ben's bed. She stared at him. Her mind flashed to the last time she had seen him. It was the day he got out of the boy's ranch when he was nineteen. He was so quiet he hadn't said more than four words that day she went to lunch with him after picking him in Gilroy. Nope, yep, can't, and didn't were his only answers to her many questions on that long, long day. She hadn't wanted to be part of the welcome home committee but her mom pressed her into it. Guilted her into it, really, saying "Arianna, you are his only family member who can do it, please go to him when he gets out!" So she was his family. But back then she had no interest in helping him restart his life because she feared she would lose too much of her own life, her life that she had worked for that was so very far away from them, from Violet and Ben. She felt that if she hung out with Ben he would drag her into an old life she didn't want. She had years without even so much as a joint and she wasn't going to risk her sobriety to help Ben. He had never been helpful to her, only a burden, and she blamed him for her mother not liking her. After Ben was born she never felt love from Violet again. She did have memories of sitting on her mother's lap and of hugs and warmth. But she also remembered there was no room on her mother's lap once Ben came along. So she had brought Ben back to Santa Cruz that Monday and left him standing in front of the county services building. She never looked back. She found out months later that Ben had gone to San Diego to live closer to Violet in hopes she would get out early from Las Colinas.

She sat as Ben closed his eyes. Her mind drifted further back. She thought about what it was like for her when her mom was arrested. Ben had flipped out and was sent to lockup. Her life had changed that day. She hadn't gone home. She'd heard the news of her mom's arrest from social workers at school. She bolted away from them at her first chance. She was on pretty shaky ground with the school anyway because she truly didn't want to be there. She only went every day to keep the cops from bugging her boyfriend. Her boyfriend Jack was twenty. He was tricky. He was stealth. He would wait for Arianna across the street from he school where she could see him from campus. She would cross the street and walk past him with only a glance and climb into his car parked half a block away or up at the gas station on the corner. He would climb into the car and they would drive off to smoke heroin and hide out at Depot Park until time to drop her off at home. Sometimes, if Violet was not home or too drunk to notice, he would park around the block from her house and Arianna would walk the sidewalk to her house while Jack slid along the neighbor's fence and into Ari's backyard. He slid into her bedroom window and would be there waiting for her when she entered.

On the day when her mother was arrested and Benny was sent to lockup, Arianna didn't go home. She climbed into Jack's car at the end of the school day, escaping social workers who had come to the school for her. She demanded he drive her out of town to San Jose. She didn't know why but she had this deep motivation to run far away from Santa Cruz. She had a weird feeling, a kind of know-ing that this was somehow bound to happen. Violet was drinking every day all day since 'The Gruesome Day' as Arianna had come to call the day when Cade and Chase had died. Benny had been a different boy since then. He never smiled anymore. He seemed angry and sullen and only talked to her to tell her to get out of his way. He had become a lot like his late father and brother and Arianna had come to distrust and even dislike him despite the fact that she felt sorry for him, too.

She had talked Jack into taking her to San Jose so they could stay together and still find dope. They parked outside a steakhouse. They took turns begging money and leftovers from people coming out of the restaurant. An hour later they were questioned by police about their begging and were taken into custody. Arianna never saw Jack again and she went wide eyed and stone cold clean and sober into the next year of her life and it was, in her opinion, hell.

Back then, the state of California wouldn't let Arianna free float in the world. She felt like she was an adult and should be treated as one. She had been acting like an adult, at least like the adult she knew- her mother, for a very long time. She smoked cigarettes and pot. She dressed to look older. She never left home without full makeup. And she smoked heroin. Daily. All day when she could. She had an adult boyfriend and they surely did adult things when they were alone. Mostly she was too stoned to care about much.

And so she was stuck at a county home for girls. It took her two months to figure out that if she would just follow the rules she might get to make choices about where she lived. That she was expected to attend high school proved to be the only way that she could gain freedom. Before long, Arianna was smoking again, her perfect tri-fecta of cigarettes, weed, and black tar heroin. It had almost killed her in a couple of ways.

She had stopped caring about her life beyond needing freedom to get to school so she could make the connections she needed to make. She had measured her time until she turned eighteen. She vowed never to use needles but couldn't stop smoking. She didn't want to stop. When the warm rush of feeling the drug made moved through her brain and body it was a magic she was sure could not be duplicated anywhere else or by anything else. She started making her way down to Beach Flats, trading sex for drugs. It was after she turned eighteen, had been kicked out of the girl's home, and was living on her dealer's porch, that she accidentally propositioned a police officer to buy sex. She was given better options than in the past by the state - inpatient drug and alcohol addiction treatment or incarceration for prostitution and drug possession. Arianna chose inpatient addiction treatment. She had just turned nineteen. The same age Ben was the last time she had seen him.

CHAPTER SEVEN

B en's voice interrupted her thoughts. "You can leave, Arianna. I don't need you here," he said dryly. Arianna walked to the whiteboard hanging on the wall. She wrote her name and number for Ben to see from his bed. She looked at Ben. She was overcome with a feeling that he needed her more than he knew, more than she knew.

"Call me when you need a ride home," said Arianna, "I'm right around the corner. I'll come right away. I don't think they will keep you much longer depending on a mental health evaluation. Have you ever had one? Psychiatric evaluation? They always do one if someone overdoses even if it is an accident."

Ben stared silently at the door.

"Well if you don't pass the evaluation then they will put you on a legal hold until more assessments are done. They can legally keep you for three days," she informed Ben, "unless you really lose it during the evaluation."

"I'm not going to lose it. And I'm not going to fail the evaluation. I think I already had it, actually. I don't need a ride home. Goodbye," Ben said with increasing irritation. He was losing his good feelings. He was starting to feel like he wanted to fix, he wanted a shot, or more pain meds ... *was that my leg? Hurts* he thought ... he felt some throbbing from his wound. "Who the fuck called you anyway? No one knows I have a sister unless maybe it's someone who knows mom. Who told you I was in the hospital?" Ben sneered.

"The hospital called me, Benny. I guess somebody at your job knew you had a sister," Arianna explained. She took a step toward the door. Once again a strong sense of need washed over her. She felt vulnerable and confused. Here she was miles from home. She seldom went farther than the next county. She rarely took solo road trips but this had been important. She could sense that Ben needed her. She needed to figure out how she could help him. *Maybe it is part of addiction recovery work* she thought vaguely. Her recovery group sponsor had been nagging her lately to do the so-called twelve steps. Ben had mentioned step seven or step eight .. something about forgiving and kindness? *I need a meeting* she thought. She said to Ben, "I think I'll go there for lunch, to your job, ok? An omelet sounds perfect for me right now. You still work at that breakfast restaurant?"

Just then the nurse came into Ben's room and interrupted Arianna. "Hi, I'm Joanna, a nurse," she said to Arianna, and then to Ben, "excuse me, I just need to get your vital signs. The doctor is going to come and do your exit interview. Looks like you can be discharged soon." She smiled warmly at them both. "Any questions?"

It was then that Ben remembered to ask about pain meds and the nagging pain returning to his leg. "What am I on? Can I get more?" Ben blurted before thinking about how that would sound to his addiction-recovery-based sister. She liked to be considered recovery-based. He was definitely not in recovery. Except for recovering from a stupid mistake. He thought briefly of leaving the hospital with the IV needle still in so he could slam some dope … it had been a long, long time since he could hit a vein. *Shit I could hit every time!* he thought.

"It's new. Methadone. Patch. It's works great for pain for you doesn't it? I know that wound you have must have been terribly painful when you first got here. Plus Tylenol. It will feel better as the infection heals. Is the medicine making you tired or sick? We can reduce it if needed," answered the nurse. She didn't bring up that Ben was there for overdosing on fentanyl.

Ben was shocked into silence. He thought *thats why I'm not craving dope.* He looked at Arianna. He was so unused to this feeling of not craving that he wasn't sure what to think. "Am I going to get a prescription for when I leave the hospital?" Ben asked the nurse anxiously.

"When the doctor comes in she will answer that question for you. I think the answer is yes we will coordinate with your current methadone prescription but it's really the doctor who knows for sure. She will be here soon," she answered. She left the room after assuring them it wouldn't be long before the doctor was with them. Arianna stood still as if trying not to be noticed.

"You can go, Arianna," said Ben as if she were a kid waiting for permission.

"Let me stay, Benny. I can help you. I want to help you. Please?" said Arianna amidst a rush of love for her brother. She hadn't called him Benny since he was a kid. "I promise not to judge or be bitchy. I just want to help you out for a few days until you heal," she pleaded. She had walked close to him. She stood next to his bed. She noticed he had closed his eyes and she reached out and put her hand on his arm.

He flinched away from her and said, "the only way you could help me right now is to get me some dope before I get out of here because I am going to be too sick to work if I don't get something. If you can't do that, get the fuck out."

She took a step back. "I can try to pick up something for you if you can set it up but shit, Ben, it's been five years since I've copped anything!" she exclaimed, "but if thats what you will let me do, then I will help you." She stared at him stonily. She had resolved to make amends to him, to try and make up for the time when she was picking up her own shit and was too busy to help him with his.

Just then a woman entered the room dressed as a panda bear. "Hi I'm Dr. Camila Travers. Please forgive the attire. We are celebrating Halloween around here for fun," said the woman as she approached Ben. "You must be Mr. Ramsey, can I call you Ben? You can call me Camila, or doctor, or whatever and I will respond." She smiled warmly. "I have some information and a few questions," she looked at Arianna, she asked, "are you family?"

"She was family," said Ben, "I mean she is family. She was just leaving I meant to say." Ben looked at Arianna with a scowl that implied she would be sorry to challenge him.

"I'll wait outside," said Arianna softly to Ben, "if you need a ride." She walked out of the room.

The doctor pulled up a chair next to Ben and sat down. "This is going to be a hard conversation, Ben, but one that we must have. You presented with some pretty good evidence that you are abusing opiate drugs. How long have you been trying to heal that wound on your leg?" she asked gently. He sensed she was genuinely concerned. He could feel a warm feeling of acceptance and caring coming from her.

He swallowed dryly. She passed him a cup of water. He had forgotten they would question him about his fucking leg. He forgot because he couldn't feel it. For the first time in weeks his leg wasn't throbbing with hot pain. He thought about what it was like these past few months trying to pretend he didn't have a gaping wound. The pain had sometimes been unbearable. He had started drinking whisky nightly. He did still make it to work six afternoons a week and managed to stand to cook short order meals in between attempts at medicating himself. He tried hot compresses, tinctures, drawing salves, and all kinds of pain meds from aspirin to fentanyl. He had been too ashamed of the oozing, ugly wound to seek medical attention. He was stunned into silence by this doctor and her seemingly genuine concern.

"Look. I know what it's like to suffer. I knew when I first saw your wound that you have been suffering, probably a lot, for at least a month," she had broken the silence with her concerned voice. "You came very close to deadly sepsis which is why there was probably a lot of pain for you. At this point, your wound is clean and should remain infection free if it is kept clean. It will hurt to clean it at first but you must. I can give you topical pain relieving medicine and I have you on a methadone patch that will also help for pain. What is your pain level? Are you hurting right now?"

Ben thought for a moment. "I don't feel pain right now," he said, "it has been since last summer .. since August, that I first got an abscess on my leg." He could feel the hot flush of embarrassment move up his neck and across his face. He stopped talking and didn't share how he had gotten the abscess while injecting heroin into his body. He sensed she knew. She could probably tell by looking closely that he didn't have accessible blood veins. That he was a junkie.

She looked at him evenly. She didn't flinch when she said, "you will be dead soon if you don't change your drug use. If no one had noticed your overdose you might have died last night. I can help you in a lot of ways. First, I can keep this quiet for you. No one needs to know you are struggling with addiction unless you want to tell them. Second, I can make sure your current methadone prescription stays in place. Sometimes after an overdose there are adjustments to your methadone dose by the dispensing clinic. Lastly, I can connect you with people who can help you." She paused and let her words hang between them. "You have a kind of head start right now because you are here. Take this opportunity and better yet, take this chance to stop using illegal drugs. You can stay on methadone for as long as you need to and live a pain free life."

Ben sat taking in this information. He marveled at how he could hear all this and not feel belittled. He had long known he had a drug problem. He referred to himself as junkie for as long as he could remember. He didn't think much beyond finding the next high. The only thing that kept him even a little on track was his job and the night runs he had committed to make. He remembered that he had been thinking of skipping a run and going to Santa Cruz when he apparently overdosed. He thought of that tree, his tree. He wanted to climb inside of it right now as the doctor typed into her tablet.

The doctor put her hand on Ben's arm lightly. She said, "I know how hard this can be. I am going to let you think for a bit on this and I'll be back in a couple of hours. I will write your discharge papers then so you can plan on leaving here in around three hours." She gave his arm a reassuring squeeze and stood up to leave.

Tears welled up in Ben's eyes and began to spill down his face quietly as he watched her stand. "Thank you doctor," he managed to say, "thank you …" He smiled weakly at her as she turned to leave the room. He wished he'd been able to finish his sentence. He had wanted to say thank you for caring but he had held his words. He was sure he would have choked on them had they come out.

Chapter Eight

Ben found himself wanting his sister to come back, which surprised him. *Maybe this near death shit is scaring me* he thought. He drifted into a fitful sleep. He dreamed about hiking into the redwood forest then climbing inside his favorite tree.

Ben could hear his sister's voice when he woke. He kept his eyes closed but tried to identify who she was talking to by what she was saying. She was speaking very softly, earnestly dramatizing her words. "It was different for me because I really did want to die. I don't think that Benny does. I went into a psych hospital for a couple weeks after my attempt. I learned a lot about myself, about my addiction. After inpatient treatment for addiction it took me seven months to get off methadone but I did it. I have been drug free ever since. I was nineteen." He waited to hear the listeners response to tell who Arianna was sharing her life story with. He opened his eyes just the slightest bit. He peered between his eyelashes. *Where are they* he thought as he tried to take in the room.

"I think someone is awake," said the doctor, who was standing with Arianna slightly out of Ben's line of sight. He opened his eyes. He tried to seem surprised that they were both there. He acted as if he hadn't heard any of their conversation. "How are you feeling, Ben?" she asked.

Arianna took a couple steps toward the door and started to say she would wait outside when Ben interrupted her with a gesture. He called to her, "you can stay Arianna, I don't care. Please stay. I'm sorry if I was mean before I just didn't expect to see you." He gestured again, holding his hand out to her. "Come sit with me," he said gently. She hesitated but took a few steps. She sat down next to him on the edge of the bed. They looked at the doctor expectantly.

"Ben, you have to decide where you want to go from here and with what medications, okay? Your discharge papers are nearly complete but I need to offer you inpatient treatment based on your admittance for opiate overdose. I think you could benefit greatly by remaining on methadone and staying in medicated assisted treatment," she paused then said, "I can refer you to a therapist. I will give you lists of personal support groups you can choose to attend to help you learn a new lifestyle. It sounds like your sister is also going to be great support. She can help you navigate the lists I will give you. I do need you to consider inpatient treatment. What do you think? It will be up to you to attend therapy and recovery support groups. All up to you."

Ben thought of what his life had been like since his mom left San Diego. He thought of his endless attempts to get high. He thought of his daily desperation that was him just going through life the only way he knew how. He tried to think of a time before heroin, before craving, before pain .. his mind was blank. His empty thoughts caused a mix of dread and hope that Ben hadn't experienced before. He was scared. He looked at Arianna. Her eyes were full of love and caring. He looked at the doctor and saw the same warm, caring look. Tears ran down his face again. "Ok. I will do the inpatient thing if I can tell my job something different, I don't want them to know I am a junkie," he said breathlessly.

"Oh, Benny," said Arianna, "you will see that you are so much more than a junkie!" She bent in sideways for a hug and squeezed him hard for emphasis.

The doctor was silently typing on a keyboard. "We can do a transfer for you to inpatient so there is no break in medication management, okay?" she asked without looking up, then continued, "they can intake you this afternoon, we can send you now. Your methadone prescription will continue as well as my supervision while you are taking it. Remember to take advantage of all the tools that will be offered to you while inpatient but call me if you need to for any reason. You are brave to do this. I commend you." She touched his arm gently. She extended a hand which Ben took gratefully. She shook his hand then walked quietly out of the room.

Ben's tears turned into sobs as Arianna turned to look warmly at him. His shoulders shook as he cried quietly. Arianna handed him a tissue. He blew his nose loudly. He thought of his job and what they would say. He thought of his mom. He knew he really wasn't any better than she was with her drinking and using dope. Shit, now he almost killed someone probably. He surely had almost killed himself. He thought of the night runs. They had been the only good thing in his life. *What about the night runs* he thought *if I don't do them no one will.* He looked at Arianna. *Maybe I can tell her, get her to do them, she would like it.* He started to panic a little, sweat ran down his back. *Maybe I can do treatment for only two weeks so I don't miss a run.* That would be his plan, he decided. He would do a short term treatment so he could still do the monthly smuggling run he had promised his mother he would keep doing. He knew it was too risky to tell Arianna about them, it could jeopardize everything. He thought of his mother. He wondered where she was and what she was doing at the moment. He hadn't wondered about Violet in a long time.

CHAPTER NINE

2016

"Go fuck yourself!" Violet yelled at the passing traffic as she tried to push her cart across Ocean Street. It was Halloween in Santa Cruz. Costumed people were getting in her way as she made her way from the methadone clinic back to Beach Flats. Every day she made it her mission to move along Ocean Street snagging leftovers from garbage bins outside the restaurants. Sometimes the burger place had food order mistakes they gave away if she got there at the right time, which she tried to do daily. It took her nearly three hours to walk the two and a half miles to the clinic and anywhere from three to seven hours to walk back to her sleeping spot.

Violet didn't think about much besides what her body was doing. She didn't think about the future. Or the past. She really didn't think much about the present. She tried hard and long not to think at all.

She had been a thinker for a short time. That had been Marta's fault. The years she spent with Marta were the years when she allowed herself to think, to feel, to be known. She had told Marta everything. Everything about her past, her shitty mothering, her shame, her love of heroin and booze. In return, Marta shared herself with Violet in ways that she never knew she could. She shared her story, her trauma, her heartbreak at losing her son and leaving her daughter in Mexico. She shared and she listened. And she learned. Marta learned things from Violet that became part of her, that could never be unlearned. Violet taught Marta the love of heroin and how to get it in prison. Violet wanted Marta to be able to escape her pain just as she herself did. They had bonded in their thousands of hours together.

Violet

Violet loved Marta. She would have stayed in prison just to stay with Marta but that hadn't been an option. Violet had gotten out six years before Marta was going to be considered for parole even though they had both been sentenced for smuggling the same year. Violet was unable to leave San Diego when they let her out because she was so lost without contact with Marta. She got a job washing dishes at a local restaurant. She tried to bide her time until Marta got out. But Marta didn't get out. She died of a heroin overdose in prison nine months after Violet got out. Violet didn't find out until Marta had been dead for almost a week and then it was only through rumor heard at her dealers house one night. "This shit is good. I heard it killed a bitch at Las Colinas."

Violet had not gotten over Marta's death. In fact, she felt bruised by Marta's death. She started drinking booze. Vodka. And she amped up her dope smoking. She started street walking to pay for it, giving blow jobs for twenty bucks. In four days time after hearing that Marta was gone, she looked like a different person. She couldn't work. She was rejected by her dealer for endless crying for dope. She started rolling around with truck drivers. She headed north toward Santa Cruz without ever saying once that that is where she was going no matter how many times she heard, "Where ya going, honey?".

She had spent nearly ten years in prison. She had then had spent time building a life that included her son. She started making the runs. Then she had lost Marta. Now she existed miserably on the streets. She had returned to Santa Cruz without planning or thought. She missed Ben. She dismissed the thought. She managed to get onto methadone so she didn't have to hustle for heroin but didn't do much else except try to find alcohol every day. Methadone and booze were her buddies now. Ben was the only one who had been around when she got out of Las Colinas Prison. He had understood her need to stay near her friend. And he had stayed with her even after Marta died, when she was at her worst, when she was strung out on heroin and methamphetamine. *He must love me*, she thought to herself, *he is the only person who I miss.* She wasn't able to think about the fact that Ben was eleven years old when she went into Las Colinas Prison.

She thought about Ben and where he might be. He probably didn't have the will to leave his job in San Diego. She knew him well enough to know that he didn't like change much. He had seemed content cooking omelets all day and smoking dope every night. He never shared his dope but Violet knew he was using. She could tell by looking at him. His shoulders slumped downward as if he carried a heavy weight. His eyes never smiled even when his face seemed to… Violet went back to her immediate task of getting where she was going. She tried to dismiss Ben from her mind but an image of him at ten years old hung in her mind.

CHAPTER TEN

Ben was relieved to be in the sun if only for a moment as he left the hospital for inpatient substance dependency treatment. He was officially diagnosed as having Substance Use Disorder. He kept looking for the word … addict … he didn't find it. He said goodbye to Arianna on his way out with a staff member. He asked her not to mention anything to his job. The doctor at the hospital had explained his methadone prescription. He learned how it would work with the local clinic. She also briefly described inpatient treatment. It sounded horrible to Ben but he was committed. He truly wasn't feeling any cravings. None. Not even one. The only time he thought about heroin was when he had to clean his wound and then it was to kick himself in the ass for his stupidity. He was beginning to think about what stopping heroin would mean to him. Yet he was unsure. When the car stopped he wanted to run but instead he stayed. He thought of the warmth he felt from Arianna, from the doctor, and the rest of the hospital staff. It was that warmth that gave him the energy to get out of the car to go into treatment.

He limped into the place behind a staff person who was carrying a clown mask. "I can't wear the mask but I want to put it on inside," he explained. The receptionist, dressed as either a polar bear or a sheep dog, Ben guessed, looked up and smiled. The man put on his mask. He did a little dance in clown-spirit then said, "here we go, folks! Last stop!" Ben smiled. He looked around. They were the only three in the reception area. Halloween decorations adorned the walls. A bowl of candy sat half full on the counter. Ben's stomach groaned. "Go ahead, have some," said the receptionist, "we can't let them go inside so we keep them out here in front of my face. Not good." She laughed, then said, "you must be Ben. We're expecting you." She came out from behind the tall counter she had been sitting behind. She extended a hand to Ben. She said, "welcome, I'm Amber. I'm going to give you a tour. I'll connect you to the right people." She reached behind the counter to grab a pet leash that she attached it to her costume. "No one can tell I'm a sheep dog! I've been called a snowman and a polar bear," she laughed as she explained. "Maybe see you later downtown," she said dismissively to the clown, "if you are down there clowning around!"

"See ya, pup," he said playfully. He took off his mask then turned to Ben. He extended a hand and said, "you are in good hands, Ben."

The two men shook hands. "Thanks," said Ben, "thanks for the ride and everything." He stood awkwardly as Amber adjusted her costume. He kept feeling waves of regret. He would think himself past his thoughts but then they would return when someone asked him a question or otherwise put him on the spot. He kept waiting to feel comfortable but it just wasn't happening. The only stories he heard about drug rehab were not feel-good recovery stories. *Especially for junkies* thought Ben *junkies don't feel good without junk.* His thoughts were interrupted by the receptionist.

"We have some paper work, then a tour and I'll show you your room. Then your medical intake," said Amber. She walked outside the reception area and gestured for Ben to follow her around the outside of the building. "Our place has many entrances. It's more of a complex than a building. You were just in the front entrance," she said as she walked. Ben followed her through another door and up some stairs. "We don't use the elevator much." They were on a landing with a conference table in the center and doors leading out in all directions. "Please sit, I'll be right back," said Amber. She soon returned with a stack of papers that Ben had to read and sign.

Another wave of regret swept over Ben. "Man, this is a lot of stuff. Are you sure my job isn't going to find out I'm here? I'm not signing away my job rights or anything, am I? I have never done this before," said Ben. Amber patiently explained. He realized that his job must know he was in the hospital if the hospital had called them looking for his family. He suspected the hospital called his job because he had no one listed as an emergency contact anywhere. He truly thought he didn't have one and never would have thought to call Arianna. It was getting close to three o'clock. He was getting exhausted. *All of this thinking is wearing me out* he thought.

Together Amber and Ben toured the small facility. At the end of the tour, Ben was left in his room to rest until dinnertime. By this time it was four o'clock so Ben had some time to himself. Or so he thought. The room had two single beds and two matching dressers. There was a chair and ottoman covered with what looked like dozens of packages of ramen noodles and some wadded bedsheets. Just as Ben was getting ready to stretch out on one of the beds the door flew open and two people rushed into the room. They started filling the pillow cases they carried with packages of noodles.

"Oh, hey! Sorry if we startled you," said a guy who seemed to be about the same age as Ben. "We're the ramen fairies! We need more treats to pass out," said one. They were dressed alike with capes made from sheets tied around their throats. They wore hats made from ramen noodle packages. One held a sign that said 'Free Ramen Dust'. "I'm Derek, that's my bed," said the same young man as he pointed to the bed that Ben was sitting on, "you can have it if you want but it will need clean sheets." He smiled at Ben.

Ben stood quickly. "I'm sorry man, I couldn't tell," said Ben. "I'll take the other bed, thanks." He sat on the other bed and tried to appear casual. Feelings of uncertainty and regret swirled inside his mind. *Ramen fairies? Sheep dog? These people are playing, not recovering from drugs* thought Ben. He was at a loss for words. They left the room as abruptly as they had come. Ben was again left alone with his thoughts.

He had almost decided to do this treatment thing back when Marta died and his mom lost her shit. But in the end he switched to using more dope and eventually fentanyl. He started to think about heroin. He could vividly remember the first time he had taken it on the day that his dad and Chase died. *Well I can kind of remember* he thought. He tried to make the memory come to his mind but all that would come to mind were memories of how painful that wasp sting had been and the sight of the balloon of heroin he had found that day. He thought of his dad but the face was blurred in his memory. He could see his dad's back in his minds eye. He pictured his dad striding up the tracks with Chase close behind him. They had almost the same gait and build. Ben had tried so hard that day to be one of them, to be a man, and in the end he was left to be the only man.

He tried to focus his mind on how the dope felt that day but he couldn't remember. The sudden urge *not* to remember that day came over him and he sat up. He stood and started pacing the room. He remembered that was one thing his mother did when she was thinking about something. Pacing. She would pace in the smallest space, just three steps over and over, until she found whatever answer she needed. Usually where to find dope. *Fucking dope* he thought *I will fucking kick this time!* He thought about what it was like to kick dope when he went into lockup. He remembered it had been pretty fucking bad because they wouldn't medicate him at that age. So he had racked up almost nine years without dope. On the day he got out of lockup he thought he wasn't going to use. But then he had lunch with his sister which was when he realized what a judgmental bitch she had become. That day, he decided to use. He sat and fantasized about heroin all through lunch with her that day.

His mind turned back to what it was like to kick dope in lockup. He felt anxious as he thought about his current situation as compared to back then when he kicked dope cold. He sighed and sat back down on the bed. He realized there was four years between that first time he ate heroin and when he had to kick cold like that. *I can do this* he told himself *it's different this time and I am not locked up.* He thought about the day he had been taken to the lockdown in Gilroy. He had been distraught not knowing where his mother was and no one giving him straight answers. He remembered trying to accept that he and his mother were both locked up within a few days of each other. He felt that it was all the fault of that social worker … *what was her name? Rose?* His memory was patchy. He could remember distinctly the feeling of needing to be with his mom. But then, that feeling had been with him for a very long time. Even when he was with her. He drifted into a light sleep with his mind filled with images and memories of his mother. He had so many questions for her.

The door opened abruptly and the roommate burst out, "it's dinnertime! Come on! We're having candy for dessert because it's Halloween!" He seemed excited and left the door gaping behind him before bounding away. Ben stood and tried to remember what he'd been told about dinnertime. He headed out. His stomach gave a roll as he smelled pizza. He followed the aroma and the sound of laughter. He forgot about his mother. He stopped thinking about that time that she went to prison.

CHAPTER ELEVEN

Violet had racked up some bad karma in the year leading up to her years at Las Colinas prison is how she had figured things. She had been ignoring her motherhood status for years. That was probably the thing that she most beat herself up about when she did have moments of lucidity. Thing is she rarely thought about her kids. Especially since Cade and Chase died. After that event her life was a blur. She started back on vodka that same night. The day that they died. It was a lot harder to block out her thoughts since then.

She was home alone that day when a police cruiser pulled up in front of her place. She had been expecting the guys and was starting to really need the dope they were supposed to be bringing. It had been hours. She was dripping with sweat when she heard a knock and got up to open the door. She startled to see a sheriff deputy. "Mrs. Ramsey, your son Ben is at Dominican Hospital. He is okay but we need your consent to speak to him for some information regarding your husband and older son. I can drive you if you need a ride," said the deputy, "I apologize to have to tell you these things. Please let me drive you."

Violet had nothing to say. She wanted to slam the door. Wordlessly, she followed the officer to his car and got in the front seat after he opened the door for her. She had not been in a police car before, certainly not in the front seat. She recoiled at the sight of the rifle mounted in the center of the car. She heard a voice call out numbered codes over the radio. They rode to the station without speaking. So many things ran through Violet's mind on that ride to the but that Cade and Chase were dead was not one of them. "Is this going to take long? I have a stomach ache," Violet asked when they were almost there, then "my husband always does this kind of thing. Can I call him?"

"I'm not sure, ma'am, I hope it doesn't take long. I'm sorry. I don't have details for you," the officer said kindly, "I'll take you back home as soon as possible."

She was led to a hospital room. When she saw Ben sitting with his knees pulled up and his head down her heart began to race. He looked up at her and almost got up to go to her. Almost. Instead he sat quietly with big tears dropping off his chin. "What happened? Why are you here? I thought you were with the guys," she exclaimed. Her mind was fogging as her body started to nag harder for dope. She sat down in a chair by the door as far from Ben as possible. "My back hurts! I can't stand here long," she exclaimed. She wanted to run out of the room and out of the hospital. She began to think she wasn't going to get her fix.

Someone said to Ben, "now that your mom is here we can get you out of here soon, ok? You will have to sleep here tonight. In the morning things will look a lot different. You can see your mom is here to check on you, ok? She will be here in the morning. We need to talk to her for a while right now." Violet looked up at him as new sobs overwhelmed him. He put his head back down onto his knees and cried, "I want dad!" Everyone left to stand in the hall outside Ben's room. The doctor stepped close to Violet.

The doctor began to explain to her why Ben had to stay in the hospital overnight for observation. She thought *so the kid had swallowed some dope!* She remembered the searing anger that washed over her back then when they explained Ben was there for swallowing a balloon of dope. *What the fuck! He swallowed my dope? Fucking Cade* she thought. Her thoughts got stuck on that point. She didn't hear when the doctor moved on to say that Cade had been stabbed and Chase had overdosed. She heard "… he tried to run down the hill carrying your older son but was unable to keep going due to his wound."

"What? I'm sorry. I am so sick. My stomach. What did you say?" Violet's mind cleared some as her anxiety grew. "What do you mean by 'unable to keep going'? What wound?" She started to tremble. She didn't see a wound on Ben. Her stomach started to heave. Someone handed her a plastic basin to vomit into but she managed to swallow and take a deep breath. "I don't feel right," was all she could say.

From that day forward her life was a blur of dope and booze. Booze was easier to get but dope was everywhere, too. Especially when she could run down to Mexicali. She could stay high for weeks after one of those runs. And no matter how fucked up she became she was not sorry she had gone to prison.

Because she had made a friend in prison. And because of that, she worked hard when she got out of Las Colinas to be a good person. She tried to be stable. She had wanted to be available when her friend got out. Back then, she was glad to see that Ben wanted to stay around. In short time, she became dependent on him. He helped her to stay on track waiting for Marta. He got her a job. He tried to help her not use so much fucking dope. Together they started the smuggling runs for Marta. Only one did time they shoot up heroin together. Violet was so ashamed it was almost enough to get her to stop shooting dope. Almost. Now she yearned to see Marta, to talk to her. Her next thought was that she yearned to nod out. She wanted not think about her life. But her mind was strong. Memories impeded her thoughts. In Las Colinas she had managed to find dope a lot but not as much as when she had access to the streets. And she never got to slam in jail. Only to smoke and smoking had long ago ceased to be enough.

Violet had been slamming heroin pretty hard in the weeks before she got arrested. She had been street-walking to trade sexual tricks for dope. Even that was too much for her in the end. But she could still drive. If she could manage to not be sick then she could run down to Mexicali, pick up whatever they wanted her to pick up, and be back home within one day if she managed to find some methamphetamine to use, too, which she always did. She hated feeling amped on meth but it would get her through twenty hours of driving. It was 600 miles from Santa Cruz to Mexicali, Mexico. Violet had made the trip in 24 hours half a dozen times before she got arrested in San Diego. The hardest part was driving the speed limit. Drive too fast and speeding is a problem. Drive to slow and get pulled over for that! So she drove the speed limit. And as long as she didn't have too much black on board (inside her body) then she could maintain speed. But if she shot just a little black she was in danger of having to pull over to nod or sleep or her speed would drift down until other drivers honked angrily at her for slowing their roll. She knew somebody that thought she was doing the right thing one time in pulling over to nap when she was sleepy but had not taken the key out of the ignition. The car was turned off but was parked in front of a residential home. The residents called the cops. The sleeper was groggy when she woke up and didn't pass a roadside sobriety test. She was arrested and charged with driving under the influence even though her car was not running just because they key was in the ignition and she seemed intoxicated. It turned out she was on prescribed medicines.

So Violet did everything she could to not attract cops. She didn't stop to shoot dope but smoked instead so she was less likely to pass out. If she were stopped she planned to say she was headed to or from San Felipe, Mexico. She was sure to always pack a vacation bag. She had an actual San Felipe address to claim as her destination where she had dreamed of staying at the Hotel Chapala. It was a beachside cabana town. She was always friendly and cheerful if asked about her travels at the border crossing kiosk. No one questioned her at the border.

One day during a long run to Mexicali, Violet was drifting into forgetfulness. Maybe even a little complacency. She was forgetting to maintain speed limit. She was forgetting to not text and drive. And she forgot to lower her pipe after taking a particularly long hit. She had been feeling invincible, like she had beat the run because she had crossed the border and made it back into California. She knew soon she would be mainlining dope and would feel really good. Her jones would be gone soon. All of that changed when she heard a voice say, "pull safely to the side of the road, put your hands on the wheel" over a loud speaker. She startled and looked up into her rearview mirror but didn't see anything. For a second she thought she was imagining things. Then a highway patrol car came up beside her and out of her driver's side blindspot. Blue lights flashed. A siren sounded briefly. Violet pulled over. She dropped the pipe. Her hands were immediately drenched in sweat, she could hardly hold onto the steering wheel. Suddenly she had to shit. Her stomach clenched.

The patrol car had parked behind her, blue lights flashing. Violet heard, "stay in your car and keep your hands on the steering wheel" over the loud speaker. Violet sat, sweating and holding her shit. *I'm going to fucking lose it,* she thought. Moments passed. An officer approached the car on the driver side. He said to Violet through the open window, "come out of the car, ma'am, slowly, and stand beside your rear tire. You were driving below the speed limit. You swerved and were not staying in your lane. What are you smoking, ma'am?"

Suddenly Violet felt like she was not only going to shit her pants but that she would throw up, too. She opened the door and tried to stand up but instead emptied her stomach on the ground beside her. She started crying.

"Come out of the car, ma'am," said the officer.

Violet stepped over her puke as she held onto the car and collapsed on the trunk, half standing. It was that one fucking hit, she knew it. She must have slowed down or crossed a line or something.

Fuck, this sucks, Violet thought and almost said. She tried to get her breath and stop crying.

A second officer was snapping on gloves as she approached Violet's car on the passenger side while radioing for a canine unit to assist. Violet could hear only certain words as her mind crowded with the possibilities. *Pipe. Not pot. Dope smoker. Tracks. Canine.* Violet started to panic. She started sweating even more, her stomach tried to eject something but there was nothing left, it heaved anyway. She didn't know where the dope was hidden and she didn't know how much was on board since the connection in Mexicali usually loaded her car while she smoked. She thought of how pissed off everyone would be and her stomach heaved again.

Violet started crying and was unable to answer the cops when they started administering a roadside sobriety test. Violet failed the test. They put her in handcuffs and into a patrol car. Violet hung her head and cried. First she cried for her next hit which she already wanted and knew she wasn't going to get. Then she cried for the punishment she knew she would get from the people who were expecting their dope. Two more patrol cars arrived, one of them a K9 unit with a skilled drug sniffing dog on board. It took the dog less than one minute to indicate something under the car … *not hidden well enough* … Violet was busted. *How the fuck did I get here?* she asked herself *How?*

After Cade and Chase died, Violet had to find ways to get the heroin she needed so desperately for herself. Cade had always been the one to make runs for the shit. Violet started making deals for dope. At first cash deals, then she ran out of cash. She sold everything she had that was worth anything. Then she traded for sex. As time went on she had to make bigger and bigger deals to stay well. She had begun to make runs down to Mexico to make pickups. *That* was how she had gotten to the point of being jailed in San Diego. Until then she had managed to keep Arianna and Ben in her custody by flying under the radar and not getting busted for anything, even for drug possession. The county knew she was a junkie because of her pregnancies but they didn't ever catch her in the act. She felt disturbingly proud of those facts.

She tried to remember where her kids were when she got arrested. Arianna had been sixteen and mostly living with a thirty-year old guy, mostly in his car. Ben was home alone most of the time. He was always bugging her and trying to make sure his mother and sister were safe, especially his mother. Violet kept dope and vodka in the house to wake up to and to put herself out at night. She didn't remember the times Ben had helped her into the shower to wash off her puke or piss.

She had gotten a 10-20 year sentence for smuggling and went to Las Colinas Prison. Back then, she didn't think for a minute about her kids. *Ben was probably at home when child protective services came for him* thought Violet.

Arianna took off right away with her boyfriend and stayed out in the world. Ben hadn't understood why he couldn't just go home and wait for his mom. Instead he was placed by the state into a foster home.

Chapter Twelve

2002

Eleven year old Ben walked away from the beach toward downtown. He knew if he walked fast, acted like he was older and knew where he was going that no one would bother him. And he did know where he was going. To Stephanie's house. He had been told his mom was arrested and he had to stay at a new home. When they got to the new home he didn't like it. He didn't want to stay. All he could think of was smoking a bowl. He looked older for his age with his downturned mouth and constant scowl. He knocked on Stephanie's door.

"Benny, I heard about your mom, hun, I'm so sorry," said Stephanie when she saw him, "but you can't be coming around here without your mom". She let him into her apartment.

He didn't know what to say. He hadn't really heard about his mom except that she wasn't coming back and he had to go live with stuck up fuckers on the other side of town, a place where in his short life he had learned to avoid because of the cruel rich assholes who live there according to his mom.

He asked, "where is she, do you know?" It was all he could think of to say. He looked toward the cabinet where he knew Stephanie kept her drugs.

"Oh honey, you don't know? She went to San Diego. She got pulled over for speeding or something and they found heroin in her car. She will be down there a while, I think. I'm so sorry. I don't know who she was going for, wasn't me," Stephanie answered. She didn't notice the kid was jonesing for a hit of her dope … she lifted a pipe and lit it without thinking. "Oh, shit! You're just a kid, I shouldn't smoke in front of you!" She put the pipe in a drawer and closed it.

"Can I have a hit? I'm sick," he said. He looked at her with a pleading look in his eyes, begging her to see his need and not his age. He sure didn't feel like a kid! He had a rage welling up in him that he had never felt. He reached for the drawer.

Stephanie let out a sort of shriek and opened the drawer for Ben. "Here." She handed him the pipe and the lighter. "It's safe, no fentanyl. I get the test strips from the county to make sure," she said. Then, "shit, there I go talking to you like you are not a kid! How long have you been using, kid? How old are you?"

He took a small drag off the pipe and exhaled slowly. He sat down on the sofa and took another drag. He passed the pipe back to Stephanie. His slight frame folded back into the couch pillows. "I'm eleven," he said, "I think I was eight the first time I smoked black. But I've been seeing it as long as I can remember."

There was a heavy silence in the room. Stephanie was realizing the danger of someone finding her smoking dope with a kid. Especially with a kid who had seen his dad and brother killed and whose mom just got popped for smuggling. She knew Violet was going down for a long time, maybe 20 years, but she didn't tell the kid. She handed him back the pipe. "You can't stay here, kid, I'm sorry, I could get in a lot of trouble!"

Ben was caught between the relief of finally not being sick and rage he felt toward the world, toward his mom, toward this bitch here reminding him he was a kid. He slipped into the comfortable feeling smoking black brought to him, knowing he would soon be suffering again if he didn't get more for later. "Can you just set me up and then I'll leave? Please? If I get sick again I don't know what I'll do. I can't go back to that fucking foster home. Can I stay here just one day?" Ben asked Stephanie in desperation as he realized his situation. He had left the foster home with permission to go walk along the coast for 20 minutes. He had been gone for 30 just now and they might be looking for him but they would never look here. They hadn't even piss-tested him. No one knew he had a drug habit like his mom.

Stephanie got up and walked over to a closet. She took out an old denim jacket and handed it to Ben. "Take this, you'll need it. I can give you a couple bowls and a pipe but if you get caught with it you found it, ok? Don't come back here for more. I know cops watch me. They maybe know your mom is my friend. You should let them put you in detox, get over this shit while you are still a kid."

"I've never been a kid," said Ben. He got up and asked to use the toilet. When he came out, there was a small bag on the table where the pipe had been before. He put on his jacket and tried to think of something to say, anything that would get her to let him stay. Nothing worked.

"I won't tell anyone I saw you except maybe your mom when I see her again. You take care. Remember, I told you to go into to detox. You should," said Stephanie as she moved toward the door.

Ben picked up the bag and looked inside. He took the pipe and small plastic bag of black and put them in his jeans pocket. "Can I take your lighter?" he asked even as he reached for it and put it in his pocket, too.

She opened the door and backed away from him. She could sense he was mad. He looked angry. His face was deep red. His fists were clenched. She forgot that he was a kid. She stepped further away from the door as he passed by her. He didn't notice that she was cowering away from him as he passed. He was as unaware of his menacing demeanor as he was unaware of his rage. And it was full on rage now. There was no break in his feelings like he had when he was around his mother and sister. Then he would get chunks of time where he was worried instead of angry. Now that was a relief he wasn't getting. He was angry and worried at the same time. He didn't know what to do so he headed for his favorite tree. No one would find him there. He started to think about his dad and his brother and the day they had died as he started to walk away from Stephanie's. He walked toward the train tracks that ran beside highway 9. He never walked on the tracks anymore, only on highway 9, ever since his dad and brother died. *Shit* he thought *they will find me on highway 9, I have to walk on the fucking tracks.*

1998

Seven year old Ben followed his dad and brother down the tracks. Up the tracks really, as they trudged away from Santa Cruz and into the forest, up the mountain. Trains ran only in summer or in December, so no train. Ben had seen the train in town. He had longed to go on it or even to wave at the people as it went by. But he had kept his thoughts and his gestures to himself. "Look at them fuckers wave to show us what we don't have," his dad had said as they watched the holiday train go by with all its lights and music and people waving.

Ben jogged some to keep up with the men. His older brother Chase was sixteen but Ben didn't realize that Chase was a kid, too. Chase had a way of acting exactly like his dad when no one else was around and sometimes even when he was. To Ben, Chase was an adult. He thought of himself as an adult, too, even though he was only seven. He didn't feel like a kid. He caught up to Cade and Chase who were just starting to climb up some rocks along a drainage ditch coming down the mountain. Ben couldn't see a trail and so tried to step only where Chase had stepped. He didn't look up or down. They arrived at a small clearing near the top of the ridge and stepped into what seemed like the coolest trail ever to Ben. They walked along for almost fifteen minutes before coming to another small clearing. Two tents stood at either side of the cleared space. The tents were camouflaged and not easy to spot, they were set up to face away from the trail and there was no sign of people.

Cade gave a low whistle and said "It's me, Cady, and my boys."

They heard a rustle in one of the tents. "Send the kid to play," they heard from inside.

"Go," Cade said to Ben. Ben stood for a moment not knowing what to do. Cade pointed and said, "Chase show him the swing and tell him to stay there."

Chase said to Ben, "come on stupid, I knew you would be a pain in the ass!" He walked across the clearing to the other tent and around to the front. Chase clearly knew the place. A tire swing hung in front of the second tent and there were kids toys about. There was a sandbox half full of weeds. Some plastic shovels were left neglected on the ground. "You heard him" said Chase, "stay here." Then he walked back the way he had come.

Ben stood and fought back tears. He felt like a man just a moment ago. Now he felt like a little kid who wanted to go home. He looked at the grubby tire swing as it hung still in the shaded sunlight. The tire was hung high and he wasn't tall enough to see if there was anything in it before he reached up to get a hold of it. He heard a snapping sound as his fingers curled into the inner ridge of the tire. He felt his fingers break into something sharp. Ben let go and landed on the ground hard, almost falling and crying out. Wasps began to fly out of the tire. He had broken a wasp nest! He felt a sting to his neck near his collarbone. This time he did scream out it hurt so bad!

"What the fuck?" he could hear voices along with footsteps crashing through the low brush. "Shut up!" said Chase as he came around the tent.

Ben could only gesture at the swing as it swung toward Chase and then his neck as tears poured down his face. He held both hands to his neck where he'd been stung. He stifled cries.

"Oh fuck!" said Chase, "come on!" He began to run back along the side of the tent and into the clearing. He tried to outrun the wasps. "Shut the fuck up," he hissed at Ben. Chase knew his dad would be angry if they didn't be quiet. No one was supposed to be living here and the only neighbors were also there illegally. No noise means no cops. If neighbors hear noise they come to shut you up. Chase waited for Ben at the entrance to the other tent, low voices could be heard from inside.

"Shhhh. What the fuck?" and "Don't bring the kid in here!" … then, "Nevermind! Come on! Zip it! Don't let that wasp in!" Ben was pushed out of the way as a woman launched herself toward the tent entrance. She zipped the tent closed as a lone wasp got caught in the screen.

"Bees in the swing," was all Ben could manage to say. He clutched at his neck. His tears had stopped but his chest still heaved with sobs. He tried to catch his breath. "I'm sorry."

Cade ignored Ben and gestured to Chase to sit with Ben. Chase sat on the floor next to Ben but continued to look toward the table next to the woman who had zipped the tent. The table was littered with trash. Cigarette butts. Candy wrappers. Piled in the center were little black plastic balls, homemade it looked like to Ben, about the size of a marble. Ben thought they were candy. Cade picked some of them up and put them in his coat pocket.

Chase groaned. "I thought we were going to do one," he said to Cade.

"Not in front of the kid," said Cade.

"Why the fuck not? Mom does!" said Chase, "she's even had him cook for her when she was shaking for booze. I bet he has shot her up! Haven't you Benny? Given mom her medicine?"

Ben looked at his dad and then quickly looked at the ground. He could feel his face getting hot. He wasn't supposed to tell anyone, especially dad.

"Figure it out and get out," said the woman flatly.

"Go sit in the corner Benny, face the wall," said Cade. He turned to the table and reached into his pocket as Ben sat and scooted into the corner of the dirty tent. He spotted one of those home-made marbles and scooped it up in his little hand. He stuck it in his hoodie pocket.

But then he had to clutch his neck and hold his breath, sucking in big breaths every few seconds. No one offered him anything to help with the stinging pain. He hoped with everything he had that they could leave soon and that the wasps weren't waiting outside to attack them all when they left. After all, he had destroyed their home. He deserved this, didn't he? He had to pee. He started to wiggle back and forth on his knees. Finally he said, "I gotta pee."

"Hold on," said Cade from behind him. There was a moment of suspended silence before Cade let out a breath with a groan. He untied the tourniquet on his arm and sank back onto the floor. Ben could hear him trying not to puke. He heard a lighter spark and knew that Chase was now cooking, getting his shot ready to use. Ben wiggled some more and pinched his crotch. He was sure he was going to let loose and pee his pants. His sobs of pain welled up and he cried out. "Shit!" said Cade to Chase, "hurry the fuck up! The kid is going to cry again," to Ben he said,"go outside and pee and stay away from the fucking wasp nests!"

Ben stayed where he sat. He had already forgotten there may be wasps outside waiting to sting him again for destroying their nest. Cade kicked at him, hitting the side of Ben's thigh. He got up and tried to stand still but couldn't he had to pee so bad. He turned toward the door just as Chase managed to empty a syringe into his arm. Chase groaned and fell back with a loud thud. Ben unzipped the tent and stepped out while waving his hand in front of his face to ward off wasps. He took three steps as he pushed down his pants … he peed, trying to aim away from the tent.

"Fuck, Cady, one kid peeing on my tent and one kid passed out! You need to get out of here. Nick has been looking for you," said the woman. Ben could hear a slapping sound.

"Get up! Shit don't do this shit! Get the fuck up!" Cade was saying to Chase. Cade tried to lift him but the teen was too heavy, he was man-sized, almost bigger than Cade was himself.

Ben could hear voices below or beside or somewhere, he couldn't tell where they were coming from. Just then, two men rounded the corner. They stepped into the clearing, seeing Ben. Ben stumbled backward and tripped over the tent behind him. He heard the tent zipper. His dad came out with Chase in his arms. He stopped when he saw the two men. He put Chase down on the ground in front of the tent. The woman came out, too, her arms up and her eyes squinting in the sunshine, *she looks like a wicked witch afraid of melting*, thought Ben.

One of the men reached into his jacket, his hand hidden from view. "Where ya been, Cady? I've been looking for you," said the man closest to Ben. Ben held back a cry as the man swatted him on the head and said, "Run kid. Get out of here." Ben ran. He didn't even think to ask his dad. He ran as fast as he could go.

He ran around the tent to the clearing. He found the rock strewn gully they had climbed up. He made his way down to the tracks, slipping and scraping his way down without looking back. He started crying, soaking his shirt. He held his stinging neck as he walked fast along the train tracks, afraid and unsure of what to do. He knew he was headed in the right direction because he was walking downhill. It had been an uphill climb following his dad and Chase. He would never forget trying to jog along uphill to keep up with the men.

Ben felt like he had been walking a long, long time. He rounded a bend and suddenly he was at a cross-street. He stopped walking. A sob escaped his chest and he started to cry again. His neck hurt so bad. His hand slipped into his pocket. He felt the little plastic ball he had picked up off the floor of the tent. So this is medicine, he thought, he put it in his mouth and swallowed it. Medicine to help with the pain.

Just then, a woman dressed in a uniform crossed a sidewalk near Ben. She noticed him. She noticed that he was probably around six years old, was crying, and he looked scared. "Hi there. I'm Judy, I drive a city bus, see my name tag? Are you ok? That looks like a nasty sting! What's your name?" she said to Ben.

"Ben," he sobbed. "I got stung by a wasp!" he added. He tried to stop crying. He wiped his face with his shirt.

"Who are you with? Can I call someone for you?" asked the bus driver as she squatted down to get a better look at Ben's wasp sting. "You are very brave for not screaming! I would be screaming if I had a sting like that. How about I call your mom or a medic to come help us get you where you need to be safely, ok?"

She must not have seen Ben wince at the thought of anyone coming, especially his mom. She stood up. Cade and Chase had not come down the mountain behind Ben. He was getting scared that his mom was going to be really angry if they all didn't get back there with her medicine. He knew that's why they had gone to the camp, to get mom and everybody more medicine, they always told him that when they left. He had seen his mom take her medicine many times. She always said she felt better after. Well, now he needed medicine, forgetting that he had already swallowed the bag of medicine he had found. He didn't know what to do. The bus driver started talking again and he realized she was talking on her phone. He took off running down the tracks and away from her as she called to him, "wait!"

He ran until he couldn't catch his breath but that wasn't very far. He was sure the woman would call the cops on him. He slowed to a walk and came to a clump of trees growing beside the tracks. There were people gathered and walking about, talking and smoking. Ben tried to be as quiet and small as possible and walk quickly by but he was too slow. His stomach heaved and he felt sick.

"Hey kid where's your momma?" someone called out to him. He started to run again and seconds later came to another street crossing the tracks. Ben stepped off the tracks and onto the sidewalk. Just then, a police cruiser pulled up next to him and two officers quickly got out. Ben tried to bolt away but one of the officers caught him with her arm around his waist.

"Hey! Hold on! I just have questions and really don't want to have to hold you, okay? We want to keep you safe. I'm going to let go of you. If you just stand right there I promise not to grab you again," the officer said as she loosened her grip. The other officer had moved to a position to block Ben if he tried to turn and run. Ben struggled against the officer's arm as she loosened her grip. He bent reflexively and emptied his stomach on the ground in front of the officers and then promptly passed out into the officer's arms.

Officers Harris and Andrade had never seen a seven year old kid passed out on dope but they sure knew the signs of an overdose. And they could see the broken remnant of the heroin balloon the kid had heaved up. Officer Harris radioed for an ambulance as Officer Andrade pulled out a nasal overdose reversal kit and emptied part of into Ben's nostril. "Possible overdose," he heard Officer Harris say into her shoulder radio, "kid looks about six."

Eleven year old Ben stopped thinking about that day that seemed so long ago as he approached the tracks and started walking up toward the forest, toward his tree. It had been four years since that day and he was a different person now. He was a man. Fatigue washed over him and he longed to be sleeping in the darkness of the tree. He felt the pipe in his pocket. He also felt the folded jack-knife he had brought that he sometimes used for burning the little pieces of smack he stole from his mother and sister. They hadn't found the knife in his sock when they picked him up from Button Street and plunked him in the foster home. He sat down on a rail to smoke.

Suddenly, he heard rustling in the bushes nearby. Then a grunt. Someone said, "I see the kid!" The bushes parted, a police officer stepped onto the tracks and said, "he's on the tracks just ahead!" He said to Ben, "hey kid! You aren't in trouble, ok? I want to help you." Ben stood up to run just as two more police officers emerged from the side of the tracks to surround him. He slid the knife into his pants pocket before they spotted it but one of the officers saw him put the pipe in his jacket. All three officers approached Ben. One of them said, "how about we all walk back to the road together. We can talk in the car. We have a social worker with us who can help you a lot." The officer put her arm around Ben and helped him to his feet. "What are you smoking? I need to have that pipe I saw you with, ok? Even if you were an adult I would want to have it, I think you were smoking an illegal substance, right? How about if you hand it over and I won't search you." Ben thought of his knife. He reached into his jacket and took out the pipe. He wanted to light it so bad. He handed it to the officer and let her lead him down the embankment to the roadside.

Ben started to cry. It wasn't that he felt like a baby that needed to cry. He was pissed! He was so pissed he could only think of how mad he was that his mom was not around. "Where is my mom?" he wailed. He sobbed and tried to hold back his tears. "I don't want to live anywhere but on Button Street with my mom!" Angry tears burned down his pale cheeks.

In the moment, Ben kept the memory going. He had never let himself think of those days ... the day his dad died. He sank back into the comfort of being pain free and thought of the day his mother had gone to prison.

CHAPTER THIRTEEN

A police car came to his house one afternoon, he was playing outside. An officer explained to Ben that there was information about his mom and he needed to come talk to the police. They told him he was not in trouble. Ben hesitated to get into the police car. An officer stood waiting by the open door. A woman seated in the backseat got out of the cruiser to stand beside Ben. The three officers surrounded Ben loosely so, in case he took off, one of them could catch him. Ben recognized the woman from the past when he went to talk to her with his mom after his dad and brother died.

"Hi Ben. Remember me? It's Terry Rose. I helped your family through some stuff years ago. It's been a long time! How old are you now? Twelve?" said the woman lightly. She knew he was eleven but was hoping to engage him in talking about himself and not thinking about his shitty situation. It was shitty in her opinion. Everyone thought he had seen the murder of his dad and brother years ago (she knew he hadn't) but he had been with them the day they died. He had been seven years old then. Most of the town had since treated the kid like an invalid as if his dad and father dying had disabled him physically. Now she had to explain to the kid that his mom was going to prison and she was going to be there for a long time. She didn't want to tell him while standing beside the road in case he bolted so she appealed to the kid in Ben. "How about we go talk for a while and get something to eat? I can explain what happened to your mom. I can help you get settled into your new temporary place. It is temporary Ben. No one is happy that your mom is gone right now, ok? Get in. Let's go eat," Terry said as she gestured toward the still open car door. Ben got into the backseat of the police car. He slid across the seat so Terry could sit beside him. She got in, closed the door, and smiled warmly at Ben.

Ben started sweating. He dreaded that he was going to be sick soon. He thought of eating a burger and his stomach groaned loudly. *If I could just get a drag off that pipe* he thought, he knew it hadn't been spent, he hadn't smoked it all. Just then the driver's door opened and an officer got in and started the cruiser. "Terry we have a one thirteen- fifty here, horse. I thought you should know," said the officer before she put the car into gear.

One thirteen- fifty thought Terry. Drugs. She knew horse was old school slang for heroin. Terry understood the officer was telling her the kid was found with heroin. *Fucking asshole mother* thought Terry angrily. She rejected her thoughts. She tried to find compassion for this kid and his family, especially his mom. Everyone was silent as they rode toward the police station.

Terry broke the silence when she reminded the officer to stop so the kid could eat. Terry and Ben went into a restaurant and got a table in the front on the glass-walled patio where two officers stationed out front could see them. Terry waited to tell Ben what she knew of Violet's arrest. She hoped to give the kid a few minutes of peace to eat before she delivered such horrible news. She wondered how long the kid had been into heroin and if he would be craving to use it. She wondered if Violet knew her kid was using drugs.

Four bites into his burger, Ben got up suddenly and said, "oh, man! I have to poop!" He looked around the patio for the restroom as if he had never been in the place. Just then a server came by and pointed into the back of the restaurant. Ben left the patio and went into the restaurant. He went into the bathroom and locked the door. He peed because he had to go bad but then he zipped up his jeans. He didn't have to poop. Instead, he left the restroom and exited the restaurant through the back door. He had expected to see police outside so he walked out with a family of four as they went through the door. He walked as if he were with them. *Can't fucking fool me* thought Ben as he took off running away from the social worker, away from the cops. He ran toward the beach. He ran until he had to stop and puke beside the music store. He climbed up onto the river levee still heading toward the coast. *They won't even look for me on the beach* Ben thought as he headed toward West Cliff Drive and the west side of town.

Ben had the overwhelming feeling of wanting to go home. He wasn't sure what he was going to do. He ran through town and practically right past the police station but no one noticed him. His strategy was working. He reached Depot Park and stopped briefly on the tracks to see if he saw anyone who knew his mom. He didn't. The only people there were two guys holding cans of beer. Ben could smell the beer. He ran on toward West Cliff Drive and didn't stop until he reached the top of the hill. He could see the surfer statue ahead in the distance that his mom used to park across the street from when she went to pray. His gut heaved and he bent over to puke up what was left in his stomach. He started to cry hot silent tears. He reached into his pocket without thinking and held his knife loosely as he walked along trying to hold back his sobs. He wanted to smoke so bad it was all he could think about. He wasn't sure where to go but kind of remembered his mom coming to the end of West Cliff Drive somewhere and buying some smoke out of a big motorhome. Ben had been made to wait outside in the rain. He wasn't even allowed to wait in the car that night because his mom's friend Jessica had come with them and she was in the car "earning dope" his mom had said.

He finally reached the surfer statue and stopped to rest behind it. He remembered his mom always said she thought it was stupid the statue faced the road instead of the waves like a real surfer would. Ben looked up at the back of the statue and thought about his mom.

Burning range welled up in his chest and rolled through his brain. He was starting to feel dope-sick. Thoughts of finding some dope dominated his mind. He started to walk again along West Cliff Drive, slipping between people as he walked. He thought he spotted the social worker in the crowd coming toward him. *Fucking bitch! How did she find me?* he thought *I'm not going with her anywhere.* He headed straight for her. She seemed to be looking past him like she didn't see him. He was confused, angry, and scared as she passed him. *She is trying to trick me!* Ben thought as he grabbed the back of her jacket. He swung around and drove his knife into her back so she couldn't follow him or take him. She screamed. Ben could hear more screams. He could feel hot tears on his cheeks and chin. He jabbed at her again but his knife handle snapped and the blade wouldn't go through her thick canvas jacket. She turned to look at him as she wrenched at her jacket that was still clutched in Ben's hand. It was then that Ben looked into her eyes and realized that it wasn't the social worker like he had thought. He dropped the knife and tried to run. Two men stepped in front of him and two men stepped behind him. The crowd had responded quickly to the terrified screams of the assaulted woman. She cried out toward him where he was cornered, "What did you do? Whhhhy?" She reached into her jacket and felt her lower back, she pulled out her bloody hand. He looked at her again, at her face. His mind flashed … *it wasn't her … not the bitch social worker coming after me* … he heard sirens and stopped struggling. Soon he was handcuffed and guided to the back door of the police cruiser. The officer opened the door and gestured to Ben to get in. Ben, defeated and sick, climbed into the car alone and started to shake with huge heart-rending sobs.

Ben hadn't remembered the stabbing directly afterward. He remembered his anger. He could remember people blocking his way. Big people. Big men. Someone had said to him in the heat of that moment, "you aren't going anywhere you little fucker." The phrase played in his mind as he sat in the police car sobbing. They can't make me go back there he thought I will leave again.

But they didn't drive him to the house on the west side. They drove him up into the mountains to a locked facility. "This is for your safety, Ben," they told him, "and for the safety of everyone else." That is when he had to kick cold from dope. That very day. He was eleven.

The scent of pizza brought Ben to the present. He tried to stop thinking of his past. He joined in the Halloween festivities at dinnertime in rehab. He stopped thinking about those events in his life but thoughts of his mother kept invading his mind.

Chapter Fourteen

2016

Violet had never meant to be arrested and thus leave Ben. As he sat crying in the back of the police cruiser thinking about his mom, she was trying to accept that she had been arrested with twenty pounds of heroin in a false bottom panel attached to the bottom of her car. *Twenty fucking pounds* thought Violet *I will never get past this! Oh my fucking God what am I going to do?* Her empty stomach groaned loudly. She had been sick since they put her in the back of the car. She knew she was going to go through some hell real soon. Her mind raced with thoughts of doom. *Probably thirty grand worth of dope, they will hurt me bad! Guess I will be kicking cold. Oh fuck, just let me die!* She didn't think about Ben. Or Arianna. She started to sweat. Her stomach clenched in her gut tightly. She couldn't catch her breath as she sobbed. She started to rock in her seat against her hands that were cuffed behind her. *I can't breath* was her last thought as she slipped into unconsciousness.

She woke to the sound of the cruiser door opening. She sat for a minute before opening her eyes *what happened?* she asked herself. Then she remembered. She was in some deep shit. Her stomach revolted. She started gagging and coughing. "Come on out," said an officer. Violet climbed out of the police car. She tried to stand up straight but her stomach kept reeling. Her head hurt. She had a craving for dope stronger than she had ever had. She felt like she wanted to curl up and die right there on the sidewalk.

Two guards stepped up to either side of Violet. They led her into a long hallway. "You are at processing. You will be able to rest in your bunk soon," said one of the officers. They took her clothing, searched her body, had her pee into a cup, and issued inmate clothing to her. "I am really sick," Violet said weakly. She followed their directions as best she could but cried the whole time, hot tears running down her face and neck. Her stomach stopped heaving but remained in a constant state of queasiness. She had no appetite and increasing anxiety. She picked and chewed at her fingernails. "Will I get to see a doctor? I need medicine," Violet said as she followed a guard down the long hallway. Just then they entered a small room that was clearly a medical office. There was a low padded table covered in paper and a blood pressure machine in the center of the room. Locked cabinets lined the walls.

"Yes, in fact a nurse is going to intake you right now," said the guard, "she will be here soon." The guard gestured for Violet to sit on the low table. Violet sat. They waited in silence. Violet didn't see a clock or calendar. There was no computer in sight. Time seemed to stand still except for Violet's nagging craving for dope. A woman came in and introduced herself as a county nurse.

"My name is Nancy," said the nurse, "I'm your go-to while you are here no matter how long you are here. If you get into a jam and you need help tell any guard that you need to see Nancy. Now tell me, how are you physically? Is there anything I need to know to help you? Is this your first time in jail?"

Violet let out a sob. When she tried to talk her words were jumbled. Her mind was reeling faster than her mouth could form words. "Yes, first time," she said, "I'm hurting. I'm sick I need my medicine bad. My back hurts so bad and my stomach, too."

"Are you on medication for back pain? I didn't find a prescription in the system or in your belongings. I see that your urine is positive for heroin," said the nurse. Heavy silence hung in the air. Nancy started examining Violet by looking into her ears. "Stick out your tongue," she said, then asked with a kind voice, "Are you pregnant or on birth control?"

"I don't think so," was all Violet could think of to say. She didn't know if she were pregnant or if the implant she had in her arm from years ago was still effective. She vaguely remembered the sex she had participated in as part of the smuggling deal she had been busted for so, yeah, maybe she was pregnant. She was pretty sure her body ejected more than one baby in the last five years. She would go three months without a period and then bleed huge dark, thick globs.

"Your urine says you're not pregnant. You don't know if you are on birth control?" asked the nurse. She listened attentively as Violet relayed her story. Then came the question Violet had been dreading, the nurse asked her gently, "How long has it been since you last had heroin? Do you normally use it every day? Do you have cravings? Do you drink alcohol?"

Violet was surprised by the gentle kindness in the nurse's voice and was able to collect her thoughts and answer. "I haven't had a drink in a couple days. I don't know how long I was asleep in the back of the car but it feels like its been a long fucking time since. I'm sorry to cuss, its a habit I can't control much when I'm sick. Can you help me? My back hurts, too, really bad."

"I can't start you on anything without the doctor ordering it, I'm sorry hun. The only thing I can get an immediate temporary order for is a shot which may help with your withdrawal. You will have to see the doctor about your back pain. I'll make you an appointment for as soon as possible but it will likely be about three weeks. If you are still here. Sometimes people don't stay long," explained the nurse. She turned toward Violet. "I'm going to give you a shot now that should help your cravings while you are here," she said, then, "if you will be here longer than three weeks then you will get a shot every month until you no longer need it. It will be up to you if you stay on it but it will make life for you here a small bit easier."

Oh I am fucked thought Violet. All she could do was nod slightly as the nurse crossed the room. She unlocked a cabinet to prepare Violet's shot. Violet quietly obeyed as she was told to stand, turn, and lean onto the padded table which the nurse was raising. She felt the needle enter her hip and she did indeed feel immediately better. Her stomach stopped clenching. But there was no rush. No payoff. No nodding out. She simply didn't crave dope anymore. She also didn't have any back pain but she had been lying about that anyway. She knew her chances of getting medicine increased if she could convince the doctor that she truly had pain. She suspected she would be here for a long time because she had been caught with so much dope. Her mind raced even as it wanted to shut down. A guard entered and escorted Violet to yet another processing point. It was well after dinnertime when Violet finally got to lay down to rest.

In two months time at the county jail, Violet was charged and tried for heroin smuggling. In that time she was able to avoid shots and mostly kick dope except for what she could find inside. And she did find dope inside the jail. She had made contact with the people she had been smuggling for and she knew she was off the hook for the lost dope. They knew she was going down for a long time. She didn't seem to get that. When she stood in court before the judge for sentencing she thought they were going to let her go or at least ship her to Santa Cruz. But they didn't. Instead, she was sentenced to serve ten to twenty years time at Las Colinas Prison. Her knees almost buckled when she heard the sentence.

On the day of her transfer, she traded what few belongings she had collected while at the jail for some black. She managed to chase most of it. She put the rest under her fingernails. But she must have chased a bit too much because Violet didn't remember the ride to the prison.

She came to consciousness once she had already arrived at Las Colinas Prison. She started to take in details of the place. She was one of four women being led into a big hallway not unlike the one at the jail. But this hallway had iron bars blocking passage at each doorway. It somehow seemed more permanent, more formidable to Violet. The other three women were as quiet as Violet as she carefully made eye contact with each of them. She could see desperation in their eyes and could smell their fear in their sweat as it ran down their necks and backs. She swallowed dryly. She hadn't seen any of them at the county jail. Two guards walked the four women into a room with a long table loaded with sets of supplies for each woman. Clothing, slippers, hygiene kits, and a small folded booklet of expectations and rules.

Violet thought about how much she wanted to smoke and started feeling anxious. *Will I get dope here?* she thought and almost asked aloud. She had heard maybe she could get methadone in prison. She had stopped accepting shots at the jail because it made her sick to use heroin if she was on that stuff. Vivitrol. But she could do those things on methadone. Sometimes she even got a little nod from methadone if the dose was high enough. *They won't give a fuck if I need medicine* she told herself *its a good thing I have some dope under my fingernails, I can eat it if I can't chase it.* The fingernails of her ring and pinky fingers on her left hand looked like they were caked with black dirt. But it wasn't dirt. It was dope. It was thick, dirty, sticky dope and Violet would eat off her fingernails to get to it if she had to. She intended to get inside and find someone with a pipe so she could swap to make connections. Her life had become in-the-moment, survival thinking in a short time and she didn't really know it nor think that she could change it.

She moved through the intake process quietly. She signed her signature when handed a pen, picked up her pile of supplies, and lined up to the left of an iron door as she was led. The four women, the new inmates, followed the guards to their assigned cells silently as current inmates looked on. Hissing, whistling, and edgy voices called out to the new inmates ... "holla" ... "new kitties in the box" ... "I wanna pet you kitty" ... "I can protect you little pussy" ... "here, kitty kitty." Violet shivered. She followed along even faster trying to push the woman in front of her to go faster, too. But there was nowhere to go except forward and then only as fast as the guards would go. The procession stopped. The women were separated into two cells. Each cell had an upper and lower bunk, a sink, and a toilet.

Violet could only nod at her cellmate. She was stunned into silence by the sheer volume of the experience that walking into prison had been. She sat on the lower bunk without thinking that it would be a sign that she was choosing that bunk, it seemed the only place to sit. The other woman quickly climbed up onto the top bunk where Violet could not see her. Violet could hear her stifled sobs. Anxiety welled up in Violet's mind as she thought of sleeping with a stranger above her. Tears came to her eyes. She struggled to hold them back. She wasn't going to cave in and be a fucking wimp here. Her children never crossed her mind.

Chapter Fifteen

Violet woke at 3 am to the sound of her cellmate using the toilet. She stayed still in her bunk for a moment trying to orient herself to the sound. She remembered where she was but she couldn't get a grasp of time. *Is it morning yet?* she asked herself *I doubt I was asleep long.* She heard a rustle. She felt a whoosh of air as her cellmate climbed back up onto her bunk then was still. Violet wanted to cry but she didn't. She held her tears like she had learned to do when she was little. She felt exactly the same lying in her jail bunk as she did when she was hiding in her mom's house trying not to be noticed by any of the people, especially the men, who were constantly coming through her childhood. She felt the pressure of a sob in her throat just above her heart. She felt it in her head right between the eyes.

She looked at her two dirty fingernails and thought about scraping the dope out from under one of them. *I could eat it* she thought, then *but I know I won't feel it. Just fucking wait, fucking dumb junkie.* It was at these times when Violet hated herself the most. Her mind replayed these thoughts as she sniffed at her two filthy, junky fingernails. Her mind turned to thoughts of her own children. Chase had been dead for five years. Violet couldn't remember much of his seventeen year life. She had avoided him as much as she could because he was as abusive to her as his father had been. The attention she had paid to her girl was sparse. Violet knew Arianna to be a drug addicted thief who only wanted to take from Violet. And then there was Ben. Violet tried to remember anything about Ben and what had been his childhood.

Her thoughts were interrupted by rustling from her cellmate in the bunk above. She heard a sob. The sob she herself had been holding back suddenly dissipated as a new feeling overcame Violet. She realized she felt sorry for her cellmate who couldn't hold back her heartbreaking sobs. She sat up in bed, pulled her knees up and wrapped her arms around her legs. This had always been the way she would sit to hide. She could put her forehead on her knees and ignore the world around her. She tried to ignore the strange new feeling she had. She didn't want to feel anything. She was hoping her cellmate would just shut the fuck up. The woman didn't look like a violent bitch, no tattoos, but Violet couldn't tell by looking if her new cellmate was dangerous. Violet said nothing. She sat quietly wrapped up, hugging herself. She drifted into a fitful sleep laced with dreams of shooting heroin, chasing the dragon and running from some unknown terror. She was still sitting up when she woke drenched in sweat. She tried to sense the time but heard nothing from the place around her. *Must still be nighttime* she thought as she stretched out. She drifted back to sleep. There was no sound from her cellmate. She stayed asleep through the night.

Noise erupted suddenly around Violet as morning at the prison started violently with a loud, mind-jarring alarm designed to awaken even the most sound sleepers. Words and groans combined with the sound of toilets flushing echoed in the cell. Violet got up to pee. When she turned around to sit down she saw her cell mate staring wide eyed from her top bunk. The woman looked away quickly, "I'm sorry" she said faintly. Violet sat and tried to relax but just could't let go of her pee no matter how full she felt. A guard walked by and yelled out in general, "ten minutes, ladies! Ten minutes til go time!" Violet finally was able to release her bladder. The smell of piss filled the space. Violet stood. She started to pace the room. She tried to be ready for go time. She turned away from her cell mate as the woman climbed down to sit on the toilet. Violet heard the sound of pissing just as another alarm sounded. The cell doors slid open with a huge clang.

The two women, Violet and her new cell mate, stood still in their cell looking at each other with wide, unblinking eyes. "I'm Vee," said Violet, "what's your name?" "Marta." Violet heard just as they were ushered out of their cell and down a long hallway to the showers. They followed the actions of other inmates. They showered with watery soap dispensed out of the wall. Everything was either built into the wall or attached to it with giant bolts. There were no shower curtains. There was no privacy. Women scrubbed at their bodies in various ways. They also seemed to be carefully watching their backs and the backs of friends. The same jeers they heard when walking in could be heard floating through the steam … "here, kitty kitty" … and "sweet pussy meat" … wafted to their ears. Vee and Marta didn't speak. They followed the routines of the other inmates and tried to stay close to each other throughout the day. It was as if they had an unspoken agreement to stick together. It was after dinner and cleaning up in the kitchen that the two women were again alone in their cell.

"Thank you!" Marta said breathlessly. She started to sob and tried to stop. "I feel like you saved me today so many times! I don't know how to thank you!"

Violet began to pace the cell. Walking back and forth seemed to calm her racing thoughts. She had been scared all day. She had relied on Marta to be there without demand. And Marta had been there. She hadn't realized Marta was also relying on her. No one who had relied on Violet in the past had been satisfied or grateful. She always let everyone down is how she felt. She was feeling a new feeling now, a rush of kindness for this woman she had just been thrown into a relationship with. *What a fucked up way to make a friend* she thought. "Look. I'm not gay. Let's get that straight right away. This is my first time in and you are right here so I stuck with you today. Don't read it wrong. You don't look like a dyke to me. But if you are don't tell me cause it will just ruin what we have started," she said as sternly as she could. She sounded more consoling than stern though and that is what mattered to Marta.

"I promise I'm not a gay! I was married and have kids," said Marta defensively, then added "a kid." It had not occurred to Marta that her cellmate would worry about her being a threat. So much else had been wrong about the last few days for her. She had been arrested for smuggling. Not only arrested, but she had been arrested, tried, and sentenced to a long sentence at Las Colinas in the span of four days. She was told she was fast-tracked for sentencing because it was not clear if she was a United States citizen. She was understood to be a citizen of Mexico who had been caught smuggling in the United States. She was trying hard not to cry constantly. She choked back a sob as she climbed onto her bunk. She had never been arrested before. In her heart she felt defeated but in her mind she was glad she hadn't been arrested in Mexico or sent back there for punishment.

Violet sat on the floor and leaned against the wall, pulling her knees up. She looked up at Marta and asked, "where are you from? Do you live in San Diego?" She remained as calm and friendly as possible and avoided the questions she really wanted to ask … What are you here for? … What kind of monster are you? … Can you see that I am a monster, too?

"Me, I don't live anywhere. I drift. I am always looking for my daughter. We got separated when she was very young. I am endlessly trying to find her. Mi hija. Mi chica," said Marta. "I was from Mexico. Sinaloa. But my search brought me here to California so here I am. It is being arrested for smuggling that has stalled my search. I had to smuggle to make money. And to maybe find my girl. I try to search the markets for her. Sex markets." Marta stopped. Her chest welled up and she sobbed. "I will not find her in here! Eh, mi hija! Mi corazón aplastado! My heart crushes!"

Violet put her forehead on her knees and tried to will away the world but it wasn't working this time. She thought about the sticky goo that the dope under her fingernails had become and realized that true, she wouldn't feel it if she ate it. *But I can feel it if I snort it* she thought. She could dilute it with water to snort it. She would offer some to her new friend. Then Marta could get some relief from her anxious thoughts and Violet could, too. *I can get more* thought Violet. She scooped her hand to catch water from the sink and started soak her fingertips in the small puddle she held in her palm. She stood up and held her hand to her nostril holding one side closed she took a sniff of the dirty looking liquid. She coughed a little but held her hand cupped toward Marta even as she felt the slight rush from the dope. *Strong* she thought *oh so fucking good.* "Here, sniff this," she said gently, "it will help you get to sleep and feel better. I snuck it in today." Marta bent her head and sniffed at Violet's palm. Nothing happened. "Close one side of your nose and sniff in really hard," said Violet. Violet dropped her hand when Marta was done and sat down on her bunk below Marta. In many ways both women changed in that instant and were never quite the same.

Marta laid back on her bunk and sighed softly. "Ah mi! What is that? I have not had cocaine before! I like it!" she said quietly to Violet who she could no longer see. Of course, she had to be there! *She must be asleep* thought Marta. She was grateful for one thing on this terrible day. Vee. She let a few minutes pass before trying again to talk to Violet but, getting no response, she herself drifted to sleep. She dreamed of Mexico. Of Sinaloa. She dreamed of her daughter. Her dreams filled with images of her child following her around the yard and house as she took care of her little family. She woke in the night thinking of them. She thought of her husband and her son and knew she would not see them again. But, *one day,* she told herself, *I will see my Martina again.* She laid in her bunk until the clamor of the prison brought her face to face with another day. She wondered if Vee would offer her more cocaine, not knowing that it had been heroin.

CHAPTER SIXTEEN

In the years that followed, Violet and Marta spent many hours talking quietly in their cell. It was late at night that Marta learned of Violet's terrible childhood and bad marriage. Late at night Violet taught Marta to chase the dragon. It was late at night that Violet heard stories of Marta's homeland and her love of Mexico. But Marta was always reserved. She didn't talk much about what had gotten her into prison. Violet only knew Marta had been charged with smuggling. She had learned that Marta was naive about drugs. Marta had not tried drugs before Violet introduced her. It was a long standing joke between them about Marta's first time and her thinking she was trying cocaine. She said she thought so only because Violet had her snort it and Marta thought only cocaine could be snorted. One night Violet connected her thoughts and asked Marta, "if you didn't do drugs, Marti, why were you smuggling? Did someone make you do it? Was it for money? For me, it was to get dope." Violet knew that Marta referred to her daughter Martina as "Marti" and she used the name for Marta only when she was feeling especially loving toward her friend. "What happened to you?" she asked Marta with a soft kindness in her voice.

Violet sensed without knowing that Marta needed to unburden herself of her story. They were six years into their sentence. Marta finally let loose. She told Violet everything, even the hard-to-hear details. She thought Violet would lose respect for her. She was sure of it. She was sure than any person would lose respect for a mother that let her child be killed. And one taken. She had gotten involved in smuggling trying to find her child amongst hard, mean criminals.

Criminals who stole children to trade them for money. Or they kept the children to sell their bodies for sex. Her child would be sixteen now. Marta ached to see her and to know she was alive. She prayed Martina had escaped being killed by smugglers. She had kept her silence because her story had been too painful for her to tell. She had only told Violet how much she ached to see her daughter. Violet had not pressed her to talk because either she was callous and uncaring or she simply didn't want to make her only friend uncomfortable. Marta had lived with it for too long and needed to talk about her life, about her daughter.

"Eh, carina, you may think different of me after I tell you my story," said Marta. It had occurred to Marta that she had felt differently about Vee when she figured out what a cold and neglectful mother Vee had been to her three kids. But she loved her anyway.

"You can tell me anything, Marti, and I will love you anyway. Even if you tell me you are gay and want to fuck me!" said Violet in attempt to lighten the conversation. She sat up in her bunk. She pulled her knees in close sensing she would need a hug during this story.

Marta began telling her story by saying, "I don't know how this is going to come out so don't ask questions. I'm going to tell it like it comes to me so I'm sorry. In my country it is different than here. In Mexico there are bad law officers who do not stop bad men from intruding on good people who live simple lives." She paused. "Please don't ever tell this story to anyone or me and my daughter will be in danger. I don't know where she is or if she is alive, you already know that. What you don't know is how I lost her. I thank you for not asking me. I am not sure I can bear to say the story now but I want to try. It is so heavy. If I tell you maybe it will be lighter in my heart. I will be able to go on hoping to see mi chica again, I miss her too much. My heart is broken."

Violet put her forehead on her knees but instead of trying to tune out the world she tuned in to the sound of Marta's voice. She listened carefully as Marta opened her heart and life to her only friend.

"I was 14 when I met my husband, he was 14, too. He was traveling through Mexico from Nicaragua on his way to the United States to find his mother. When he passed through Sinaloa we met. We fell in love. It broke my family's heart when I got pregnant before they even knew I had an interest in boys. I was still 14 when I had Carlos. He was my oldest child and only son. He was my firstborn which is important in my culture and in my husband's culture. Miguel, Carlos' father, stayed in Sinaloa and tried to build a life with me and our new baby. He gave up the quest to find his mother. But it was hard for a man from somewhere else to make a living in Sinaloa. Then we had another baby, our Martina. My husband could hardly earn anything tending fields. That is what he was doing the day that a trio of ugly men came to our house. Miguel and Carlos were plowing the ground together in the field neighboring our house. Carlos was seventeen. I was in our house with mi chica when I heard a gunshot." She paused here and began to sob lightly. Violet knew the sound of Marta's sobs well. She waited patiently for Marta to return to her story.

"I looked toward the field in time to see my son crumpled on the ground. One of the men held his hand up toward my kneeling husband and I heard another shot. My husband fell. He also laid on the ground not moving. I screamed," she paused for a long time, "I wish I had been silent."

Marta didn't need to tell Violet why she wished she had been silent. She could sense Marta needed to finish telling her story so she again waited quietly. She cleared her throat softly so Marta would know she hadn't fallen asleep.

"The men came toward me so fast I didn't have time to run! They were on me like dogs in heat. I didn't resist. I didn't," she sobbed,"because I thought if they finished fast enough they would leave before they found Martina playing in the backyard. I prayed she wouldn't come inside the house and see these two dogs raping me. But she must have heard their cries of lust. I looked up to see her face. Her brown eyes open wide. She was crying. That is the last time I saw her. I was hit in the back of the head. I lost my thoughts! They knocked me unconscious then left me for dead. They took Martina. Mi chica! They took her." She stopped talking. Her breathing was heavy and labored. She paused her story, sobbing softly.

"I am sorry I could not tell you, Vee, I am scared you will not understand what I had to do next," she continued so faintly that Violet almost did not hear the words, "I started meeting those very same men or men like them. I approached them to buy and sell children." She sobbed openly for a moment before explaining, "I thought if I could become a child seller then I could find my girl. You see, Mexican police do nothing for people like me. Especially in Sinaloa. I found out she had been taken to Mexicali but then I lost the trail. I went to Mexicali. I worked myself into a position amongst child sellers who were bringing kids across the Mexican border into the United States. I got arrested on my first run." Her sobs continued.

Violet stayed quiet. She stood next to the bunks and put her hand on Marta's shaking shoulder. The kindness and compassion that she felt as she let her friend's story sink into her mind filled her with a warmth she had never felt. She knew Marta to be so stable and sweet. She was never upset. Violet wanted to scoop Marta into a hug. She wanted to tell her everything would be okay. But everything was not okay. Six years had passed since Marta had been able to search for her girl. Marta still didn't know if Martina were alive or dead.

CHAPTER SEVENTEEN

Martina was very much alive. And she did remember her mother. She remembered her laugh. She remembered her smiling face. She longed for her mother's hugs. She wanted to hear her laughter and kind the words that she remembered her mother saying. What she couldn't have known was that her mother lived right there in San Diego County just like she herself did. As Martina was living and growing and longing for her mother's hugs, her mother was living close by and was thinking of her constantly.

Martina had memories of her mother that were mostly pleasant. But lately when she thought of her mother she thought of her mother's tortured and crying face from the last time she had seen her. And so she tried not to think of her mother because it would make her cry. When she thought of the day she was taken from her mother she could only remember pieces of the experience. She remembered hearing noise come form the house that she had not heard before. She remembered her mother's face. But she could hardly recall the face of her father. Her brother was only a distant memory fragment.

She remembered what it was like to arrive at Colonel Lopez's home because Señora Lopez had been so kind. Martina had been so scared of the colonel. She hadn't understood why she had to leave her brother, father and mother. Her mind returned to that troubled time … *Did she have a brother? Where is my family? I want to go home but don't know where home is* she thought.

Even after years of living in a stable home in San Diego Martina was sometimes overwhelmed with a childlike desire to go home. She knew she did have a home. She had a safe place to be. She had people who loved her. But she still wanted to see her mother and to feel her hugs. She threw herself into her studies. She vowed to become a strong worker for human rights. She shuddered at the thought of the day she had been made to leave Señora Lopez to come to the United States. The memory was easier for Martina to recall than the first tragedy- the day she was made to leave her family.

She tried again to recall her feelings. She remembered the backyard where she was playing that day. She had made a fort in a sandbox with a sheet and some sticks. She was very proud of her work. She remembered dancing with her dad and brother on the hard dirt beside the sandbox that morning before the men started working in the field. She remembered the music her mother played on the radio for them to dance. She tried to remember more of her mother but the memories were fleeting. Instead she thought of Señora Lopez. It was her face that Martina kept seeing. Señora Lopez had always been calm, she never raised her voice. She never showed any sign of weakness or fatigue. The five years Martina lived with Señora Lopez were blurred in Martina's mind. She remembered the long days working to exhaustion. She spent all her time with, and was ordered around by, Señora Lopez's daughter Marcia. Marcia was always strict and mean to Martina. She resented that she had to care for "mami's naco", as she referred to Martina. Marcia did everything she could to make Martina's life hard. But Martina was resilient. She was patient and strong. She worked hard. So hard that no one could say she didn't, no one ever caught her idle.

The men who took Martina from her home that day were looking for teenage girls to sell or trade for drugs. They didn't want to take a girl so young as seven years but they had to bring something to be traded so they took Martina. They traded her in Mexicali. It happened that a colonel needed a house maid at the same time Martina was just arriving in the city. When her kidnappers attempted to sell her the colonel's wife heard of the girl and thought one so young could be trained properly to do her bidding as a house maid. Señora Lopez was right. Martina's days were spent doing endless amounts of polishing floors for the first months. Gradually she became more trusted in the house and was allowed to do laundry which meant not being on her knees all day. She was known to obey and complete all her assigned tasks. She anticipated Marcia's commands. By the time she was ten Martina was going to the markets on her own with open ended return time. She became an expert at quickly choosing what she needed in the markets. She discovered the value of time as she began to explore the city.

Martina had come to expect that she was going to always live with Señora Lopez. It was in her nature to make the best of her situation, a trait Martina had inherited from her mother. No one talked to her of school or education but she had an appetite for knowledge that soon led her to the city's libraries. The library closest to her home was her favorite and the one she went to the most. It was her favorite because it was not only a library but also the Instituto Nacional de Antropología E Historia. Martina spent many days visiting the library. She most loved to study how people lived in many different cultures. She always sought to read how different cultures value their children. She didn't know until she was much older that she had been trying to make sense of her own life. Trying to understand why her life had changed so much so fast on that last day she had seen her mother.

In time, Martina became complacent about returning to Señora Lopez's. She began to stay out in the city longer as if she herself were Marcia Lopez and could do as she pleased. She had begun to think more about her family and her mother. She wanted to search for answers. It was on one particularly emotional day for Martina that her life once again changed.

She had been reading at the library about the bonds that form between mothers and daughters across cultures. She had just turned thirteen but was not told about her birthday because no one around knew when she had been born. Menstruation had come late and she had only recently learned about that. No one had warned her it would happen. The image of Marcia smirking when she cried out in distress to find blood on her dress was burned into Martina's memory. As much knowledge as she gained at the library, she was ignorant to the path that was directly in front of her.

One day, Martina was startled to see Marcia on the sidewalk outside the library when she came out. She had thought no one knew she was going to the library. She stopped walking. Marcia looked at her with a chilling smile, her teeth bared like fangs. Martina shivered. Marcia turned to yell toward a car parked nearby, "ahí está ella! There she is!"

Marcia Lopez had known since Martina arrived that Martina would be discarded when she became a woman. She had seen it happen to other girls before Martina. She had overheard conversations between her mother and father about the usefulness of women. Marcia had learned to bide her time and wait until the day came when blood started to flow.

Señora Lopez emerged form the car. She advanced toward Martina with targeted malice. She grabbed her by the elbow and seemed to hiss at her, "entrar! Get in!" As she pulled Martina toward the open car door. Martina was thrown into the backset. The door slammed shut. Señora Lopez had not followed her into the car. The car started to roll. Martina thought to look at the driver. A dark haired man sat behind the wheel staring wordlessly ahead. He drove quickly away from the library. She twisted in her seat to see out the back window to watch Señora Lopez and Marcia embracing as she was driven away from them. *Wait!* She wanted to yell *I won't go to the library again! I promise! I'm sorry!*" But she was unable to yell. She could only choke on sobs that welled up from her chest. She started to scream. She tried to open the car door. Her cries grew louder when she realized it was locked. The driver ignored her wails. They pulled into an open garage and the door lowered behind the car. Martina's panic increased as she was cut off from the sunlight. Darkness descended about her like a blanket she could touch. Lights suddenly came on. She struggled to find her way out just as the car door opened. She was pulled out of the car.

She was thrust from her kidnapper's grasp into the back of a van. Three other girls were already in the van filling the small space with their crying. Not one word was said. Martina was stunned into silence. She could only sob quietly as she stared at her shoes. There were no windows in the van. No door handles. There was slit the size of a small book in the front of the space where they sat, captured. The van started moving. The girls' crying took on a whine. The stink of urine and sweat filled the air as fear manifested in their bodies uncontrollably. They hadn't been rolling for long when the van stopped. Knocking and thumping sounded on the side of the van. The girls grew quiet. Except for Martina.

Martina let out a scream for help that nearly deafened the ears of the girl next to her. "Ayuadame! Help me!" she screamed, "Ayuda!" She didn't stop screaming until the van door opened and sunlight poured into the back of the vehicle.

A loud voice proclaimed, "you are safely in the United States of America. We are here to help you." The girls were ushered out of the van. They were led into the waiting arms of individuals with blankets. Martina was warmly welcomed into a new country.

Martina did not return to Señora Lopez. Instead she found herself in the custody and compassionate care of The Coalition to Abolish Slavery and Trafficking, lovingly called CAST. Martina was placed in a family home outside San Diego, California to await reunion with her parents. She had not known her last name nor did she witness the murders of her brother and father and so she thought them still alive. She had lived in Sinaloa "sinnylowa" she remembered. She also remembered her mother's screams each time she relayed her story to her social worker and then to her foster family. She longed to see her mother.

Soon she was enrolled into local public school. She began classes in speaking English. Language came easily to Martina and she was soon caught up with her contemporaries. Still no one was able to locate her mother, father, or brother. Four years passed. Martina thrived in the family environment. She loved school. When she was seventeen she was contacted by the Mexican State of Sinaloa-they had finally sent confirmation that her father and brother were dead. *Maybe I will seek their story someday* she told herself, then *now I have more room in my heart for hope to find mami.* When she turned eighteen she made a vow to herself to spend her life working toward helping children reunite with their parents. She graduated high school and enrolled in college. She set her sights on achieving a degree in cultural anthropology. She wanted to find answers to questions she didn't know she had.

What Martina also could not have known was that her mother never stopped looking for her. It could be that she and her mother brushed arms on the busy streets of Mexicali when they were both there. Maybe one day on the way to the library she had walked beside her without knowing. She could sense deep in her thinking and heart that her mother loved her very much. She was busy in school and was nearing the end of her third year in college when thoughts of her mother started to arrive constantly in her mind. She asked herself *why am I thinking of my mother so much? I should be thinking about earning money for school.* Marta wondered if her mother were thinking of her, too, at that very moment.

CHAPTER EIGHTEEN

Marta sat alone is prison and could only think of Martina. She allowed her mind to fill with memories from the days when Martina was hers. She longed to hold her and smell her hair. She wanted to hug her so close that they became one person. Then she would never miss seeing her again. Violet had been released from Las Colinas, she had been gone for two months. No one had been assigned to share her cell. Marta was glad. In the time since Violet's release she had been finding and using heroin more every day. She knew Violet would be really angry so she didn't tell her anything about it in her long letters she wrote and sent daily. And because Violet wrote back daily it was almost as if they had a conversation going but it was so lonely for Marta. She could barely get through her daily duties. Twice she came close to losing her coveted kitchen position due to her apathy. She just didn't have any energy to put into her day.

Violet had been the one to keep Marta going. Violet would remind her often that she would one day see Martina again. Together they would talk for hours to plan their scheme for finding and rescuing her from traffickers. Now it seemed they wouldn't get to execute their search because Marta was still locked up. Her mind ran in circles *... how am I still locked up? I need to find my girl ... only seven years left to my sentence ... will they let me go like they did Vee? Please God ... I need to hold my girl ... why can't I? Please God ...*

She soon learned that smoking dope brought her the only relief she could get from her loneliness and rumination. She could smoke some dope then nod out for hours. Vee had called her a lightweight.

She had advised Marta not to use dope but she just had to get relief from her relentless thinking. Vee had described to her the danger of smoking alone. Vee told her about fentanyl and to never, ever use it under any circumstance because it could kill her. Vee had even told her that she wouldn't know if her dope was laced with fentanyl in attempt to scare Marta away from dope altogether. But it didn't work. Marta had started to use daily and stopped caring if she survived or not. She had given up hope on being released. She had come to believe that she would not see her daughter again and that her daughter must hate her, the mother who let her be taken. This thought, that her only daughter must hate her, filled her mind as she crouched down in a corner of her cell one night to smoke some dope. She had a tiny chunk of black, a piece of foil and three matches.

Martina shook off the feeling of sadness that had lately descended upon her usually cheerful thoughts as she got ready for her first shift at her new job. She had worked and held many voluntary positions that taught her a lot but it was time for her to earn some money to support her dream to go to graduate school. She had never thought she would work as a waitress but everyone she knew told her it was the best way to make cash. She found a job she could walk to so she wouldn't have to ride buses like she did to get to school. Besides, no buses ran at five in the morning which is when her shift started at the restaurant. She had agreed to work early morning until noon so that she could have time to get to school. She locked up the small room she rented and headed to work.

The restaurant seemed barely lit as she arrived. Then she saw someone moving inside. A light came on just as motion sensor lights lit up the front door where she stood. A man looked at from inside and she smiled. She waved. He continued his task and ignored Martina. She sighed. *He must think I'm a pushy customer* she thought *not a new employee.* She knocked on the glass door. He walked out of sight.

Moments later someone came running up the side of the restaurant startling Martina out of her bewilderment. She screamed a little before recognizing this was the man she had seen through the restaurant window.

"Hey! Sorry to scare you," he said, "we don't open the front door until six sharp. You must be the new waitress? I'm Ben. I cook." He started walking back the way he'd come. "I'll show you to the back door, come on. Employees almost always use the back door."

Martina followed Ben into the restaurant. She tried to apologize for distracting him from his job but he dismissed her. "No problems here," he explained, "Tracy is usually late. She will be the one training you I think. Have you worked in a restaurant before?"

"I haven't. This is my first restaurant job," Martina answered, then asked, "Have you been here long? Do you like it?" She joined him in the task of cracking eggs into a large bucket. Her natural ability to help others whatever the task at hand put him at ease.

"I like it here, sure. The team is tight. I like that there are only eight hours of the day we are open to the public," he paused, then exclaimed with a laugh, "I crack eggs all day! I crack twelve dozen on weekdays and twenty five dozen on Saturday and Sunday. I am the King of Cracking! I like your technique, by the way, you have already passed me with your two handed cracking."

Martina was taking an egg in each hand and cracking them simultaneously on the counter then opening them into the bucket. It seemed to impress Ben that she could crack an egg in one hand. She smiled and shrugged. "I have cracked eggs more times than I can say," she explained, "I learned when I was very young."

Just then a woman entered the back door. She was clearly in a hurry. She was out of breath and rushing. "Oh shit. I forgot about you," she said to Martina, "give me a minute." She walked out of sight.

"You will get used to Tracy," said Ben, "she is always in a hurry.

She's been here for a long time. She will get you up and running. I bet she will have you taking tables by the end of today. You can ask me anything. Anytime." He smiled and started to whisk the raw eggs as they finished cracking them. "You increased my cracking potential! Please join me in cracking again soon! Next show tomorrow morning at four thirty." He lifted the bucket of eggs and retreated to the giant cooler as Tracy came into the kitchen.

"Ok! Let the show begin," Tracy exclaimed cheerfully. She handed Martina an apron, a small pad of paper and a pen. "Take notes if you want to. Have you done this work before? We hardly ever have positions open but Dolly had to quit so I guess you got lucky. Dolly is coming back but it will be months. Are you planning on staying here a long time? Why us?"

"I love the food here. Plus I live across the street," answered Martina. Just then a harsh knock happened on the window near where they were standing. Martina was startled. She hadn't noticed anyone outside but now she could see what looked like a woman knocking sharply on the glass.

"Oh shit! That's Ben's mom," said Tracy. She went quickly to the door. She opened it a crack. She hissed through the crack, "go away Violet. Come back in forty minutes and I'll give you breakfast. I didn't even start coffee yet. We have a new girl. No more knocking! Go!" The woman stomped away slowly, gazing open-mouthed at Martina through the window. She seemed very old but Martina couldn't explain that. Her appearance put her at around sixty but her demeanor indicated a much older person. Her shoulders slumped. Her greying hair hung limply to her waist, some of it caught in a zipper. She seemed to take each step with huge effort. Tracy said to Martina, "She worked here for a couple of months but then she started drinking at work, couldn't stop. Crying all the time. Ben used to be close to her. They were even working on some Save the Kids project.

He got her the job here. Then she had some friend die. She flipped out. I give her food if she shows up here before we open. Come on I'll show you how to get the place up and running." The rest of the day was spent teaching Martina the tricks of the restaurant trade. In the end Martina especially liked three things about her first day … she liked rushing around while acting like she was not in a hurry, she liked talking to customers, and she very much liked Ben.

Ben had liked meeting Martina. He had been cautious lately in trying not to become interested in anyone. Everyone in his life told him to stay away from relationships. For the first time he had some sobriety racked up. He had been feeling tenuous about his status lately. He found himself questioning everything. He had stayed on methadone after his hospital stay. He had managed to stay away from heroin. His leg wound was healed. He was back at work full time. He tried hard to connect with what everyone called the recovery community but he was having trouble. He felt he could never truly share his feelings. He was still taking methadone which made him feel like he wasn't really drug free.

He was down to twelve milligrams of methadone daily. He liked the counselor he had to see at the clinic once per month. He was learning a lot. He was going to group support meetings every week. Sometimes twice or three times if he was off work which was usually only on Tuesdays. He didn't want to end up like his mother. So he stayed sober. He worked hard at changing.

Then he met Martina. Something about Martina triggered a deeper sense of being alive in Ben. From the moment he saw her in front of the restaurant that dark morning when he had been expecting to see his mother, he knew Martina was unique. He found himself hanging out around her just to hear her talk. He fell in love with her smile. He tried to earn that smile as much as he could.

Throughout the day Martina smiled easily at Ben. She beamed when she looked at him with her eyes wide. She found herself learning from him even more than from Tracy. By the end of that first day, as Ben had predicted, Martina was waiting tables on her own. Soon Ben and Martina were dating. They started routinely opening the restaurant together six days a week. Violet didn't show up at the restaurant anymore, she had disappeared.

Ben had been tapering down his methadone dose with a goal of stopping altogether. He wanted to tell Martina about it. He felt that telling her would probably help him be accountable for his behavior. But he still couldn't tell her. He didn't want her to see him as weak. That's how methadone made him feel. Weak. As if he wore liquid handcuffs. He had to submit to the dose or else he would suffer. He had told Martina so many things. He told her about Violet. He told her about Violet's long prison stay and her loss of mental health after her friend died. He mentioned he was glad she hadn't come around begging from him lately. He told her about his dad and brother. He told her the tragic story of his being locked up for years. But he hadn't told her about his addiction. Or about the night runs. He was so torn about what to share with her. He sensed she might understand why he was doing these things he had to do to survive but he didn't want to worry her. She was working hard in school. He knew she kept a lot of stress to herself.

Martina recently shared with him that she wanted to move to Santa Cruz before he had the chance to tell her he planned to never go there again. She knew he had been born there but didn't really understand how hard it was for him to consider living there because she didn't know about his drug use. His former drug use. And his current use of methadone. He felt confused. He consulted with his counselor at the methadone clinic to outline a plan to taper off methadone. Ben wanted to be done with methadone clinics forever. He reasoned if he could return to Santa Cruz without having to use anything, not even methadone, then he could maybe be the partner that Martina deserved. But what would he do about the night runs? His only choice was to tell Martina about them. He hoped she could help him figure out what to do. He hadn't been able to tell Arianna about them when he was just going into treatment. He was still on his own in making sure the runs happened. And they had to happen.

Night fell as Ben and Martina finished their take-out dinner in Martina's rented room. Martina could tell Ben was tense. He didn't want to sit. He kept changing the subject away from any questions she had. Ben's vague explanation about why he had to go away for the evening hung in the air. He told he he had to pick up important cargo that had to be moved. Which was true. He had no explanation as to why he had to go out so late. He couldn't bring himself to lie to Martina. He longed to tell her what he was doing and his stress was written all over his behavior so to speak.

"Look," he said solemnly, "I have to tell you some things, ok? Let's walk. Can we walk? It's easier for me to talk if we walk." He put on his jacket. He held a sweater out to Martina. She put it on and followed him out of the house. Ben walked past his parked truck to the street. He turned to look at Martina. "I have to tell you some things, Marti, I'm sorry to have not told you before now," he started to explain, then "if you can't forgive me I understand but I think you know what kind of person I am. I would never hurt anyone, especially a child." He put his arm around her. He started walking again pulling her close.

"You are starting to worry me, Benny! You can tell me anything, please," Martina exclaimed as she stopped walking. "Why are we out here? Let's go back to the house," she said.

"I have to be somewhere at ten tonight. I want to tell you about it. I think you will understand but I'm not sure. Honestly, Marti, there is a chance you won't like what I have to say," explained Ben. "We're right here at the restaurant. I have my keys. It's eight thirty.

Let's go in and sit for a few minutes, okay?" He had the door open before Martina could answer. She followed him into the restaurant. They headed to the back of the place to sat in the kitchen out of sight from the windows.

"Back when my mom was in prison she met a woman who had been convicted of smuggling kids. Hold on," Ben said as Martina stood. She turned away from him. She stood with her back to him. "These were kids being smuggled into the United States to be reunited with their mothers. With their families because the kids had been taken from their families. They were sold into slavery as house maids, field workers, and even as sex slaves," he paused, "when my mother got out of prison she told me the story of her friend. She told me how her friend got caught smuggling while looking for her own daughter who had been taken. My mother made contacts when she got out of prison trying to find her friend's daughter. She started to bring kids into the restaurant to eat and then drop them off with people who tried to find the families." He stood and stepped to stand behind Martina. He put his hands on her shoulders and turned her body so that she was facing him. He looked into her loving eyes. He went on, "I continue to do the work after my mother could not continue," he paused again, his gaze beseeching her to understand and to love him still, "each week I bring at least one child from the border to a drop place nearby here. Often, there are more than one. Sometimes it is a family of five. I never know until I get to the pickup spot." He stopped talking.

Martina let out a wail. She started sobbing. "Oh, Benny," she exclaimed, "I love you so much! My heart breaks for these kids! You know I am in college to become someone who helps people. What I haven't told you is that I want to work with the very kids you describe. I was one, Benny, one of those kids." She collapsed against him, sobbing. "I was taken from my mother and family when I was seven and made to work in a private home until I was twelve. I was on my way to being sold when I was rescued and put into foster care."

Ben breathed in the scent of Martina's hair as he embraced her tightly. A sense of relief washed over him as she melted against him. "I met the people I do this for through my mom. They swear secrecy because they operate underground in Mexico, Guatemala, Honduras and other places where it would be dangerous for rescue groups to operate openly," Ben explained. "I have a pick up tonight. Do you want to come with me? It might be very emotional for you, maybe you should consider that before answering." He pulled back from her. Once again looked into her loving eyes and, yes, the love was still there. He was suddenly thrilled. He hugged her close and said, "come with me, Marti, and I will come with you to Santa Cruz!"

Martina pulled away from Ben, startled. She had recently been bracing herself for the changes that grad school would bring. She had learned through Ben's few stories about his childhood in Santa Cruz that he seemed to have lost his love of the place. She was planning to go up there and stay four days a week to complete grad school and commute to be with Ben the rest of the week. She nodded. "Yes," she said, "I'll go."

The night seemed especially dark when they rolled up to a locked gate in Ben's truck a few minutes later. It was not yet ten o'clock so they had a little time. Ben was unsure what his colleagues would think of him having a companion but he was willing to take the risk. As much as he needed to keep these runs going he needed to pass it on to someone else so he could leave the area. He was reasoning, and taking a huge chance, that letting Martina in on this would help his colleagues find other connections. If his colleagues were to meet the people who rescued Martina, Ben believed, they could help even more children reunite with their families. Martina had a lot of contacts.

"Wait here," said Ben. He got out of the truck to unlock the gate. He rolled it open wide. He returned to the truck and drove it through leaving it open behind them. They drove into an open warehouse bay door that started to close behind them.

Martina felt a wave of panic as memories of being sold flooded her thoughts when she heard the door raise. Seeing the door was not what alarmed her. It was the noise of it raising. She stiffened in her seat. She remembered who she was with and calmed herself. She knew she was safe with Ben. She didn't scream as she had back then. Back then, she had screamed to save her own life and now she was silent to save the lives of others. She stayed in her seat.

Ben knocked on the side door of a white van parked in front of the truck. Martina saw what looked like a grown woman get out of the door. She left it open for Ben. Ben turned to gesture for Martina to come. He waved one hand at her as he held onto the side of the van door. He put a foot up getting ready to climb in. Martina had no time to think. She got out of Bens's truck and followed Ben into the van. He slid the door shut and climbed into the driver's seat before Martina could focus her eyes in the dark van interior. Ben started the van and drove out of the warehouse into the night.

Ben drove for twenty minutes then pulled into the garage of a modest home. Martina looked at Ben. "Stay here," he said. He got out and opened the sliding door to let everyone out. Martina watched as Ben led them into what looked like a comfortable house. He was back in the van moments later. Martina met Ben's eyes and said quietly, "thank you." They rode back to Ben's car in silence.

CHAPTER NINETEEN

In the time since he overdosed, Ben had come to understand life in a new way. His own mortality hung foremost in his mind these days along with newly found compassion for other people. He was a naturally kind person but was deeply impacted. He couldn't easily reach out to people. He hadn't been able to stay at inpatient treatment for more than a week. But he had picked up the tools he needed to get started fixing his life while he was there. He had new understanding of his own accountability and that changed his life in ways that made it possible for him to be a boyfriend to Martina. Now he was considering being much more than a boyfriend. He knew if they went to Santa Cruz together that they would become family and it scared the shit out of him. But he had learned how to handle his fear. He thought of his friend and mentor who he had made in treatment. Now they were friends who liked to have semantical arguments about words. Words like *sponsor. Sobriety.* And *friendship.* He wondered what Jack would say about his moving to Santa Cruz ...

Ben had met Jack at his first ever recovery support group meeting while in treatment. It turned out that inpatient treatment meant having meeting after meeting about choice making and how to make better choices. Plus a lot of talk about what Ben learned to call recovery. To Ben it was simple. Admit mistakes. Find strength to make different choices. Be accountable for your choices, apologize for past mistakes. Do your best to learn from mistakes, set solid examples for people, especially loved ones. In that first meeting Jack had pegged Ben as someone who wouldn't be around long so he had reached out pragmatically.

"I know you don't want to be here," said Jack to Ben directly after that first meeting. They were standing in the room where the meeting had just ended. The meeting had been jovial and almost silly because of the Halloween costumes people wore. After the meeting, Ben was unsure of where to go and was standing by the coffee looking for sugar. He could only see non-sugar sweeteners which seemed to increase his craving for sugar. "Here," said Jack, "suck on this, it will help." He handed Jack a cough drop. Cherry. Ben opened it and put it in his mouth. Menthol burned Ben's sinus as he sucked.

The two men were silent as the remaining people left the room. Jack broke the silence by asking, "do you want another one?" He handed another cough drop to Ben. "Keep it for later. I'm going to be here tonight until eleven but am not back for a couple of days," Jack paused, "I'll write down my phone number so you can call me if you need to even if you aren't here when I get back." He sat quietly for a moment. When he started talking again it was if he had known Ben for a long time. He spoke with compassion, telling Ben his story. "I've been working here for six years. I grew up with one parent who was addicted to heroin. I've always thought if I had a mom maybe life would have been different. But then I hear all the stories from people with moms, so go figure. Hearing people's stories- about their lives, not their drinking and drugging stories- helped me to see that I wasn't alone as I felt down in my deepest self. Thing is, I still do feel alone in this world," he paused.

"I first took heroin when I was ten," continued Jack, "trying to follow in my father's footsteps I guess. I ended up streetwalking, hustling tricks. Shooting up five, ten times a day. Lucky for me I got stopped in my tracks before fentanyl came around or I would likely be dead." Jack stood and started to clean the room as he continued, "I got stopped in my tracks when I found my father with my girl-friend together in bed one night. They had overdosed. I can't forget the gray color of their faces."

Ben absorbed the story. He wasn't sure why Jack was telling him these things but he sat and listened anyway. He sensed it was important to his success. He was stunned by Jack's revelations. He felt guilty about wanting to know more. "That's terrible," was all he could think to say.

Jack continued, fast forwarding his story, "something happened in me that day when I stood so close to death. I kicked cold. Well, I made a kick kit. I'm not supposed to bring those up but I am thinking you know all about that? You have been close to death. Maybe time for you to kick? Can I ask you about your methadone?" Jack asked.

"I'm trying to taper off but it is fucking hard," exclaimed Ben, "I'm down to twelve milligrams. I have tried kicking cold but never made it. Especially off methadone. I thought maybe being in here would help me. But I hear it takes a longer time to kick off methadone. Can we go outside?" He stood and folded his chair, adding to the chairs Jack had folded and put along the wall.

"Sure, let's go," said Jack as he led Ben out a side door into a small fenced space with two wooden picnic tables. "I know what you are going through right now," said Jack, "because I had the same feelings about being here. Stick around for a few days. Learn as much as you can. Maybe you will come to enjoy groups. I didn't." He stood to moved away from Ben's smoking cigarette. "But I did learn to make better decisions. I changed the things I did everyday. Most importantly, I didn't use heroin. You will kick off methadone I bet. Like I said, stick around a few days," he started to leave the room, "we should go. Thanks for listening to my story."

"I am going to stay," said Ben as he followed Jack out of the room, "as long as I can." He avoided the Halloween party going on in the common area. He went to his room. He was relieved that his roommate was not there. He climbed into his bed. He pulled his knees up and hugged himself. He let his tears flow. He cried because he was ashamed. Ashamed of himself for being a junkie. Then he cried for heroin. He wanted to run from the place. He wanted to go find some dope. Instead he thought of the kindness he had felt when at the hospital and also since being here. He stretched out on the bed. He buried his face into the pillow until he fell into an uneasy sleep. He was aware when his roommate came in because of the rustle of noodle packages. He slept through anyway until being gently prodded awake the next morning.

By the time Ben saw Jack again three days later he was a lot more comfortable with the routines at the facility. Ben also knew he was going to leave. Jack had been right about Ben not being the kind of person who could stay inpatient for nearly a month as the program prescribed. Ben had resolved not to use heroin. He had made a plan to exit treatment and change his ways. He set plans to be tapered off methadone by January. He consulted with his clinic counselor about the plan. He felt physically better than he ever.

Five days after going into treatment, Jack sat next to Ben after a group meeting. He asked, "how's it going, man? It's good to see you today!" Ben felt a feeling of familiarity which baffled him. The compassionate respect that Jack demonstrated to Ben, and to everyone, impressed Ben more than any other moment or person since he had come into treatment. "I thought you might bolt away soon. When do you leave?" Jack asked in a non-condescending voice.

Ben had been bracing for people's judgement about his decision to leave treatment. He had been expecting people to be condescending. Few people were. It seemed only those there for a couple days were harsh judges of Ben. He had heard various opinions about his exit. People told him "it won't be a problem for you because you aren't really clean" and "methadone is dope". He couldn't wait to get out but was glad Jack didn't settle heavy judgement on him. Ben could sense Jack was genuine in his concern. "I'm leaving in the morning," answered Ben. "I tried hard to stay but I need my privacy bad, man. Do you know what I mean? Inpatient treatment is not for me. You were right that I am like you and don't like groups." Ben smiled. He hadn't smiled in a few days and it felt good. He added pensively, "people in here don't seem to like methadone much."

"I know," acknowledged Jack, "it has been something we've worked on as a company to educate people. People feel either strongly against learning about methadone or they understand it can help people. I bet you can be one of those people who demonstrates methadone can help you." He handed Ben a card. "My number. Call me anytime. If you need someone to hang with or just to talk to when you kick methadone call me. I'll get you out surfing or something. You can do this, man."

Ben thought of Jack as he made plans to talk with his counselor the next day.

CHAPTER TWENTY

B y noon the next day Ben was sitting in the lobby at the methadone clinic waiting for his counselor to take him back to his office for the required monthly hour of counseling that was prescribed with his methadone. His last few hours at the inpatient facility had crawled by. He had made agreements, in writing, with Jack to report immediately to his methadone counselor to try and taper down his dose. Ben was getting into the habit of thinking of his painful, almost-septic wound every time heroin came into his mind. His mind was filled with jargon and slogans from treatment … one day at a time … stuck with him the most. One day. And so on that first day he waited to make change happen.

Ben was called to the front desk. "Dennis is running ten minutes late but will be out soon," said the receptionist, "Can you wait or should I take a message and reschedule your appointment?" She glanced down at her computer screen and waited for Ben to answer.

"I'll wait, thanks," answered Ben. He sat back down in the lobby.

"Hey! I know you!" Ben heard from the man next to him. Instantly Ben felt exposed. He didn't want to be recognized by anyone who knew him from work. He had thought he was safe because he worked in the kitchen, in the back of the restaurant. "Aren't you Vee Ramsey's kid?" asked the man.

Ben took a closer look at the man. He could vaguely remember him from the days before his dad and brother died. "Um, ah, … yea, Vee," was all he could say. Dennis came into the lobby just then. He called to Ben to join him.

"I'm sorry about that, Ben, I had a phone call run over," explained Dennis, "I'm really sorry." Ben glanced back at the man who had recognized him. He nodded.

"Tell Vee I said hi! Is she here in San Diego? I never thought she would leave Santa Cruz," said the man. He waved Ben off as he went on to talking to the next person who sat down.

Ben followed Dennis into his office. He took a familiar seat across the desk from the counselor. Dennis offered Ben the lead in the conversation by asking, "how is your leg?" He sat back in his chair to listen, ignoring the computer. He did have signatures to get from Ben but he was more concerned with how Ben was feeling than anything.

Ben sighed. "I'm done with methadone, man, I need to do a faster taper plan," he said, then "I want to be off by the end of the year. That gives me two months." Ben relaxed into his seat. He had thought all night long about how best to approach the topic with Dennis. He had been tapering down his methadone dose for a long time but the goal was always, for Ben, so he could feel the delicious nod of dope again. He had started in the methadone program when his mom first got of prison in attempt to help her stay away from dope. In his opinion, he was still wearing the liquid handcuffs of methadone. He was sure he wouldn't be able to make any real change unless he somehow shrugged off those cuffs.

"Let's do it, then," said Dennis as he reached for the documents he would need to collaborate with Ben to plan a methadone tapering plan. As up-to-date as the clinic had become there were paper documents the prescribing doctor had to sign. "Can we go through the Tapering Readiness Inventory again?"

"Look. I'm ready to go down. Start there. I want to take a pretty big drop then wait a week or so to see how I feel. Down three milligrams every three days to six. Do it," said Jack, "I will go to twelve step groups every day this week after work. I will find a program sponsor and work the steps as you describe. But can you keep your promise to hear my fifth step if I decide to share?"

"Of course I will," answered Dennis, "maybe you will find a sponsor in the community for taking the fifth step. You need to build more into your plan than twelve step meetings. What if you feel sick? Can you afford to miss work?"

"I won't miss any work. I know I can stop my taper at the dosing window if I need to. I have stomach meds. I have muscle relaxers. Yes, prescribed to me. Years ago but still. I get restless legs all night long when I'm kicking dope if I don't do something. Yes I am trying to change my mind about that! I know what you're thinking," said Ben.

Dennis slid the tapering plan document across the desk to Ben. "Three down every three days to six. You know where to sign. Now, checklist. You have a job. Check. You have a safe place to live. Check. You want to build sober support. What are you going to do with your time outside work? You have to find something to do that is just for you. Something fun. Or engaging. Or both," he paused, "maybe you could take up hiking or motorcycle riding. Or both." He smiled warmly at Ben and said, "I know you can do this, man, I'm honored to know you." He extended his hand to Ben. The two men shook hands.

That same day Ben started thinking about how much meaning Martina was bringing into his life. They would be living together very soon. He also thought of the two men who had helped him the most in the last month- Jack and Dennis. He thought about methadone and how there seemed to be a divide between the two sides of treatment. Inpatient treatment hadn't seemed compatible to his methadone program. That had irritated and confused Ben. He went that evening to his first twelve step group meeting since getting out of inpatient treatment.

"Hi, my name is Jordan and I'm an addict," said a man at the front of the room. "Welcome to the Evening Serenity Seekers Meeting." The man took a seat behind a table facing the rest of the room. Ten or so people sat around the room at various tables. The smell of coffee wafted to Ben.

They were meeting in the basement of a county building, an old morgue Ben had heard. Ben had forgotten it was Sunday and was surprised when everyone prayed together. He had been hoping to avoid overly religious meetings (a suggestion from Jack). *At least the meeting wasn't in a church* thought Jack. He sat in the chair closest to the door. He tried to pay attention. The topic was the fourth step. Ben was catching phrases from people around the room as they shared … *searching and fearless moral inventory* … and *need a sponsor for this* stuck in Ben's mind. He thought of Dennis and their conversation about the fifth step. *So this is what Dennis meant I should share … my inventory.* Ben started to listen more intently. By the end of the meeting he was thinking of his timeline for tapering off methadone. He would do his fifth step in Dennis's office during their next scheduled counseling meeting. Ben was planning to be off methadone soon. He wanted to be discharged from the clinic by the end of December.

Ben began to write when he got back to his place. He didn't have paper in the house but found a grimy sticky note pad to make his inventory list. On the first page he wrote 'Things I did wrong and feel guilty about'. He stopped to think. He had always been so careful not to hurt anyone yet he felt like everything wrong was somehow his fault. He felt like the stabbing that had happened was a freak accident because he couldn't remember it. But he definitely felt guilty about it. He had all the long time he was in lockup. He had therapy in lockup about the incident. He had written letters of apology to everyone involved, including the people who held him that day after the incident. He had never stolen anything except for dope from his mom but that wasn't stealing so much as forced sharing. He would snatch some of her dope after she nodded out. He always checked to see if she was breathing. He made sure she was on her side so she wouldn't choke on her own puke if she vomited in her slumber. He thought about how much he wanted to tell his mom how sorry he was for all the things he had done. He started writing again, one thing each on their own piece of paper, seven tiny pages …

1) Not able to save my mom and sister from abuse 2) Let my dad and brother die 3) Started using heroin 4) Started drinking alcohol 5) I stabbed someone 6) Still not able to save mom 7) Still using, but not now.

Ben believed the one thing he had done in the world that he couldn't forgive himself for running when that man said to run the day his father and brother died. Somehow Ben had fixed in his mind that he could have stayed to save them. He had no way of knowing that Chase had died immediately after shooting up dope in the tent. He was probably dead when he hit the ground. The sound of the deadfall thud seemed burned into Ben's mind. For the first time during this inventory process, Ben started to crave dope.

The craving started in his body and then consumed his mind completely. He was glad he slept at his place instead of Martina's as he was increasingly doing. His thoughts dropped back to a time when he first slammed fentanyl into his veins. *I want that so bad,* he thought suddenly. He started to feel it deep in his spine. He was alone. It was late. But still not late enough. He wasn't going to be able to get methadone until early morning. *I better get used to this* he told himself *if I'm going to get off methadone.* He looked at the clock and thought about calling Dennis. He knew Dennis reported to the clinic at five-thirty in the morning and he didn't want to wake him … it was two-thirty. He swallowed some ibuprofen to help him relax which helped a little. It seemed that just swallowing the pills helped him calm down. He took a long shower then paced quietly until it was time to head for the clinic. He had made it through the night without going out to get dope. He let himself feel a little proud even as his anxiety grew.

He watched Dennis ride up to the clinic on his bicycle. He took a chance that the counselor wouldn't mind him approaching him in the dark. The sound of his truck door closing echoed in the morning air. Dennis turned to look at Ben. "Hey, Ben! I thought I would see you this morning," said Dennis, "I thought about you all night. How you doing, man? Still want me to submit that taper plan today? You look upset. Come on in, I have an hour before I have to meet with anyone." They went into the clinic.

When they reached the privacy of Dennis's office, Ben began to talk. He felt as if he'd never had so much to say. His thoughts were jumbled and it caused him to speak too fast, "I went to a fourth step meeting last night. Wrote mine when I got home," he paused, "then out of nowhere I couldn't stop craving to shoot fentanyl." He collapsed into a chair by the door as if he didn't want to commit to coming all the way into the office.

"So, did you?" asked Dennis. He took a seat. He waited to hear what Ben had to say.

Ben took a moment to catch his breath. He stood up and moved to sit in the chair across from Dennis. "No," he smiled weakly, "I made it through the night with a huge jones. I haven't slept. But I didn't use." He could hear people moving in the hallway outside the office. He knew the methadone dosing window would be opening soon. But, he didn't want to appear desperate in front of Dennis because he truly did want to go forward with the plan to taper off methadone. He didn't want Dennis to think he wasn't stable enough to beat this shit.

Dennis looked squarely at Ben. "You have to identify your trigger. Knowing your triggers is an important part of the Tapering Checklist that we didn't get to yet. What happened last night? What were you writing about? If you identify what happened, what triggered you to think about using, then you will be better prepared to handle it when thoughts of using come up again. You can learn to avoid triggers."

Ben put his stack of post it notes on the desk in front of Dennis. Dennis picked it up and read to himself the first note *Things I have done wrong and feel guilty about.* He did not flip to the second note. Time was passing quickly. "Hold on," said Dennis as he signed into his computer to check his schedule, "we need to spend more than fifteen minutes on this. Can you get your methadone dose now and come back at seven to meet with me? If you fall asleep before then I can meet you at one. You might want to dose, then go get some sleep. I have no appointments at seven. If you aren't here by seven thirty I will look forward to seeing you at one. You can call me if one doesn't work out." He stood. He handed the stack of notes to Ben and gestured toward the door. "Taper starts tomorrow," said Dennis as they exited the office.

"I'll try to come back at seven," said Ben as he left. He checked in at the front desk to wait in the lobby to get his twelve milligrams of methadone. *I can do this* he told himself *I can get loose of the liquid handcuffs.*

What Ben didn't understand yet is that it wasn't methadone that was causing the feeling of being cuffed. His own thinking was holding him back from making changes to the way he lived life. But he was beginning to make changes each time he made the decision to do something different from what he had always done. He was beginning to understand the need to take a look at his life. He sat in his truck flipping through the pages of his fourth step inventory.

He could feel the methadone working in his body. A familiar sense of relief mixed with defeat engulfed him. Somehow the familiarity was not the same. There was an element of unfamiliarity. This time Ben was not afraid to go forward into his unknowns. He went back into the clinic just before seven.

CHAPTER TWENTY-ONE

Dennis was surprised to see Ben when he entered the clinic lobby at seven. "Hey, good to see you! I thought you might need to sleep some," said Dennis, "come on back." He ushered Ben into his office and gestured for him to sit.

Ben sat down and pulled the stack of notes out of his jacket pocket. He had been thinking about his wrongdoings but was having trouble describing the guilt he felt. "I can't pin it, man," he started to say to Dennis, "it's like I feel guilty for just being alive .. like everything I have done in life is wrong but I don't know how to write that down." He paused and stood up to pace across the small office.

"I think you should start with what you did write down," said Dennis.

Ben stopped pacing and sat down again. He pulled off the top piece that read the first note, "things I did wrong and feel guilty about". He crumpled it then held it in his palm as he read the second note … he read aloud, "not able to save my mom and sister from abuse," then paused. He sighed then explained to Dennis, "I used to watch my dad abuse my mother. He would yell and take swings at her that she usually managed to dodge. My older brother used to treat my mom the same." Ben stood and started to pace again … three strides in one direction then turn to take another three strides. "My sister used to try to stop my dad. She would yell, cry, and scream." He paused again. "I didn't," he said quietly as he sat down and leaned toward Dennis. He held back tears, "I didn't do a fucking thing but watch from behind the couch. Not a fucking thing." Tears began to roll down his face. He felt like he had been running. His breath was heavy.

Dennis sat quietly. He waited for Ben to catch his breath. He knew from experience that he could not contribute to the narrative. He fully understood that Ben may need to seek the help of someone who could help him with the lasting affects of growing up in a fucked-up home so to speak. He also fully understood that the expression of these things would liberate Ben so that he could seek help if he further needed to work out his issues.

Ben looked at the second note he had written in haste the night before ... *let my dad and brother die* ... and he began to sob. "I can't say this one. I just can't," he whispered between gulps for air, his sobs consuming him, he continued slowly, "I know this is true but have never said it to anyone, not even therapists all that time in lockup after the stabbing." He stopped talking. He stood and began pacing the small office again. "I told you about my first time with heroin. Eating it that day my dad and brother died? What I didn't say is that I think I ..." his words seemed to hang in the air between the two men, "if I hadn't run that day then maybe they would be alive." He sat. "If I hadn't been stung or made so much noise those men would not have heard my dad. They would not have come to kill him. I fucked everything up that day. Chase jacked too much dope because I was bugging dad. I was being a fucking baby." His shoulders shook as he cried. He took a deep breath then said, "if I had stayed there they would have killed me instead. My dad would have had time to fight those men and to save Chase." He sat quietly. He tried to calm down.

Dennis and Ben sat together in silence. Neither one spoke for a few minutes but the silence was not uncomfortable. Dennis was first to break the silence, "thank you for sharing this part of your life with me, Ben. I think you will be surprised by how much lighter you will feel, this has been heavy on your mind. You are hard on yourself," he paused, then said, "maybe someday you will talk with a therapist about this but for now I have to say that, Ben, *it is not your fault that your dad and brother died that day.* You were a kid. Think of any kid when you are being hard on yourself, realize how small you were. You were unguided. You were making the best choices you could for a kid in your circumstance. Now you are taking steps to forgive yourself, let's go on."

Ben took a deep breath. "Dope and booze," he said as he looked at the next two notes, "I've chosen over and over again to use dope. And you know my booze story. I can only think I didn't kill anyone with all the times I drove drunk or blasted on dope." He crumpled the three notes he had just read. He looked at the next one *I stabbed someone* it read. He had written the three words in tiny print unlike the rest of his notes but he hadn't noticed until that moment. He tried to read it aloud but the words, "I stabbed someone" were barely legible. He realized he had no emotional connection to the stabbing except that he was angry at his mom for getting arrested that day. He couldn't remember the stabbing. He cleared his throat and said loudly, "I stabbed someone." He had relayed the story to Dennis in the past when he explained his years in juvenile lockup. He felt like he could leave the statement hanging. He had tried a lot of times to feel something about the stabbing but all he came up with was his anger. He crumpled the note. He glanced at the clock realizing he had only twenty minutes before he had to go. "I tried to help my mom when she got out of prison. You know that's why I'm even here, why I didn't stay in Santa Cruz," he paused, then "I'm not sure why I feel guilty about this but I do. We were doing really well for a few months, me and Violet, there's a long story I won't go into now because most of it you know. What you don't know is how bad I feel that she fell apart and went back to Santa Cruz. I didn't follow her or try to help. I was disgusted by her. I feel really shitty about that."

Ben thought briefly about the last time he had seen his mom. She had been outside his job tapping on the window but was gone when he opened the door fifteen minutes later to hand her a breakfast burrito. Since that morning he had tried to ignore his thoughts when they turned to her.

"Violet had some things going that I have been doing since she left," said Ben cautiously, "she wanted to help her friend Marta find her daughter who had been stolen from her in Mexico. Marta had connections to some people who move … other people." He looked again at the clock. He started talking in a rush … "this has been a way for me to make things right with Vee. It was, it is, something that I can do. I feel good about but somehow I know I am not doing enough." He looked into Dennis's eyes and said, "I am a middle person, an interceptor, who takes kids who are smuggled into the country and gets them to other people who will try to connect them with their parents." He sighed. "I know this is a good thing except that I don't like sneaking around or keeping secrets."

He looked at the last note he had written … it read 'still using, but not now'. He thought about the deep craving he had to use heroin just a couple hours ago. He thought about how methadone had helped him in the moment.

"I can't save Violet," Ben started again, "but I can save myself." He crumpled the last of his notes. "I know you have to get going I can't say enough how much better I feel even as tired as I am." He had never told Dennis of his night runs smuggling kids. He could sense that Dennis was taking in his words. Ben stood.

"Let's meet as often as we can until you are done," suggested Dennis as he stood, "thank you again, Ben, you're a good man. Let me know how the taper goes if you need to otherwise I'll see you next week. Think about what triggered your craving last night, we'll talk about it." The two men shook hands tightly. They leaned in for a half-hug before exiting the office together.

Many times Ben had left Dennis's office feeling good. Sometimes feeling great. This time he had a deeper sense of satisfaction than ever before in his life. He was physically exhausted. His mind kept spinning around the things he had shared with Dennis. In the past he was ashamed when he talked about his life but this time he didn't feel that way. He drove home as carefully as he could making it home just before he felt like he was going to fall asleep driving. He set his alarm to wake him for work the next morning and fell into a deep, restful sleep. He dreamt about his mother.

Violet was especially grumpy as she made her way up Ocean Street. She looked seventy years old but her body was not yet fifty. She was in menopause. Hot flashes plagued her constantly. Especially if she didn't get booze. People thought she was bad for being a junkie but oh my fucking god if she didn't get a drink she would probably flop out and die. That's what she called her alcoholic seizures … flopping out. She witnessed a friend flopping out one night, twitching and shaking on the ground, and from then on that was her term. If she didn't get a drink her body would drop to the ground and spasm like it was dying. And maybe it was. She trudged over to the liquor store. She had only been back in Santa Cruz for a little while but it felt like she had never left. She made her way back to her sleeping spot and fell into a fitful slumber.

Violet was dreaming about a big, cheesy omelet when a barking dog woke her from her fitful sleep. Memories of working at the restaurant with Ben cooking came to mind. Her stomach groaned. It was dark. Dew had not yet settled on Vee's tarp so she figured it was around three or four in the morning. *Shit* she thought *it's too fucking early*. She couldn't get the omelet out of her mind. And Ben. She could barely remember the last time she had seen him. She thought of the last thing he had said to her, "I'll be right back with your burrito". She wanted to turn back time to that moment. She would have stayed right there waiting by the back door of the restaurant. Instead, she had walked around to the front. She had knocked on the door meaning to get coffee from Tracy. Her heart almost stopped when she looked in the window. She thought she saw Marta standing inside. What she didn't know was that it was Martina. She couldn't take her eyes off Martina that morning as Tracy hissed at her through the door to go to the back door. Sadness and anger descended on Violet as if a heavy shroud had been put around her. She was deeply sad that she couldn't see or talk to Marta ever again. She was angry at herself that she had ever turned Marta on to dope. The new girl at the restaurant had looked exactly like Marta. It triggered grief deep within Violet. She couldn't handle it in the end.

Violet started to drink and smoke herself all the way back to Santa Cruz. In the present, she groaned. She sat up and started to get ready for her long hike to the methadone clinic.

CHAPTER TWENTY-TWO

The sound of his alarm growing louder eventually broke Ben's deep sleep. He had been dreaming of a time when he tried to pick Violet up from the driveway but he was too small. She was still on his mind when he realized he would have to rush to make it to work on time.

He hadn't told Martina anything about his so-called recovery program. He didn't want to draw attention to his details as he called them at this point. Methadone was a soon-to-be-left-behind detail. He felt so good, so unburdened after his confessions. The fifth step had been good for him. Telling Martina about his weekly night runs- and Dennis, too- had left him lighter and happier than he had felt before in his life. Martina and Ben had talked into the next day about the possibilities for Ben not having to do the runs anymore. Martina wanted to connect Ben with her friends and colleagues at her former job. She wanted him to know that what he was doing was noble, commendable, and he should be recognized and supported. She had told him, "no one should have to do this alone. I love you so much." He believed her.

Martina had not slept. She had spent the few short hours she was in bed thinking about the future while feeling mired in the past. She couldn't stop thinking about her mother. She had so many questions. The one she had asked herself many times, that she couldn't stop thinking about, was *did she look for me?* This question was always hanging in the back of Martina's thoughts. It was her motivation to get involved with social work. Now she was elated with the information Ben had shared with her. Her mind was on fire with ideas about how to connect her colleagues to Ben's. She wanted to build an even bigger safety net for helping children. She turned her thoughts to the present. She forced herself to get ready for work.

Ben was cracking eggs when Martina arrived at the restaurant. She had a flashback memory of her first day a short time ago. It was then she remembered that Ben's mom had come to the restaurant that morning. Tracy had said something about Ben and his mom had some kind of Save the Kids plan or something. She wanted to ask Ben about it. She planned to ask him all the way to work but when she saw him so happy she just couldn't ask. She didn't want to bring up his mom. Violet had not come back to the restaurant even once as far as Martina could remember since that first day.

Martina joined Ben in cracking eggs. "How are you feeling, Benny? Did you sleep?" asked Martina, "I never did fall asleep." She smiled at him. She met his glance with love and admiration. He didn't answer immediately so she kept talking, "I am excited we will be going to Santa Cruz! School starts for me soon up there. Want to take a trip to Santa Cruz this weekend?" She waited for Ben to respond.

"We have to cover our shifts here. Maybe next weekend? It's easier for you to be gone than me. I have to work on finding another cook. Maybe I should let the restaurant know I plan to leave," he answered, then "I need to get someone to do the night runs." He went about getting the kitchen open as Martina got ready for her shift. He glanced again at Martina. She was standing quietly apparently lost in thought, she stared out the window.

"I will call my friend Miranda today and we can start talking with them about your situation, ok? I am sure they can help you pass on this task. I have to ask ... did you and your mom work on this? Tracy said something about a Save the Kids program or something?" Martina had decided to ask Ben about Violet. She was worried Ben would close himself off from her. She worried he might shut down but instead he sat down at the counter as Martina made coffee. "Where is your mom?" Martina asked.

Ben started talking softly, "I think my mom is in Santa Cruz. Maybe I will see her, maybe not. If she is drinking then she may not be okay with me coming around, I don't know. I know I haven't said a lot about my mom, I'm sorry," he paused, "it's hard for me to talk about her to anyone." He started helping Martina with her opening chores. "I don't really know my mom," Ben said quietly, then "I didn't live with after I was eleven. Before that I don't remember her being around much. She was drunk a lot. The most I heard her talk was when she was wanting heroin. She used to tirade and yell until she got her fix." He walked to the front door to unlock it for the two people outside waiting to come in for breakfast. He winked at Martina and said, "time to go! We have a long, tiring day to face!"

Together, Ben and Martina worked toward closing time with a mixture of fatigue and excitement. Both of them needed the deep connection that was growing between them. Martina wanted to cry for Ben over his lost relationship with his mom. Ben wanted to find Martina's mom who she so longed to see. That they could fill a void for each other brought them closer to anyone ever before.

CHAPTER TWENTY-THREE

Violet couldn't stop thinking about Ben as she made her way along Ocean Street in the pre-dawn shadows. She planned to spend the two dollars she had on scrambled eggs because she couldn't stop thinking about eating a cheese omelet. She had finished off the vodka she had before she headed toward the methadone clinic intending to beg some money from someone to get more. She begged two dollars from a woman leaving the all night diner. She got a scrambled egg with cheese and they let her fill her mug with coffee. Violet was grateful but still could not stop thinking about Ben even after she ate. She continued on toward the methadone clinic asking people for a few bucks whenever she passed someone. She had gathered eleven dollars when she got to the clinic. She felt rich. She felt even richer after talking her methadone counselor into asking the doctor for a dose increase. Violet had been very careful lately not to show up at the clinic for methadone if she had been drinking vodka. Today, of all days, they had not breathalyzed her. She got her full methadone dose. Then she spent an hour with her counselor. The counselor had helped Violet to fill out a methadone dose increase request based on her report that the "shit is not holding" to stop her cravings for twenty-four hours. She was excited about getting more. More meant less for Violet. Less thinking. Less feeling. Less being aware of all the damage she had done to people. She thought to herself *if it goes well I will be nodding out in the sunshine tomorrow about this time.* She headed to the liquor store to spend her eleven bucks. Nodding out on methadone was really hard but with enough on board she knew she could maybe even check out for good like Marta did. She went into the liquor store for her booze.

Now here it was morning again. Violet didn't remember anything after leaving the liquor store. She did remember that she had bought a fifth of vodka instead of her usual pint. She had splurged all her money. She stepped up from the bottom shelf a notch so the booze itself was probably stronger. She remembered sitting down near the river to have a tipple as she liked to call it. An afternoon tipple. She woke up, or came to consciousness, two days later in the local alcohol detoxification unit with no recollection of how she had arrived.

Violet tried to move but her arms and legs felt heavy. She groaned. She could hear movement across the room. She tried to open her eyes but her eyelids were too heavy. She groaned again. She heard more noise as someone approached. She felt a blood pressure cuff squeeze her arm. The pressure seemed to give her the power she needed to lift her eyelids. She peered through her eyelashes into the room. She spotted a person sitting outside her doorway. She couldn't tell if it was a man or a woman. *This doesn't look like a hospital* thought Violet as she opened her eyes wide to take in the place. She was in a room with six beds but she was the only person. She tried to sit up but managed only to groan louder. The person outside her door came toward Violet; she could see it was a man.

"Hi, I'm Gabe," said the man to Violet, "here, take a sip." He helped Violet to sit up in bed. He handed her a cup of water. Violet swallowed it quickly then held the cup out for more. "Sure, all you need," he said as he filled her cup from a small pitcher. "I see you haven't been here before?" Gabe asked, then went on without waiting for Violet to answer, "you aren't in our records. You are at the poison detoxification unit otherwise known as detox. How are you feeling?"

"Like a fucking truck hit me!" Violet exclaimed, "and like my bladder is going to burst!" She tried again to swing her legs over the side of the bed.

A woman came into the room. She said, "Hi I'm Macy. Can I help you get up? I mean, do you mind if I help?" Macy stepped in beside Violet's bed. She said, "here, grab my elbow." Violet grabbed onto Macy with both hands. She was able to get her balance. Macy said, "the bathroom is behind that door. Sorry, it's not well marked."

Violet headed for the door Macy indicated which was about ten steps across the room. She tried to mutter thanks but she was afraid she was going to piss herself. *Fucking detox* thought Violet. She had heard about detox. In the past she had gone from hospital stay to outpatient methadone clinic patient. She had not previously been to detox. She tried to gather her thoughts. She remembered that big bottle of vodka she had bought. She berated herself as she pissed *I must have really fucked things up ... fucking drunk junkie.* She took a breath. She splashed some water onto her face before heading back to her bed. But the bed was stripped of blankets. All the beds were empty. It was then Violet realized she was still in the same clothes. *That's why I don't feel like I'm in the hospital* she thought *no gown.*

Gabe leaned into the room from a hallway and said to Violet, "come on out. No one gets to sleep all day unless they just got here. You've been here two days." He smiled. He held a hand out to Violet.

Violet ignored the helping hand then said, "well I sure as fuck have to sleep some more! I feel like I have weights on my brain!" She stepped into the hallway. It was then she noticed other people in the place. It looked like maybe a dozen people in various states of consciousness were lounging in chairs or couches. She started walking slowly toward an empty recliner chair sitting in the corner. She curled up and got as comfortable as she could manage. In a lot of ways she was more comfortable than she had been in a long time. The chair cushions were soft and were soon warmed by her body. Someone came by and draped a blanket over her. She felt almost hugged. Warmth began to generate deep within Violet that day. She began to thaw. She slept in the chair until she was roused to come to eat lunch.

Chapter Twenty-Four

B en and Martina sat down in the break room after their exhausting shift to share a cheese omelet- one of Ben's favorite meals. Ben had been thinking about who he could train to replace him. He had been talking to his coworker about taking the job. He suspected Martina wasn't taking him seriously about leaving for Santa Cruz so he surprised her when he said, "Miguel wants my job. He'll be here at seven for his shift. I think he will be a great lead cook and kitchen manager."

Martina stopped eating. "Really, Benny? Wow," she exclaimed, "that's awesome! I think he would be great!" She wrapped her arms around him in a huge hug. "You can get work in Santa Cruz that you will like," she said as she hugged him tighter, "let's plan a road trip. Three days off, maybe four. You deserve it!" She kissed him quickly. She scooped up the last bite of omelet before sprinting out of the break room.

Ben spent the day automatically filling orders with his mind on the changes he was about to make. He was thinking he should give his sister a call to let her know he was planning on coming up to Santa Cruz. He hadn't seen her since the evening when he was released from the hospital. She had wanted to give him a ride to inpatient treatment but he had to take so-called insurance approved transportation so a staff person had driven him. He remembered Arianna had been really glad he was going into treatment. He hadn't talked to her since the day after he left the place after not completing the whole program. He figured she assumed he was failing. But he wasn't. He was down to eight milligrams of methadone. He wasn't feeling any cravings. No pain. He was *feeling fucking great* he thought.

Fucking great Violet thought *I need a drink.* She got up from the chair where she had been sleeping since lunch. She made her way across the room to stand looking out the window. She was trying to figure out where she was in town so that when she got the chance she could skip out of this place. Staff had informed her she could stay up to six days to make sure she didn't go into alcoholic withdrawal. She was invited to go into inpatient treatment, was in fact strongly urged by her methadone counselor, but all she could think of was getting out. All she needed was information and an open door. And shoes.

Arianna was driving on Ocean Street when she caught a glimpse of a person she thought was her mother. It wasn't. She sometimes did see Violet trudging along but this time Arianna was mistaken. Her mind kept returning to the time she had seen her mother when she was released from prison. Arianna never understood why Violet didn't want to live in Santa Cruz. She had driven down to San Diego thinking she was going to be bringing Violet home with her. That hadn't happened. Instead she had fought bitterly with her mom about using heroin. Arianna had driven off angrily. Violet was slumped on a bus stop bench the next time she saw her. Arianna was positive who that had been. She had thought the woman looked dead. When she got close she could see labored breathing under a dirty sweatshirt. It was definitely Violet. Her mom. She hadn't disturbed her sleep but stared for a moment. Feelings of shame washed over then as it did now while she was thinking of Violet.

Three years of therapy plus self-help groups and I still can't think about her without losing it thought Arianna. She sighed. She had become reclusive. *I spend too much time with myself.* She had come to a point in her life when she wanted to make some changes. She had recently realized that the routines she lived with were the only structure she had. She longed for adventure even as she couldn't imagine being more daring than grocery shopping at three in the morning. She longed for a partner ... someone who would be glad to see her. Every time. Unlike her family. And her mother. *Shit I don't want to think about her* Arianna proclaimed.

Just thinking of the word 'mother' caused Arianna to feel anxious. She had taught herself how to think through her anxiety. Normally she could change her feelings but today it wasn't working. She tried to call to mind good thoughts of Violet. She could remember a time, way back in her memory, when she laid her head on her mother's pregnant stomach. She remembered looking up to see the curve of her mother's chin from underneath. She recalled the smell of tobacco in the long hair that tickled Arianna's nose. She didn't really hear anything but she said "yes!" when Violet asked ,"do you hear it?" *Things sure did change after Benny came along* she thought *seems I always think of him whenever I think of Vee.* She cleared her mind as she pulled up to stop for a snack. She reasoned a full dose of chocolate cinnamon ice cream on a sugar cone would help her not to think of those times.

She got her ice cream and found a seat near the window. As she was enjoying the moment her phone rang. Ben's face appeared on her screen. *Damn the universe is weird* she thought as she answered Ben's call. "Hey, brother," she said with genuine warmth, "how are you doing? I was just thinking about you!"

"Hi Arianna. That's funny! I was going to call you yesterday but didn't get the chance until now. Maybe you felt me thinking about you. I'm coming to Santa Cruz soon. I thought you should know. You might spot me getting ice cream or something. I have a girlfriend, Martina, who is going to be in school up there so we are going to move up. I don't know if you met her we weren't dating yet when you were down here," said Ben.

Arianna was glad to hear from Ben. She remembered the warmth she had felt for him in the hospital. It wasn't fair to him that she had been angry when he left inpatient treatment. "I'm sorry I stopped calling, Benny. Your life is not my business. Please forgive me for being an asshole?"

"Done," answered Ben, "forgiven." He paused. He could almost feel the question Arianna had in mind. "I know what you're thinking. No dope. Not since the overdose. I'm coming off methadone, too. I plan to be done by the time we move up there. I'm close. Down to eight milligrams."

Arianna's relief at hearing Ben's words was huge. "Oh, Benny, thats great! That is so cool. I am stunned. I don't know what to say," she paused. "I'm sorry for doubting you. I know how hard it can be to change. When are you coming? I have to work but can be around some. A girlfriend! Martina? Sounds familiar. She works with you right?" She felt like she could go on questioning him but she stopped. "I'm so happy for you. I don't have room at my place but I can get you a discount at the hotel near here."

"Don't worry about that we have a place that Martina found. I'll call you when we get there," he hesitated, then asked "Have you seen Violet?"

Arianna was caught by surprise. She couldn't answer right away. It seemed like Benny was looking into her mind when he called during her thoughts about Vee. "Not for a few days," she answered quietly, "I try to spot her at least once a day. My office looks out on Ocean Street. But I haven't seen her for three days now. I think she might be avoiding me."

"It's okay. We're only staying two nights. I'll talk to you Friday. Thanks, Arianna," said Ben, then, "Thanks for everything. I'm sorry if I ever hurt you."

"Hey! That sounds like some twelve-step stuff!?" exclaimed Arianna, "you never hurt me Benny. I hope I never hurt you. I am really sorry if I did. Talk to you on Sunday!" She ended the call. She finished her ice cream with a warmth that couldn't be chilled.

She thought of where she had heard that name *Martina*. The name sounded familiar to Arianna but she couldn't remember where she first heard it. *Maybe her mom? I think Violet had a friend named Martina* thought Arianna as she drove home. Then she remembered the woman her mom was friends with in prison had a daughter named Martina. She planned to ask Ben about it then next time she saw him.

CHAPTER TWENTY-FIVE

"Violet?" said a woman's voice, "hi, I'm Carmen. Can we talk some in my office?" She helped Violet to gather her blanket as she gestured for Violet to follow. "I see that you haven't been here before. I want to make sure you know all your options, she said as she closed the door, "you've been here for forty-eight hours. Your body is adjusting to not getting alcohol. How are you feeling?"

Carmen waited patiently for Violet to relax enough to answer her question. Violet couldn't help an angry outburst when she did finally speak, "I feel as shitty as I look which I know is pretty fucking shitty. My body is not adjusting to not having alcohol. In fact, I'm going to head out soon. I want to be done with this whole show!"

"Okay. You can do that. I can help you even. But what if you stayed the whole six days to get some rest?" asked Carmen, then, "you can stay on methadone. We can help you get off alcohol. Right now the doctor has you on a small benzodiazepine dose. And you got less of that today than you did yesterday. Tomorrow you may feel a lot better than shitty. Lasagna for dinner tonight."

"I'll stay for dinner but I don't know after that. What about all my stuff? I have stuff," her voice trailed off to nothing. But in her mind she couldn't bring to mind a single thing that she wanted. She had to admit that she truly had nothing. *Except* thought Vee *maybe a chance to get some rest.* She hadn't rested since she shared a cell with Marta. Of all places, prison was the place she longed to be most of all.

Carmen broke the heavy silence by asking Violet, "can I call someone for you? A friend? Family? You can get someone to bring

141

your stuff." She glanced at the clock then stood. She said, "we should head to dinner. Do you want to go together?" She held an elbow out for Vee. Vee reached out. She let Carmen help her.

"Nah. Nobody thinks of me these days," answered Violet.

Ben sat thinking of Violet after talking on the phone to his sister. He could picture Arianna spotting Violet from her office window. Santa Cruz was a small town to the people who lived there. Everybody knew everybody else's business. Ben thought of Arianna watching for Violet. He wondered how Arianna kept it quiet that she used to be a junkie. *Maybe she doesn't* he thought.

His leg was completely healed but he kept a bandage on to help him remember where he had come from. The bandage also reminded him of what his goal had become, to get off methadone. He had been going to counseling weekly. He would take morning break to run, literally, to the clinic and back for his daily dose. He made sure to go when Martina was very busy so he could avoid telling her about his dependence. He thought again of Arianna. He felt good about looking forward to seeing her.

Arianna sat thinking of Ben and wondering at him having a girl-friend. She wondered if he had told his girlfriend he was an addict. Or about Violet. She thought, *does his girl know about our drunk junkie mother?* Anxious thoughts overwhelmed her as she stopped for even more ice cream. This time it was for a quart to take home. She needed a much larger dose than one cone. She went into a store to grab some but was nearly knocked over by a man running out.

"Shit! I'm sorry," he said as he dropped something. He steadied himself by holding Arianna's arms at the elbow. A container of chocolate cinnamon ice cream rolled between them on the ground.

"I was headed for that very kind!" said Arianna before thinking about being grabbed, and held, by a stranger. She shrugged a little. He let her go. His hands had felt nice on her skin.

"I am so sorry. I was trying to rush. I didn't see you. Can you forgive me?" He asked, then, "this is the last of this kind. I haven't had it but it sounds most awesome. I would be happy to have it a different time. You can have this one." He said as he picked up the dropped ice cream. "I had not seen such cool ice cream flavors as here in Santa Cruz!" He smiled broadly and held the ice cream out to Arianna.

Arianna was speechless. *Too many coincidences today* was all she could think as she stood staring at this beautiful man who had just set ice cream at her feet. And not just ice cream but her very favorite kind.

Violet sat eating ice cream with Carmen at a long table where the facility staff and patrons gathered for meals. It wasn't a kitchen. Or a dining room. More of a break room with an extra large table, a toaster oven, two microwaves, a coffee machine, and a fridge. Meals were brought on tall steel rolling carts to be heated up in microwaves. Staff simply went into a big walk in fridge to roll out whatever meal was scheduled. Violet was thinking this would be a good place to swing by to beg for leftovers. She had decided to stay at least for the next day to see if what Carmen said was true about her feeling better soon. She knew that vodka, or vitamin V as she liked to call it, was fucking her up. Waking up in detox was enough for her to stop to think about what was happening. Booze hadn't been a problem for her for a long time but this last time she picked it up it bit her in the face. Now she was trying not to think about booze.

Violet took another bite. "This chocolate ice cream is good but have you ever had cinnamon chocolate? I love cinnamon chocolate," said Violet.

"I have! I love it," answered Carmen, "its hard to find, easy to make."

"You can get it a few places. Fucking awesome," exclaimed Violet, then, "I used to take my kids for ice cream on the first of every month like clockwork no matter how much money I had. My girl always loved the cinnamon chocolate as much as me."

"That sounds like a good time," said Carmen, "I would have liked that growing up. Where did you grow up?"

"Shit I was still a kid when I got here so I guess I grew up here in Santa Cruz," Violet hesitated, "but I was born in Alabama. My three kids were born here. That's something." She gave a half smile but it didn't reach her eyes. "My oldest son died here when he was seventeen. My other son lives down in Santee outside of San Diego. My girl lives here in Santa Cruz." She stood and stretched. "I do feel a lot better. I will stay a couple more days."

"Can I call your daughter for you?" Carmen asked. She let the question hang in the air. She was pretty sure she had asked loud enough. She had not missed that Violet's daughter lived in Santa Cruz.

"You are determined aren't you?" Violet asked rhetorically, then "you can call her if you tell her it was your idea to call, not mine. I doubt she will believe I am kicking booze. You'll have to find her though, Arianna Ramsey last I knew. I doubt she will ever marry. She wouldn't change her name if she did. She's one of those super-feminists? Not gay I don't think. Just doesn't like men much as far as I can tell."

"I will let you know when I find her," said Carmen, "I'm off work tomorrow but will call as soon as I get back. If you are still here. Can I give you a hug?" She smiled at Violet as she asked then opened her arms wide.

Violet stepped in to get a hug and finally, after many years of not being able to shed tears, she began to shake with sobs. Tears spilled from her swollen eyes and ran down her reddened cheeks. She felt the tight squeeze of Carmen's hug which melted her resolve. She tried to think back to a time when she could feel this kind of emotion.

She remembered one time when she was pregnant with Ben, Arianna had crawled onto the couch to lay her head on Violet's belly. She remembered the feel of the four year old's heat as she held her ear close. She had looked up with big, soft eyes. A rush of loving warmth engulfed Violet back then as it did now. She used to get warm, loving feelings for her daughter. She hadn't realized she missed that feeling. She found herself hoping Arianna wanted to see her after all this shit. After so much time.

It had been a few days since Arianna had last seen Violet struggling along on Ocean Street. She found herself badly wanting to see her. When she left the ice cream store the other night with a stranger, Violet had come to mind. In a way, she wanted to flaunt her recklessness to her mother. She wanted to brag about what she had done. Everyone thought she was so straight-and-narrow. Her heart raced a bit as she thought of her night with Keith.

She had agreed to go home with him to eat ice cream. She stayed until nine the next morning. She had ice cream alright. And pot. And sex. She was still elated from the experience even as she noticed Violet's absence. She was hoping for another date with Keith on Sunday. She looked forward to almost nothing else. She also was sure he wouldn't call. She wasn't sure if she was going to tell Ben about the date. Or fling. Or whatever it was. Probably not.

I think I'll hit a nooner thought Arianna as she left her office, meaning to attend a noontime recovery meeting. She decided to walk the distance to the meeting to try and spot Violet along the way as she had in the past. Violet was not around. Arianna spent her lunch hour wandering. She never did go to a meeting. She was feeling guilty about smoking pot. Many of the people she knew in recovery groups smoked pot, and cigarettes, but she had always been on the abstinence side of any argument. Now she wasn't so clean. But she was thrilled. It was if a pressure had been lifted from her mind. Even her usual feelings of disgust toward Violet were missing. She hoped she could find Violet before Ben and his girlfriend came to town. Maybe she would stop by the methadone clinic to say hi to a friend she had who worked there. She wouldn't be able to ask about Violet but maybe she could run into her. *I'll stop by there tomorrow* Arianna noted to herself.

Chapter Twenty-Six

B en sat in his truck outside the methadone clinic. He had driven over instead of running because it was his day off so he wasn't on break from work. He told Martina he was helping a friend move furniture. He needed time to go through the process of picking up methadone doses that he could take some with him to Santa Cruz so he could avoid the clinic there. He sensed it was going to take him a while to pick up his doses based on the line outside the clinic. He got into line.

He hadn't thought about using heroin in a few days. He was sleeping better every night. He was talking to Dennis about trying to stretch out, or even miss, his methadone dosing time to see how he felt. It was almost time for him to stop methadone completely. He was less scared every day as he started thinking about setting a date to stop like Dennis suggested. The clinic allowed him to take two doses home with him every week. Just as he was leaving the clinic the same person who recognized him in the clinic lobby before spotted him and yelled out, "hey, Violet's kid! The survivor!"

Ben looked at the man. His throat froze, he was unable to speak. Instead of responding, he left the clinic. He practically ran to his truck. "Survivor'

" is what his mother's friends had called him after he lived through the tragedy of losing his dad and brother. It was also what his mother had called him from then on. She never called him Ben. As he drove home he tried to recall a time, even one time, that his mother had called him by his name. Sometimes she had called him *leftover,* he remembered.

Thoughts of his mother filled Ben's mind. He thought of how when she got out of prison, she had accepted his help. She had called him 'my benefit'. Not Ben. Not Benny. She came close to saying his name a few times in the past when she was drunk but instead called him benzo. She would say to him, "there's my Benzo" or "come on over, Benzo". At some point Ben learned the she got more excited about actual benzos, or benzodiazepine pills, than she did about him. Violet called benzodiazepines the second best downer. Ben wasn't sure if her first best was booze or heroin. Or him.

He drove back to the clinic after thirty minutes to wait out the process in picking up his medicine. The man who had called out to him was gone. He was so ready to be done with methadone. He thought about his future new life as he drove to meet Martina. He was meeting her at the restaurant for breakfast before they started packing for their trip later in the day. He was feeling a little sick to his stomach. He was down to six milligrams of methadone daily. He cracked open a bottle of stomach medicine he bought at the drug store. He took a swig of it without measuring. His stomach groaned. The thought of eating caused him to wince as he went into the restaurant.

Martina sat at the counter engrossed in conversation with a woman also sitting at the counter. "All of them are really good," she was saying as Ben approached. He assumed she was talking about food as both women had menus in their hands. He sat next to Martina. He gave her a kiss on the cheek. Martina smiled at him and said, "Hi Ben! I am ready to go! I'm excited to be going on a road trip," she said as she threw her arms around him.

"Hi, Marti, " said Ben, "did you eat yet? We could leave early if you want to, I'm not hungry." He tried to seem calm. But his unease was growing. He was kicking himself for not telling Martina about his dope use. He felt his stomach clench tight like a fist in his gut.

"Maybe we should get something to take with us? You might be hungry in a couple hours," said Martina lightly. She gestured to Tracy to come take their order.

Tracy approached the counter carrying a take-out food bag. "I made you guys a picnic, a little bit of everything! Including coffee," she said. Ben felt a wave of relief sweep over him. *Tracy knows me so well* he thought. He took the bag of food. He started to pay for it. Tracy insisted they go … "on the house," she said as she ushered them out the door. Ben's stomach medicine started working as Ben and Martina were headed home. A wave of relief helped Ben to relax. He started looking forward to driving to Santa Cruz which felt good. He glanced at Martina. He felt a wave of warmth with his relief. *I could get used to this* Ben told himself.

Martina was excited to get on the road. Within an hour she and Ben were rolling north with plans to stop to eat their picnic along the way. "I have never been to Santa Cruz," exclaimed Martina though she knew Ben already knew she hadn't. She chattered about what she had read about the city. She had applied to a masters program at the university in Santa Cruz without visiting, she was that sure Santa Cruz was where she wanted to earn her degree. She felt drawn to study cultures. Especially how cultures could develop into child abusing, sex trafficking cultures that separated children from their parents. For Martina, the desire to study Cultural Anthropology in Santa Cruz was undeniable. In a few short weeks she would be living a dream while working toward finding her mother. She also felt huge waves of love and respect for Ben because of the work he had been doing by himself in keeping kids safe. The two of them hadn't fully talked about the possibilities. Martina sensed she shouldn't push Ben into talking about their plans until he was ready. Santa Cruz was Ben's childhood home. He didn't talk much about his childhood. Martina could sense he was apprehensive about the place.

Time rolled by slowly for both Ben and Martina as they drove. They talked about the views they passed. They talked about the non-celebration they were planning to share on Christmas and New Years Eve. They talked about their shared dislike of so-called holidays. What they didn't talk about was family. Pleasant silence filled the car. They drove for hours, stopping briefly to eat their picnic. When they got closer to the city Ben started talking slower. He seemed guarded. They maneuvered off the highway.

"This is Ocean Street," he began to explain, "my mother spends a lot of time on Ocean Street." He was quiet for a moment. "She used to, anyway. Arianna's office is also on this street, coming up on the right side. I told her we would see her Sunday so we can focus on finding a place. I hope it's okay if we meet her then. It won't take long. Just lunch," he said as he gestured toward the building they were passing, "that's Arianna's job."

"I really want to meet Arianna," said Martina lightly, then changing the subject, "I think we will like the place I found. We won't have to look at a lot of places. Maybe only this one." She took in Santa Cruz as Ben drove to the room Martina had reserved. It was hard for Martina to think of Ben's family even though she couldn't help thinking about them a lot lately. She was confused about the relationship between Ben and Arianna. *If I had a sister I would hug her everyday* thought Martina. She remembered seeing Ben's mom outside the restaurant her first day of work but then didn't see her again nor did Ben talk much about her. When Ben told her about the night runs, as he called them, she had learned more about Violet. Otherwise he was silent about his mom. Martina definitely admired Violet for her efforts to help kids. She longed to talk with Ben about it. She was trying to choose the best time to bring it up.

Martina realized she was in love with Ben. She was sure he felt the same way about her. They seemed to share an easy coexistence when they were together. He had been staying at her place almost since the day they met. They constantly considered each other which is something neither one of them realized they needed. No one had considered her like Ben did. He asked her opinion on everything. They checked into their hotel.

Once the car was unloaded they headed toward the coast on foot setting out to watch the sunset. Martina was excited to see the ocean. Her mind filled with very early memories of going to the shore with her mother. She tried to recall her father and brother to the memory but she wasn't able to place them. *Maybe they weren't there* thought Martina *I will ask her someday.* She could only recall her mother going into the salty water with her to help her to float.

Ben was thinking he was glad they had stayed close to the harbor. They walked along hand in hand. Ben didn't know much about this part of town so he wasn't worried he would have memories about the place that would crash his good mood. He hadn't thought about methadone or withdrawal since they were leaving in the early morning. He was feeling strong. Walking with Martina was lifting his mood, too, and he was feeling grateful. They got to the beach in time to see the sun slip out of sight. Violet crossed his mind. *I wonder how she is* he thought in a moment of warmth toward his mom *I hope she is okay.*

Violet sat thinking of how much she wanted to leave. She was almost done with a six day stay at the withdrawal unit of inpatient treatment. Everyone, staff and other patrons, were trying to talk her into going through the program as they called it- the twenty-eight day program she could go to immediately. On one hand she was happy to be warm and fed. On the other hand, she wanted to be free. *Fuck it* she thought *if I don't like the program I won't stay at the program.* She signed her way into a longer stay. The day was nearly over when she got to the room she would be staying in for the next month. The double windows of the room faced the coast, overlooking the street. She watched two people walking hand in hand toward the beach. She watched their backs as they receded from her view. *That looks just like my Benny* she thought as she laid down to stretch out on the bed. She was asleep in minutes.

CHAPTER TWENTY-SEVEN

Arianna was trying not to think about Violet. She forced herself to think of something else. Then she would catch her eyes searching the sidewalks along Ocean Street as she walked home. Just as she was leaving work her phone lit up with Keith's name. *He's calling me* she thought excitedly *I thought I wouldn't see him again.* She answered the call breathlessly. "Hello," she rushed, "hold on I'm crossing the street." She rushed to cross Ocean Street. She clutched the phone to her chest just as she noticed the truck coming too fast toward her. *Oh fuck* she thought *he isn't going to stop.*

Keith was sure Arianna hadn't meant to cut off their call. The short time he had spent with her had been the best time in his life. He was sure she felt the same. She had sounded glad to hear from him when she answered the phone. He tried to call her back but her phone went to voicemail. He decided to drive by her job to see why she had ended their call so suddenly.

He heard sirens wailing as he turned onto Ocean Street. He approached the crosswalk he thought she would have used. Emergency vehicles blocked the way. He was waived to the side of the road. An ambulance raced away from the scene. He decided to follow it. He sensed Arianna was in trouble. He knew that he could get past the doctors at the emergency room since he was a doctor himself who has license to practice in the hospital. He hadn't told Arianna he was a doctor because he didn't want to scare her off so-to-speak. It seemed to him that in the past women treated him different once they knew he was a doctor. For Keith, he hadn't become a doctor to make a lot of money like a lot of people thought. In fact, he was in significant debt probably until the end of his life because of his degree. He was young for the job at thirty-two, he knew, which is why he was at the emergency room a lot. He was sent on errands other doctors wouldn't think of doing.

Keith had become a doctor in order to change the world. It was that simple. He wanted to impact people in meaningful, lifelong ways. He had recently completed a fifteen year path to become a psychiatrist. Sometimes he went to the emergency room to help people in crisis. He was familiar with the staff. He knew he could find out if Arianna was in that ambulance.

In all the time that Arianna lived in Santa Cruz she never became close enough to anyone that she could list them as an emergency contact. She was deeply ashamed of her so-called next-of-kin- Violet. She would not have expected Violet to rescue her from anything anyway. Not that Violet had a phone or was reachable. They had a common last name but it was an unusual one. Arianna's phone got smashed when it hit the ground after the collision. Based on her identification she carried, she was identified but she remained unconscious. One of the nurses knew Arianna from recovery groups but even she didn't know anything about Arianna's family. One of the mental health doctors had also identified Arianna. He was awaiting news of her status.

Chapter Twenty-Eight

Ben and Martina walked back to their room in silence. They were exhausted from their long drive. They were further tired out by the long walk. That, combined with darkness coming on quickly, they were asleep soon stretching out to rest. Ben tried to ignore thoughts of panic about how morning might turn out for him. He knew where the methadone clinic was in case he decided he needed help. He convinced himself that if he felt sick he would just take the doses he had. Or tell Martina that he was sick. *I don't have to tell her why* he thought was his last thought before a fitful sleep that granted him rest for a few short hours. He had two, six milligram methadone doses with him but was trying to avoid taking the stuff.

He woke at three in the morning with his stomach in knots. He gulped some stomach medicine. He slipped out of the room to get some ice to eat. He slipped back in. He sat in the bathroom in case Martina woke up. He planned to claim he was shitting. Or puking. He jammed his fists into his stomach trying to make it stop flexing. He was sweating. By four he had taken stomach medicine which had helped his stomach to relax. He stood up to listen for Martina. He got into the shower. He blasted himself with hot water until the steam blocked his sight. He turned off the water. He stood in the steam thinking about the changes he was making. He was determined to not take the methadone he had brought with him unless it was dire.

Ben thought of Martina. He knew he was in love with her. He thought about her all the time. When he was awake, he wanted to know that she was happy. He wanted to know what she was doing.

If he thought she was hungry or bored he wanted to change that for her and make her life better. When he was sleeping, he wanted to know she was safe with him. He wanted to help make her dreams come true which was exactly what brought him back to this city that he had never stopped loving. He had only lived in Santa Cruz for those first years of his life He had been torn away suddenly but that didn't stop the feeling he had of deep connection to the place. He was counting on not being connected to the drug world here since he hadn't ever been strung out in Santa Cruz. He wasn't worried about booze- he had seemed to outgrow any thoughts of drinking even a beer since his leg had healed- but he was worried about what Violet would say and do when she saw him.

Violet woke suddenly with a dream fresh in her thoughts. Her brain had been playing some early memories from when she was pregnant with Ben. Memories of how much she wanted to be a mom to him filled her mind. She recalled how that hours after she found out she was going to have him she vowed to be a better mom than she had been to Chase and to Arianna. *I sure fucked that up* thought Violet. She had lasted about three weeks before she started smoking a little dope every night to relax. She hid the pregnancy as long as she could from the methadone clinic but once they knew she was knocked up she started smoking every morning and afternoon, too. *At least I didn't shoot dope when I was knocked up* she thought *smoking can't be as bad.*

She shrugged off her thoughts as she rolled herself over. She was alone in the room. She vaguely remembered someone coming into the room in the night but the two other beds looked the same, as if no one had slept in them. A door stood open and she could see into the hallway. "Hello," Violet called out weakly. No one answered. She tried to drift back to sleep. Her body needed methadone though so she made her way out of bed.

Violet realized she was finally having a morning without thinking about booze first thing. Now it was methadone. But she didn't think about methadone the way she thought about booze. Methadone was mostly a body thing … she would start to sweat, maybe get some stomach cramps. Booze was a body *and* mind thing for Violet. When she was on booze her first thought would be of whatever container of vodka she had saved from the day before. Sometimes she couldn't remember what she had saved or where she had put the bottle. *I don't have to think about that today* thought Violet. She allowed herself some good feelings.

She made her way to breakfast by following her nose. Soon she was caught up in learning the routines of the place. She would get her methadone every morning before breakfast as early as six. She had signed a methadone taper plan at intake that put her on track to be safely off methadone in two years. She knew she could change her plan anytime based on if she felt she was in danger of relapsing into heroin use. By the end of her first morning in treatment Violet was getting comfortable. She started to feel grateful. She was especially grateful for methadone which took the edge off her demeanor. She was beginning to smile at people.

Ben was deciding to take half of his morning methadone just as heard noise from the other room. He changed his mind yet again. *Fuck it* he thought *I'll ignore my fucking stomach.*

"Benny?" Martina called from just outside the closed bathroom door, "are you okay?" She tapped on the door a couple of times.

"Yea, I'll be right out," Ben answered. He opened the shower door to let out the steam. "I couldn't sleep," he said lightly, "I thought a shower might help me relax." He smiled at Martina as he came out. He stretched on the bed.

"I think I'll take a shower, too," she said as she went into the bathroom,"it's almost six." She turned on the shower leaving the bathroom door open. The sound of the shower soothed Ben into a fitful sleep. He dreamed of his mother. It was the day she got out of prison in his dream. Violet was happy to see him that day. Her smiling face was in his mind when he woke a half hour later.

Keith had arrived at the hospital behind the ambulance. But he hadn't approached. He knew the medics were probably very busy. He just had to know if this was Arianna. He went into the front of the hospital to make his way to the emergency room internally winding through the halls. No one questioned him. By the time he made it across the hospital the person just brought in was being assessed for injuries so he wasn't able to see her. He checked into the computer and confirmed that it was Arianna. He planned to stay with her until she was awake.

CHAPTER TWENTY-NINE

B en and Martina set out to see their prospective home around nine on Saturday morning in good spirits. It was an unusually warm day for early December. The place Martina had found for them to see was unusual. They would rent the second floor of an old three story house for a great rate. The odd side was they would share the first floor kitchen.

Martina loved the house from the moment they arrived. It was yellow. There were airy balconies on all sides. She didn't mind that it was downtown on a busy street. The street was tree-lined and there was a bus stop in front of the house with a direct line to the university. She thought maybe Ben wouldn't mind not having a kitchen since he had spent so much time cooking for work. Besides they could use the downstairs kitchen anytime. The top floor attic was occupied. The owner lived on the third floor with her cats. They could have two bedrooms and a bathroom on the second floor with locked access to ensure privacy.

Together they decided to take the place since it seemed ideal. Neither one had been looking forward to the search. By noon they had signed the paperwork and scheduled a move-in date. Martina's excitement was contagious. Ben allowed himself to go-with-the-flow so to speak, he tried to catch Martina's enthusiasm. He chugged another dose of stomach medicine. Ben was feeling good about the day- for him it was moment to moment because he was coming off methadone. Martina was feeling good about everything.

"Can we explore Santa Cruz? I've been reading about places to go see," said Martina lightly, "I found a place where monarch butterflies gather. Can we go?" They were sitting in the car outside their new home. Uncomfortable silence began to fill the space between them for the first time as Ben didn't answer. Martina shifted in her seat. She opened the door to let in some fresh air. "We can do something else," she said, "I'm open to whatever you want." She smiled.

Ben started the car. Martina closed her door. "I know just where you mean," said Ben, "we can grab some sandwiches, have a picnic, see the bugs." The uncomfortable silence dissipated as they laughed together. Ben started driving toward the west side of town where he knew of a park full of trees that attracted monarch butterflies. He hadn't been to this part of Santa Cruz since the day his mother was arrested. They stopped for sandwiches.

Ben's appetite for food was gone but he made a huge effort at feeling normal for Martina's sake. He was careful not to drive on West Cliff Drive yet, which had been the scene of the stabbing, he wasn't ready. He hadn't told Martina of the stabbing or his years in lockup. She knew he didn't like to talk about his life. When they were done with lunch they walked into the park Ben knew about but it seemed they were too early in the season to see the butterflies. Signs indicated that in a couple months the butterflies would arrive. Ben promised to bring her back to the park in January.

They could hear waves crashing as they neared the end of the butterfly trail.

"Let's go see the waves," said Martina excitedly, "it's so loud!" She headed toward the beach without waiting for Ben. This was an apex for Ben. *On the other side of this beach is West Cliff Drive* Ben thought to himself *maybe I will remember something I want to stay forgotten.* He was trying hard to find the ability to move forward. He started toward Martina, downhill onto the sandy beach. He let the sight and sound of the ocean fill his mind. The sun warmed them as they sat in the sand.

"Maybe we should head back today so we can get some rest before we have to do a night run," suggested Ben. It would be dark soon but they could be back in Southern California by midnight, reasoned Ben. "Arianna will understand," he continued, "she knows we'll be living here soon. We can have lunch with her then." In the back of his mind Ben knew he was trying to avoid spending more time on the west side. He was afraid to walk on West Cliff Drive.

Martina, who had no idea that Ben didn't want to walk along the cliffs, started walking toward the ridge where the road began. "Sure. We can head back tonight that's cool with me," said Martina, then, "let's walk the long way back to the car." Ben followed.

They walked along in silence taking in the beauty and fresh air. Ben found himself wondering if Violet ever walked on West Cliff Drive. He tried to imagine her as he had last seen her, strung out on dope, unable to keep her eyes open with no apparent interest in the world. He was grateful he didn't have any memories coming up as they walked along. He decided he should tell Martina about what had happened thinking she might find out from others which would be ugly, he thought. He didn't want to the the chance that she would be upset with him.

"I have some memories of this road," Ben started, he looked down the cliffside to the churning ocean as they walked "and some stuff to tell you that I should have probably already told you…"

Martina was quiet. She took his hand. They walked slower. She tried to let him know by her warm touch that there was nothing he could say that she wouldn't forgive.

"You know my mom was in prison," Ben began, then, "I was just a kid. No one told me anything that day." He paused. He realized that he didn't remember exactly where the incident had happened. Walking along the drive was not triggering the trauma which he had feared. "Let's turn here to head for the car," said Ben. He continued with his story, "the day Violet was arrested I was put in a foster home somewhere around here. I ran from there. I thought I was being chased. I was eleven. I was scared." He stopped talking. His mind suddenly flooded with memories of feeling threatened.

"I had a knife with me," Ben started, then he rushed, "I stuck a lady with the knife I had because I thought she was trying to catch me. I stabbed her. She didn't die. I spent years in lockup for it." They walked along in silence. "When I got out I moved down south to be near Violet," Ben said quietly, "I'm sorry I didn't tell you before."

Martina squeezed Ben's hand. She stopped walking. She turned to face him. "I love you Ben Ramsey," she paused to look up at him, "you did what you had to do. I know you wouldn't mean to hurt anyone. It sounds to me like the impulse of a scared boy." She pressed herself to him and hugged him tightly. "You aren't violent, Benny," she said, "I know. You didn't want anyone to die. And no one did." She released her hug as she turned to urge them along. "Let's get going," she said, "we have some driving to do."

Ben called Arianna to leave a message for her that they wouldn't be around on Sunday. It was not unusual for Ben to leave her messages so he didn't think twice about not speaking directly to her. He felt so much lighter after talking to Martina about the stabbing. Even lighter than he had after doing his fifth step with Dennis. He smiled at Martina as they checked out of their room early to head south.

Ben was relieved to be heading back. He still had one more night run. *One more time* he thought *then the whole thing will be legit.* The night runs were the one nagging thing that Ben dreaded. But he trusted Martina. And Martina said she was going to bring in good people to take over so that no one would get into trouble. He knew what he had been doing, the night runs, they weren't wrong. But he also knew it was sensitive. He knew if he wasn't intervening for these kids then they would be trafficked. Sold to the highest bidder.

He had so many mixed feelings about the night runs. He was burdened by them. But then he also had gratitude that he had been able to share his burden with Martina. He needed to get some help. He was glad to have an end in sight. He did feel good about helping so many people find their way home. *Probably the only thing I've done for other people* he thought. Martina was setting Ben up with people who would be going with him on his next run. People that Martina trusted. On a darker side, he was beginning to realize that he had some bitterness that Violet had even got involved in that shit. If Violet hadn't started up the night runs then Ben would never have been involved. He wondered where she was or if she was even alive.

CHAPTER THIRTY

Violet found herself feeling more alive than ever. She was gaining newfound interest in people's lives that she hadn't previously experienced. There was a dozen people with her at inpatient treatment with various lengths of time without drugs or alcohol. Plus she talked with the staff. Between meetings and counseling she spent most of her Saturday in conversation. Talking with people reminded her of Marta- who she thought of daily. *Its kinda funny* she thought *I can only make friends when I am locked in with people.*

It was her first Sunday morning in treatment. She was now only taking methadone. She was feeling better every hour. She spent free time playing cards and listening to music. She avoided thinking about the future for the most part. But memories of the past kept intruding on her thoughts. She thought of her own kids. She couldn't help comparing herself to Marta's story. *Marta lived for her kids* thought Violet *my kids didn't get a mom like that.*

She took out her notebook to try to write what she had just been thinking. Carmen had her focusing on being aware of her thoughts. The point was for Violet to be nicer to herself. Carmen had told her that if she could change the way she thought about her self then maybe she could be nicer to herself. And if she could do that she would be nicer to others. Including her own children. Especially her own children. She wrote *I was a shitty mother.* She snapped her notebook shut. She wondered where her children were. She wondered if they thought about her.

Carmen had tracked down Violet's daughter on Friday but she hadn't approached her. She hadn't wanted to interrupt Arianna's weekend plans. She hadn't found Arianna's personal phone number, only her work address. She had planned to show up at her public job space around noon on Monday.

Keith was sitting next to Arianna in a hospital room thinking of how quickly he had fallen in love with her. He was sure his feelings were there before this tragedy. He knew she wouldn't want a knight-in-shining-armor kind of guy. He also knew she might be pissed if she woke up to find he was there. He was practically a stranger.

There was a rustling next to him. He looked toward Arianna as her eyes opened. She tried to clear her throat. Keith helped her to take a sip of water. She held his gaze. He could sense her relief that he was there. "It's okay, no need to talk. Do you remember we were talking when ... well you got hit by a truck." He stopped. He held her hand in both of his.

"I am so happy to see you looking at me," he started, then, "I am a doctor here but not like you think. I'm a psychiatrist. That's how I got in. I came right away to where I thought you were walking. I followed the ambulance here." He stopped talking. *She might not remember* he told himself *shut the fuck up and let her answer.*

Arianna sipped some water then tried to sit up. She laid back on the pillow, groaning. She cleared her throat quietly. She avoided looking at Keith.

"Look," started Keith, he hesitated. Arianna looked at him. Her gaze gave him the strength to talk. "I am so sorry this has happened to you. I wish I could turn back time. I would have called you just five minutes later. Maybe you would have been able to get out of the way," he paused. He continued softly, asking, "do you know what I mean? Do you remember?"

Arianna managed to sit up to take another drink of water. She started to shake with sobs, her shoulders giving way to her distress. "I do remember! It happened so fast," she said breathlessly between sobs, "it was not your fault! I shouldn't have even looked at my phone."

She let loose of her tears. She cried out, "I'm so sorry!"

"Oh honey," Keith said as he wrapped his arms around her shaking shoulders, "it was not your fault either. The guy was drunk. He failed to stop. I think he will probably pay a pretty big fine that might include some jail time. I can't say enough how glad I am that you are here talking to me now." He squeezed her gently.

Arianna let herself be engulfed by Keith's warm, loving arms. She leaned into his hug. She let her sobs go until there were no more sobs to let loose. He held her tightly. Quietly. "Thank you," she said softly. "What day is it?" Arianna asked, "I feel like I missed a whole week."

"You were hit twenty days ago," answered Keith, then in attempt to lighten the news, "you successfully avoided the holidays." He tried to laugh but his throat was too dry. His eyes were wet with tears as he gazed at Arianna.

Arianna began to cry, too. "I was supposed to have lunch with my brother! He must think I hate him! He was bringing his new girlfriend to find a place in Santa Cruz. I was going to see him for the first time in a long time," she paused, "I was going to meet her for the first time."

"Can you call him?" Keith asked, "you can use my phone if you need to. Your phone was destroyed." He was quiet. He released his grip on her. He reached for his phone.

"Thank you so much. I feel like I know you," said Arianna, "thank you." She tried to catch her breath. She realized she didn't have Ben's number. She found herself holding Keith's phone but with a loss for words. She handed it back to him. "I'll have to find the number," she mumbled, "maybe Violet has it. I wonder where she is?"

The days were passing quickly for Violet in treatment. She had no choice but to accept that Arianna was not around. Carmen had tried to stop by Arianna's job but was told she was off work until after the holidays with no indication of where she had gone. Carmen left a note.

Violet stretched her arms up as she thought of Arianna. Her only daughter. *She is better off without knowing me* thought Violet *I haven't been a good mother to her.* She let her mind drift to the past. She thought of how Arianna was always singing when she was a kid. She would sing to Violet's belly when Violet was pregnant with Ben. Violet realized she didn't know much about Arianna or her life story. Sadness clouded Violet's thoughts. But she didn't panic, she was learning to go through her feelings instead of stamping them out with booze or drugs. Her thinking was slowly clearing.

Violet no longer thought of booze first thing in the morning. She was sleeping eight or more hours every night. She was eating more than she ever had by her own reckoning. Even methadone had taken a backseat to her thinking as she had come to trust the relief it brought to her daily. She was grateful not to have to struggle to the clinic every day to get her methadone dose. In fact, she was grateful for so many things that it brought tears to her eyes to think of how lucky she felt. She was especially grateful for Carmen. Talking with Carmen was lighting up a part of Violet that she had only felt when she was with Marta. And now, after many hours talking with Carmen- sometimes two hours a day- she could think about Marta without feeling heavy guilt.

Thinking about Arianna was a different story. Violet felt that Arianna's absence from work, and from the holiday time, was directly meant to hurt Violet. In the past Arianna had always managed to find Violet on the holidays, especially New Years Eve, to share the changing of the year. Sometimes they would call Ben. Violet tried to think of Ben. *Ugh* thought Violet *I can actually feel on my chest the weight of the guilt I have about how I have treated that kid.* She turned her mind to the present. She went forward with her day. So much had changed in the short time she had been inpatient. She was ready to transition to the next phase of her recovery as Carmen called it. Violet was going to move into a home with six other women who were also kicking dope or booze. She would be heavily involved with inpatient treatment but from the outside, attending support groups. She would be meeting regularly with Carmen for therapy.

Violet was feeling scared about transitioning out of the safe cocoon that inpatient treatment had become. Lately her moods were changing almost hourly from happy to completely dejected. She made her way to the nurse for her methadone then headed to breakfast thinking of her scheduled meeting with Carmen soon after. *Carmen will help me through this* thought Violet *I can do this.*

I can do this Arianna thought *almost done.* She stood and turned around as the doctor had asked her. She was getting one last exam before going home to rest a few more days before returning to work. She felt disoriented. She was confused most of the time even as she worked to accept that she had missed the holidays. She felt like she was coming out of a blackout drug binge. And, in a lot of ways, she was indeed coming off drugs. She had been in an induced coma for three weeks due to head and spine injuries sustained when she was hit by a truck that was traveling thirty miles an hour. Now it seemed she had recovered fully. She had been working hard in the days since she woke to get back to independence. She was almost there. Her mind filled with thoughts of eating out. She dreamed of sitting in a restaurant. Her stomach audibly groaned. She blushed.

"Someone is hungry," said the doctor, "you need something in your tummy." He kept typing into the computer in front of him as he talked.

Arianna felt a rush of embarrassment. *Why is he treating me like a toddler? I am clearly not a child* she thought angrily. She took a deep breath. She turned toward the door. She was trying not to appear too eager to leave feeling like that would hold her back somehow. As if the doctor would change his mind about her discharge because she wanted to leave so bad.

"We are almost done," the doctor said as he stood, "I'll be right back with your discharge paperwork. I'll hurry. Most people are really eager to leave, don't worry." He smiled warmly as he left the room.

Arianna was relieved that it was all in her thinking that he was being anything other than professional. *He probably has little kids at home* she thought as she let him off her moody hook. Her stomach groaned again. The doctor came into the room with Keith close behind.

"You sure you don't want to stick around for lunch? We can extend the discharge time," the doctor asked. He immediately added, "I'm joking, I'm joking." He laughed.

Arianna gave a nervous laugh. "I am ready to go. Am I okayed to go? My ride is here," she said as she smiled at Keith.

"You are all set. Everything we talked about is printed here," he paused as he handed her a thick folder, "usually one of the nurses would see you out but the kind doc here is going to be your escort." He gestured toward Keith.

Keith smiled then stepped briefly into the hall. He rolled a wheelchair into the room. "Hospital policy is that you ride out," he said as he smiled at Arianna. She quietly got into the chair with little regard for the banter between the two men as they headed down the hall together.

Once they were settled into the car Keith turned to Arianna with a serious face. "I have to ask you something," he said gravely. He waited a moment. Arianna fidgeted in her seat.

"Well ask me," she blurted out, "your scaring me!"

"I'm sorry, I didn't mean to scare you. It's my dry sense of humor I guess," he paused, "I'm truly sorry. I just need to ask where to go? Where do you live? I was trying to make light of the fact that I haven't been to your home before, yet, I love ..." he stopped, then said softly, "I love you."

Tears made Arianna's eyes shine as she smiled back at him. She was speechless.

"Which way do I go?" he asked lightly. He started the car.

"My house happens to be a block from where I was hit," she said quietly, then added "you can park anywhere around that street because I don't have a driveway." She was suddenly reminded of her mother. She had never told Violet she lived so close to her job and to where Violet was likely to be passing daily. She knew that if Violet knew where she lived that she would soon find her mother sleeping in front of her place. Or in her bushes. *Stay in the present* she told herself. She felt a rush of warmth. She was grateful to have Keith in her life. It felt good to be taken care of. She looked over at him as he calmly drove her home. "Thanks for helping me," she said, "it means more to me than I can say."

Arianna started to think about calling Ben. She was worried that he wouldn't be reachable. She knew when they last spoke that he seemed skeptical about them being friends. Now almost a month had passed. She hadn't talked to him. He no idea that she had been in a coma. She practiced in her mind what she would say to him if he answered his phone. They had gone months, years even, without talking. She hoped he was okay.

CHAPTER THIRTY-ONE

Ben was feeling good about his move to Santa Cruz. In three weeks time he had tapered off methadone completely and was, for the first time in his adult life, drug free. He had swung into an attitude of not wanting to take any drug which was something Dennis said might happen. Sometimes the cratered scar on his leg would ache with a phantom pain. Ben was learning to think it through. He learned to dispel the pain in short time. He didn't mention to Martina that he was a junkie. *Was* he thought *I am not a junkie now*.

In the same three weeks time, Ben and Martina had packed their belongings. They were heading north. Martina had left that morning in her car. Ben took one last look to make sure back of the truck was locked before climbing into the driver's seat of the rented moving van. He started the truck. His phone rang. He looked at the unfamiliar number and decided to answer only because he was waiting to hear from restaurants he had applied to work for in Santa Cruz. "This is Ben," he said when he answered.

"Oh, Benny, it's Arianna! Please don't hang up," came his sister's voice into the truck cab, "I was in a car accident." She paused. He could hear her try to stop crying. She asked, "are you still there?"

"Arianna! Shit! What happened to you? We thought you had decided you didn't want to know us," Ben said as he turned off the truck. "Are you okay? Wow. I'm not sure what to say, Arianna, I am glad you called," he said with kindness.

"I wasn't able to call you. I've been in the hospital since the last time we talked," she paused, then added breathlessly, "I got hit by a truck." She sobbed quietly. She was so relieved he had answered. She took a deep breath. "I was literally hit by a truck while I was walking across Ocean Street. I've been in a medical coma as my brain healed from the trauma. I got out of the hospital this morning."

"That's terrible! I am so sorry to hear that happened to you! Are you going to be okay? I mean, well, you are home?" Ben wasn't sure what to say. He had so much he wanted to say. His heart swelled with love for his sister but he wasn't sure what to do with the feeling. "Damn," was all he could say, "damn."

"I'm so glad you answered, Benny, please know I didn't mean to not call you," said Arianna, then asked, "where are you guys? Are you still moving to Santa Cruz? How is Martina?"

"We are. Martina is up there now. I am rolling out in the moving truck as we speak. I thought it might be a job prospect calling when I answered the phone," said Ben, then "I have a lot to tell you! We will be near downtown in a funky old house. You can meet Martina, too, probably tonight! How are you feeling? Do you still have all your arms and legs?" He was trying to lighten the heavy conversation. Again he felt a wave of love wash over him toward his sister. He tried to send the feeling through the phone.

"I do," Arianna laughed, then said dryly, "I have everything except for twenty something days of my life." She was feeling a wave of gratitude as the conversation went on. She had been home less than an hour. Keith had brought her home then left to pick up take out food. She had called Ben right away. She followed Ben's lead in trying to lighten the mood. "I sure wish I had one of your breakfast burritos right now," said Arianna, " but soon I will! I will let you go so you can get rolling! I will be home whenever you get to town. This is my new permanent phone number, call me when you get here. You are in a moving truck? I know people who can help you guys unload."

"I'll call you around five or six," said Ben, then, "Martina will be glad to hear you haven't decided to ignore us, she was worried that you didn't like her. I have been telling her I thought maybe you were wanting to avoid Violet. Have you seen her? Mom?"

"I've been out of it Benny. I haven't seen or heard from mom," said Arianna quietly, then, "I was looking for her daily before the accident. I think she will turn up somewhere. I plan to look for her."

"Fuck. I'm sorry, Arianna, I forgot. You know me. My memory is shit," said Ben. He had forgotten she was in a coma for three weeks. "I love you," he said softly, "I'm glad you are okay. See you tonight!"

"It's okay, Benny. I can't wait to see you! I love you, too, little brother," she said lightly. She could hear Ben starting the truck just as she heard Keith come through her door with their food. She beamed a smile at Keith as she put down her phone. She explained excitedly to Keith how her conversation had gone.

Ben put the truck in gear and began to roll away as yet another wave of warm feelings washed through his mind. *I do like this feeling* he thought *I think this might be love.* He glanced at the restaurant as he drove by on his way out of town. *Maybe I will start my own breakfast place* he thought. He let his mind wander through possibilities.

Violet tried hard to keep her thoughts positive as she made her way to her new home. The place was walking distance to inpatient treatment. Carmen walked along beside Violet. The walk was beautiful. Colorful beach cottages with overgrown flower gardens lined the street. The house she was moving into was painted bright green with a raised vegetable garden in front of a wide porch. They stopped to munch on cherry tomatoes before walking up to the front door. It looked like a home. *This doesn't look like a halfway house for drunks* thought Violet.

"Are you sure this is the place? It doesn't seem right," said Violet.

"Yes, this is it," said Carmen as she opened the door and went in, gesturing for Violet to follow. Inside, the house was quiet, sunlit. "I have been here many times," said Carmen, "it isn't always quiet, believe me, some of the women here have kids who visit. There is a playground and a tree fort for them out back. Don't worry, Vee, no kids live here." Carmen had seen the look on Violet's face at the thought of having kids around. Carmen knew that Violet was working on the guilt she felt about how she had mothered, or hadn't mothered, her kids. It was on Carmen's schedule to be in touch with Violet's daughter when Arianna returned to her job after the holidays. It happened that Violet was moving into her new home just days before Carmen would be able to reach Arianna. They looked around the kitchen and living areas as a young woman came and introduced herself to Violet.

"Hi I'm Jane, one of your roomies. There are six of us here now," she smiled, then continued, "your room is the smallest room but it is also the most private." Jane showed Violet around. She helped her to find her spot on the chore list and cooking schedule. "Don't worry about cooking though, we can order pizza if we want on the nights we have to cook. Sometimes we have pizza five nights a week," she laughed as she explained the house.

Carmen made sure Violet had a schedule to follow. Violet would be reporting to the inpatient facility every morning and afternoon for counseling and to participate in outpatient therapy groups. She would get daily rides to the methadone clinic until she earned take home doses of methadone. Plus she had to stay on a plan to taper off methadone safely. She was expected to go to recovery meetings every evening unless she was sick. And she had to attend house meetings twice a week. Carmen could tell Violet was overwhelmed by the move. She put her hands on Violet's shoulders and looked into her eyes.

"You can do this, Violet," Carmen started, then continued, "I think you will like it here. You can go into your room to get privacy if you need to. You can reach out to any one of these women who live here if you need to talk. Especially if you find yourself thinking about using or drinking. Your schedule will keep you busy."

Violet felt a rush of warmth. She wasn't used to people caring whether she lived or died. Carmen had been the kindest person she had known since Marta. Her heart wrenched as she thought of Marta. *I wish Marta were here* thought Violet. She took a deep breath. "I'll see you in a couple days," she said to Carmen. She ushered Carmen to the door. Once Carmen had gone, Violet stretched out on her bed. She tried not to think of the past. Violet knew Carmen would be contacting Arianna soon. She was worried about the rejection she felt she would likely get. She felt raw. She was scared. She had always run out for booze or dope when she felt like this but now she had choices. *God damn choices* she thought vehemently *I don't want to think about it*. She fell asleep.

Arianna woke to the sound of her front door closing. She had been sleeping on the couch. She opened one eye to look around the room. She sensed she was alone then opened both eyes wide. Keith had been here when she fell asleep. She saw he had left a note for her. She smiled as she read his kind words. 'See you tonight' he had signed the note. She had asked him to be around when Ben and Martina came over. She was glad he had said he would. She was itching to go to her office for a few minutes to check in. Her doctor and Keith both told her to rest but she wasn't going to listen. She had hours until dinnertime. She was out the door within the hour headed to her office. It was a beautiful sunny day. She felt wonderful to be outside. She avoided the crosswalk where she had last walked in her neighborhood, where she had been hit. She looked for her mom even as she told herself that wasn't her goal.

CHAPTER THIRTY-TWO

Violet stayed in her room the whole first day she was in the halfway house. She felt confused. Part of her wanted to be there so she tried to figure out just what she was halfway to. Another part of her felt she was halfway free to go get some booze or some dope. Then she would think of Carmen and the agreements she had made with her to try new things for a couple of months. A light knock on her door brought her to the present. "Hey it's dinnertime," a soft voice called out.

She made her way to the kitchen. She was surprised to see only three boxes of pizza -no people gathered at the table. No pressure to join people eating together. Violet felt relieved and sad at the same time as she grabbed some pizza. She headed back to her room.

Every time that she caught herself thinking of leaving the house she made herself stop. She was trying to follow Carmen's suggestion that she make a list of things she was grateful for but Violet had not started the project. She went with two housemates to a recovery meeting in a nearby church but did not feel comfortable. The meeting was full of 'old-timers', people who had been coming to the meetings for a long time. Violet could not relate. She had trouble just listening. She was glad to get back to her room that first night. She opened her journal for the second time to start her list. The first thing on her gratitude list was her bed. She fell asleep thinking of Arianna and the good times they had when Violet had been sober, or on methadone only, those few short years.

Ben was thinking of how much he enjoyed having a clear mind. Since he had stopped methadone he spent about a week dealing with short periods of thinking about heroin. After that, he had felt free as never before. It wasn't even that physical cravings were gone but instead just that his thinking didn't turn to using dope like it used to. Sometimes his mind would begin to trick him. Thoughts like *no big deal, Benny, why not* crossed his mind. That first week he had called Dennis when he had those thoughts. He found if he kept very busy then he didn't even think about anything but the task at hand. Planning and working toward moving to Santa Cruz was definitely keeping him busy. Now here he was rolling toward his destiny, so to speak.

He thought of his sister. He was relieved to hear from her. He was surprised by her news. He had thought it was rude of her to just ditch the lunch date they had made. But she had ditched him in the past so he shrugged it off. He had explained to Martina the he and Arianna didn't know each other much. He looked forward to seeing his sister and introducing her to Martina. He also looked forward to having help unloading the truck.

Arianna noticed that everything in her office had been placed on shelves. Her desk apparently had been taken over by whoever stepped in to do her job when she was absent all those many days. But her inbox was there and it was full. She noticed on top of the pile a small note that said, '*social worker Carmen Perez came by about Violet*', there was a number but nothing else. No date. She took the note when she left for home.

She decided to call the number right way when she got home. A pleasant voice answered the phone, "this is Carmen."

"Hi. My name is Arianna Ramsey. I have a note that you wanted to talk to me about Violet Ramsey? She is my mom," she paused, "I've been out of the office and just today got your note."

"Arianna! Thank you for calling. We, me and your mom, have been waiting for your vacation to end," said Carmen, then, "your mom will be so glad you called."

"Where is Violet?" Arianna asked. The question hung in the air. *I can't call her mom* thought Arianna.

After a moment, Carmen answered carefully, "Violet is currently in a halfway house for women recovering from addiction. She has been in treatment for almost two months and is doing really good."

Arianna was silent. Carmen continued, "your mom wants to see you. Do you think you could visit with her? She is working hard at settling in to the halfway house. She's been there a few days."

"I want to see her, yes," answered Arianna. "I was in the hospital for a while and am home now. I was hit by a car. How do I get in touch with Violet? I mean," she hesitated, "my mom. I can stop by there later today." Tears welled up in her eyes as she thought of seeing her mom. And seeing her sober. Sober!

"I will find out when is the best time to stop by," said Carmen, "thanks again for calling, Arianna. Please call her house if you want to, I'll text you their number. As soon as I find out I will text you best time to visit, too. Violet doesn't have a cell phone or we could text her. Best to call the house if you want to talk to her." Carmen was quiet for a moment, then said, "I am so sorry to hear about your accident. Thank you for sharing with me. Do you want me to talk to your mom before you call her?"

"That's okay, thanks. I want to call her myself. Thank you for making the effort to contact me," answered Arianna, "we had been out of touch for a while. I am surprised and excited to hear that she is in treatment! Wow. Go Vee. Thanks again for calling."

"Of course," said Carmen, "Violet is really working hard. I am sure you and I will meet soon."

Arianna left her office with renewed energy. She walked home with a lightness she hadn't felt before. She crossed Ocean Street like she always had without thought of the accident. Only a brief flashback of remembering the moment when she answered the phone. She shrugged off the thought. She brought to mind the plans she had later to have dinner with Keith. Ben and Martina, too. Then she thought of her mom. The prospect of seeing Violet, and seeing her sober, was something she had never thought would happen. *Maybe Keith can drive me over to see Violet* she thought.

CHAPTER THIRTY-THREE

Violet sat thinking of this new feeling of warmth that was with her more often than not. She had just finished attending a recovery meeting. The topic at the meeting had been forgiveness. She had realized in the meeting that the person she hated the most, the person she most needed to forgive, was herself. All morning she had been caught up in thinking about Arianna. Her thoughts circled back to how she had failed to be a mother to Arianna. Then she would think of Ben. And then Chase. *I failed them all* came to her mind, then *but maybe I can change.* She had started to talk about them, her kids, to Carmen. It was too late for her to make it up to Chase but maybe she had a chance with Arianna and Ben. She was sitting on the front porch in the sunshine when a car pulled into the driveway. She didn't recognize the car or the driver but when the passenger got out of the car she could see that it was Arianna. Tears welled up in Violet, her chest heaved. Arianna waved at her and called out, "Hi!" As she made her way onto the porch. Violet sobbed.

"Oh, Arianna! I was just thinking about you," Violet almost screamed, "Arianna!" They hugged on the porch. Both women cried. Their shoulders shook together as they embraced.

"I am so sorry I wasn't around for you, mom," said Arianna, "so much has happened. I was in the hospital. Car accident. I got out today. But you! How did you get here? I am excited for you, Vee, you look great."

Tears rolled down Violet's face. "I can't remember the last time you called me mom," she said, "even though you called me 'Vee', too." She laughed and sobbed at the same time. "It is so good to see you. An accident? Fuck! Are you okay? A lot happened to me too but mostly I had a blackout. Woke up in detox. They detoxed me off booze and talked me into staying. Here I am," said Violet. She opened her arms to gesture around the place.

"Sounds like we both had near-death experiences," exclaimed Arianna, then, "I know someone else who had a near-death experience. Benny." She put a hand on Violet's arm as if to steady her. "So much has happened in just a couple of months," said Arianna, "Ben had an overdose. He is alive, it's ok. Don't panic." She gave Violet's arm a squeeze then said as warmly as she could, "he is sober, too. Even off methadone. He is moving here with his girlfriend. Here! To Santa Cruz. I haven't seen him since before my accident. I haven't met his girlfriend yet. She is the reason Ben is moving here." They sat quietly for a few minutes. They shared comfortable silence. It was if the two women needed to be in each other's presence, no words were necessary.

"Wow, I had no idea," said Violet, "A girlfriend? I didn't know he was seeing someone. We lost touch when I left. But you know that story. Marta died. Fuck! I can't believe there was another overdose." She sat. Arianna sat next to her. They heard a car door open and close. A man approached. "Keith! I'm sorry to make you wait," said Arianna as Keith approached the porch.

"Hey, no problem," said Keith, "I just got a call and have to report to work. I can walk over there if you want or maybe you could drop me off? If you don't feel like driving I get that. You should go home and rest. Hi, I'm Keith." He held a hand out to Violet.

Violet shook Keith's hand as she introduced herself. "I'm Violet," she managed.

Arianna looked at Violet. She seemed awed by Keith's presence, she gazed at him. She nudged Violet and asked, "do you want to get some dinner tonight? I can drive."

Reality seemed to settle into Violet's thinking as she answered, "I have to stick around here. I've been here two days. We have to wait a week to gain freedom." She laughed then said, "you can come eat here but I can't go out yet." An awkward silence started. The silence this time wasn't comfortable. Both women fidgeted as Keith started to walk off the porch. He tossed some keys to Arianna.

"I'll jog over to the job," he smiled, "I'm close by. Call me if you need to. I can catch a ride home. I'll get my car from your house tomorrow. I hope your meeting with your brother goes well. I wish I hadn't been called into work. Nice to meet you Violet!" He took off jogging.

"That man loves you a lot," said Violet to Arianna after Keith had gone, "I could see it in his eyes." She looked at her daughter. She had not felt intuitive much in the past but this time she felt it deeply. She could sense the love Keith had for Arianna. If felt good. Steady. Like she should feel this for her girl. She thought of Marta, about how much Marta had talked about her daughter. Violet wanted to be a good mother like Marta had been. She felt a sob well up. She reached out for Arianna. Arianna took Violet's hand and pulled her into a hug. She squeezed her mom tightly.

CHAPTER THIRTY-FOUR

Marta was thinking of the last time she had hugged her daughter. It was the evening before Martina was taken. She had grabbed up her girl before bedtime. She took a big sniff of her hair. She loved to sniff her daughter's hair. Especially at the end of a long day. She took a deep breath trying to imagine the scent of her girl. So many years had passed but memory of the aroma was as fresh as yesterday. She turned over in her bunk. She fell into a fitful sleep. She dreamed about her daughter, her life in Mexico, and her years with Violet. She felt so small. So alone. She didn't know why Violet had stopped writing. It was small comfort to pray. She tried everything to make her nights less nightmarish. *Please god* she thought *I know I am unworthy ... if I could just know that my girl is okay.*

Martina was feeling lost. She was struggling to meet the deadlines the university had placed on her. She was also trying to manage the move. She was having trouble letting Ben take the reins on any aspect of the event. So here she was waiting for Ben to arrive with the moving truck. She had talked to him that morning but not since. It had been almost eight hours. Soon she heard a truck beeping as it backed up. *Finally* she thought *he is here!* She went outside to guide Ben as he parked.

Controlling every situation had become a huge problem for Martina. She just had to have the last word. Or the only word. She was beginning to realize she was her own problem. The move itself was showcasing some of her worries. Martina once had a conversation with a coworker about her need to be in control. They concluded that because Martina was so suddenly out of control when she was taken from her mother she just couldn't allow that vulnerability. *I will let Ben do this* she told herself *it's his home, too.* Ben was coming up the driveway.

"Good news," he said, "my sister called. She had been in the hospital and couldn't call us. She is going to come by with some friends to help us unload the truck."

Martina was surprised by the news. She was also a little worried that strangers would be helping them but then she didn't want to, and couldn't, do the heavy lifting. "That's great! I am glad she could call. But how tragic, a car accident! Is she okay?" Martina asked. *I really have to learn to loosen up* thought Martina.

"She says she is. How about we unload once help gets here? I think it will be soon, maybe a half hour? I need to call Arianna," Ben said as he walked toward the house, "how's it going for you here? I missed you last night."

Ben is right thought Martina *we don't have to start unloading this second.* She smiled at Ben as she followed him into the house. She reached for a hug from him as soon as she was close. "I missed you, too," said Martina as she squeezed Ben tightly, "I don't want to be away from you again."

"No pressure there," said Ben as he laughed, "I don't want to be away from you again either, Marti." He squeezed her tightly then held her at arms length. Their eyes met. He kissed her briefly. He grabbed his phone. "Let's get the show on the road," he exclaimed excitedly as he called his sister.

Arianna's was getting back home from seeing her mom. She had made plans with Violet to visit again after dinnertime. She felt exhausted and elated at the same time. She took a couple ibuprofen, the only drug she was currently taking. *What a trip* she thought *to think of Benny and Vee both sober.* She called two friends to recruit for unloading Ben's truck then took a hot shower before calling Ben. By four she was parking Keith's car on the street outside of Ben and

Martina's new home. She could see the moving truck already backed up to front porch.

Arianna was surprised to find she was nervous about seeing Ben. Meeting his girlfriend was a big deal. She had never known Ben to date. As far as she knew he never did. The house was huge but not imposing. A wide front porch covered with potted plants and cushioned chairs made the place inviting. A small gate separated the porch from the sidewalk. She went in and could see people gathered in the kitchen. She recognized Ben as she stepped into the room. Tears welled up for Arianna. She held them back as she watched Ben as he bent to give Martina a hug. He spotted Arianna as he pulled back from Martina. She could see gladness in his eyes when he smiled at her. Arianna was happy to see that Ben was glad she was there.

"Hey," Ben called out, "Arianna! Aw .." He held out both arms. Arianna let her tears flow as Ben hugged her close. "Wow, I am so glad you are okay." He led her to the kitchen table where a few people were sharing a pizza. "Want some?" Ben asked.

Arianna laughed as she wiped her eyes and caught her breath. "Sure, smells great," answered Arianna, "if there is enough."

"All yours," a man said as he left the kitchen. Others started to clear the counter.

Arianna recognized Martina as the woman she had seen at the restaurant where Ben worked. She approached her with as much warmth as she could. She held out a hand. "You must be Ben's lady," she said awkwardly, "I'm his sister. I'm happy to meet you."

Martina grasped Arianna's outstretched hand with her two hands. She, like Arianna, emanated warmth as she said, "Arianna. I can't say enough how glad I am that you are here. You must be exhausted, sit! Here, have a slice, I'll join you. Ben is going to start unloading. We don't have all that much."

Ben left the house to unload the truck. The two women sat together enjoying pizza for a few minutes. Both women could sense the excitement in the house. Martina took Arianna on a tour of the place. She explained the communal type living, the shared kitchen. Then they went out to help Ben unload the truck. Arianna's friends had arrived to help unload. In short time Ben and Martina were moved into their new home.

Martina and Arianna were instant friends. They chatted about everything from Santa Cruz to what types of vegetables to grow. Ben enjoyed seeing the two women engrossed in each other as they worked bringing stuff up the stairs. Arianna drew Ben into the conversation when she brought up Violet.

"I have interesting news," started Arianna, "Ben you aren't going to believe this … Vee is in recovery. No more booze or drugs." She paused to wait for the words to sink in for Ben. "The whole time I was looking for her before my coma she was in treatment. Now she is in a halfway house. She moved in a few days ago. I found out when I got out of the hospital. I went to see her today."

Ben sat on the stairs where he had been standing as if the news swept him off his feet. In some ways it had done exactly that. He had become accustomed to dismissing thoughts of Violet because he felt like there was nothing he could do for her. He looked up at Arianna. "Wow," he said, "I don't know what to say. Wow."

Arianna gave Ben's arm a squeeze. "I'm going back to see her tonight," she said, "she just moved in so she can't leave except to recovery meetings. Do you want to come with me? You and Martina? We could take the truck back then go see Violet. I'll bring you guys back here."

"Yes," said Ben loudly, "hell yes! Sober me wants to meet sober Vee! Ha! Now I'm a poet." He stood. He stepped onto the landing to grab Martina for a hug. "Just kidding. I am really happy about the news, Arianna! Wow. Let's get going."

CHAPTER THIRTY-FIVE

Violet had fallen asleep after Arianna left her place. She woke up to someone shaking her shoulder. "Hey Violet, wake up," said a woman's voice, "your family is here to see you. They are out on the front porch."

"What? Who ..." started Violet but the person had already gone away. She sat up. *Family? What fucking family? Must be Arianna* thought Violet. She had been sleeping soundly. She had to shake herself awake. She made her way downstairs to the front of the house. She stepped onto the porch in the dusky light. The slanting sun blinded her momentarily. She looked at the figure closest to her. She felt faint as the figure came into focus. *Marta?* Her eyes were tricking her. She couldn't help but exclaim, "Marta!" She fainted.

Ben rushed to catch Violet as she folded, managing to help her slowly to the floor. He crouched in front of her saying her name, "Violet? Hey, Vee ... it's me, Ben."

Violet was only passed out for a moment. She roused at the sound of Ben's voice. "I am so sorry," cried Violet, "I was sleeping. I was dreaming of Marta. I swear I just saw her standing here!" She let Ben help her to her feet. She squinted up at him, the sun still blinding her. He stepped in front of her to block the sun so she could see him. Tears started to roll down her face. "It's good to see you," she said between sobs.

"Surprise," said Arianna brightly, "Ben lives here now, Vee, with his girlfriend. I know I already told you this but I didn't say when! I wanted to surprise you." She gestured for Martina to step closer.

Martina had stepped off the porch. She felt like she had somehow upset Violet. When she heard her mother's name she almost fainted herself. *She said my mother's name when she saw me* was the only thought in her mind. She was frozen in place, unable to react to Arianna inviting her to meet Violet. She was shaking.

Ben made sure Violet was sitting then walked over to Martina. He asked, "are you okay? You look scared, I've never seen your eyes so wide. What can I do for you, Marti? Want to come sit down? I'm sorry for the drama I should have warned you a little more." He scooped her into a hug. He could feel her tremble. "You're shaking," said Ben, "oh sweetie, what can I do?"

"She called me Marta," said Martina into Ben's shirt as he held her, "my mother's name is Marta."

"It is? Damn," said Ben, "Marta was my mom's friend in prison. But this is unbelievable! It must be a common name? I mean, is Marta used a lot in Mexico?"

"I don't know," answered Martina. She pulled out of his embrace just as Violet approached.

Violet was staring at Martina. Her mouth was moving, she appeared to be talking but no words came out. She croaked, "I'm sorry." She started crying. She gestured to Martina then said to Ben, "I'm sorry it's just that she looks like Marta!" She turned to Martina and said, "I don't mean to scare you. You remind me of someone from my past. You look so much like her I thought you were her."

Martina took a deep breath and said, "my mother is named Marta." She wanted to go on. She wanted to say that she had not seen her mother in decades, that she longed to hug her.

"Where is she? Your mother?" Violet asked, "maybe my friend is related to you. You look just like my friend." Her voice trailed off.

Martina looked at Ben. She looked at Violet. She decided to reveal her story to Violet and anyone who was listening. She sensed that

Ben was at a loss for words. Arianna had stepped off the porch to join the group as Martina started to answer Violet.

"I don't know where she is. I was taken from my mother when I was very young. I ended up living with a family in San Diego. I have been searching for my mother since I can remember," said Martina, "I learned years ago that my father and brother were dead but have never learned what happened to my mother."

"Oh my god! It can't be," cried Violet, "my Marta had lost her husband and son but was searching for her young daughter. She was arrested trying to follow smugglers who had taken her girl!" She cried deep, heaving sobs. "Maybe you are the daughter of my friend. Oh god. San Diego?" She bent over. She put her hands on her knees. "This is too much!"

Ben put a hand on Violet's shoulder. "Do you want to go sit on the porch? Wow, this is a lot for all of us," he said.

The four of them made their way to porch chairs. No one spoke. There was a growing current of excitement amongst them. Yet they also shared an underlying sadness that throbbed like a broken heart. Marta had died in prison. They all knew that. They knew that Violet had left San Diego after Marta died. They also knew that Violet blamed herself for Marta's overdose. And for her death.

Martina was first to recover from the shock of the situation. She realized that Violet must be sensitive about so many things right now. She decided to be practical to avoid drama. "This is a lot to be sure," she said as she leaned toward Violet, she put her hand on Violet's arm before saying, "if this is true it is really great news! I have wanted to know where she is for so many years, Violet, that this could be life-changing for me. Maybe you can rest easy on my mother's behalf because you found me." She wiped her face as tears started to roll down her face matching Violet's tearful shine. "She would be really happy about that I know. *If* I am hers."

Arianna spoke up, "Let's contact the prison. Maybe having details will help. I'm thinking that Martina can get details about Marta. She is family. Do you guys remember how hard it was to find out anything about Marta's death because none of us are family? You could get some answers, too, mom. I know you never got to say good bye or even read an obituary."

Violet was catching her breath. Her face shined with tears but her sobs had stopped. She looked closely at Martina, gazing into her eyes. "Yes, I see Marta in you, I do," she said, "I'm so sorry to stare. Damn."

"I don't mind if you stare, Violet," said Martina, "I hope you are right. I hope we are talking about the same Marta. Prisons don't close, right? Let's call them now." She smiled warmly at Violet.

Arianna had calmly been looking up Las Colinas prison as the conversation unfolded. "I have the number, the prison," she said loudly, "do you want to call now Martina?"

"Yes! Call them," exclaimed Martina, "I am ready to find out if this one-in-a-million possibility is true!"

Arianna put her phone on speaker. Anticipation mounted as the call was transferred from one place to another by confused prison employees. The call ended up going to the prison warden's office in the end. Their anticipation deflated when they were told, "no information about inmates can be given over the telephone. Family status has to be verified in person, at the prison. Please make an appointment to visit the prison." So they did. They made an appointment for the next day. The group was quiet for a few minutes after the call ended.

"I'm going to do some research. I can comb death certificates or obituaries with focus on the prison," said Arianna, breaking the silence, "write down everything you know about Marta. About your mom, I mean." She handed Martina a pad and pen.

Ben, who had been quiet for a long time, looked at his mom and said, "this is blowing my mind. Just blowing my mind. How are you feeling, Violet? Are you okay? Can you come with us tomorrow? Maybe you can get special permission or something to be gone all day if you are with us."

"I keep thinking of her. Marta. Her face. Especially her smile," said Violet, "you have her face. Her smile."

Martina began writing the information about Marta. "I don't have much information. Just first and last name. Her birthday is April 4, 1968," she said.

"You are hers! I know it! You have her handwriting," Violet practically screamed, "and her birthday was April 4. I'm not sure of the year but, shit, it must be!" She started pacing on the porch. "I will try to get permission to go. I will leave this fucking place if they don't give it."

Ben stood to step in front of Violet. He interrupted her pacing. "We can plan this. It will work out, I promise," Ben said, "Look. Let's talk to whoever we can tonight. It's getting late. We can try to leave first thing in the morning. Our appointment is not until two-thirty." He put his hands on Violet's shoulders. "Can I give you a hug?"

Violet folded into Ben's embrace. She shook with heartrending sobs. She pulled away to look up at him. She cried, "oh, Ben." She collapsed back into his embrace. It was the first time she had spoken his name. "I am so glad you are here," she said quietly.

Ben felt like he could save the world. The rush of warmth he felt toward Violet as he embraced her was comforting to him in a way he had not felt before. He wanted to erase her pain. He looked at Martina. Tears streamed down her face. Ben felt another rush of warmth emanating from deep inside. He pulled Martina into the embrace. Arianna put her arms around them to cry with them. Ben reached around to include Arianna in the huddle.

CHAPTER THIRTY-SIX

By seven the next morning the four of them were on the road south. Violet had arranged with her sober house to be gone all day as long as she stayed with her family. She also had to attend a recovery meeting at some point in the day. She got her methadone dose before leaving town. The group planned to find a meeting for Violet somewhere near the prison. They talked about having omelets but their stomachs roiled with nervous anticipation. Neither Ben nor Arianna had spent so many hours with their mother. Certainly not sober hours. Violet was quiet, much quieter than they had ever seen her. Arianna rode quietly, too, only asking an occasional question. Ben said nothing.

Martina's voice filled the silence. She told stories of her mother. She told stories of Señora Lopez and the library that she loved. She talked about how much she wanted to make realistic, lasting change for suffering people. She kept her stories sweet. No talk of being taken, no words of resentment, no blame. She already had a growing love for Violet. She didn't want Violet to feel responsible for her mother's death but she knew that Violet did. So she told light-hearted stories of her life to try to cheer up the grimness of their trip.

Because they shared the driving, soon they were near the prison. No one wanted to stop to eat. They decided to arrive early in case there was an entry process. They planned to enter as a group to support Martina getting information as a family member. They entered the prison lobby to sign in. When Martina got to the window she said politely to the uniformed person, a man, behind the glass, "hello,

I'm here about my mother, Marta Rodriguez? I have a two-thirty appointment. I'm early, I'm sorry. It's my first time here."

She wasn't sure if the man had heard her. He continued to hit keys on the keyboard in front of him. Just when she was going to repeat her words, the man looked up and asked, "name?"

"Marta Rodriguez," answered Martina.

"I meant your name," he said dryly.

"Oh. I'm sorry. I'm Martina Rodriguez. Her daughter," said Martina.

He turned back to his computer. "I don't see you on a visitors list. What do you mean you have an appointment? With who? Visitors usually just show up, they don't need appointments. Mostly on weekends," he said.

Martina was at a loss for words. *Visitor?* She tried to explain that she hadn't seen her mother since she was a kid and that she wanted to find out anything she could about her to confirm she had the right Marta Rodriguez.

"Look," the man said, "have a seat. I will see if I can get you on her list." He left his desk before Martina could respond.

She was stunned. *Who is he going to ask? It can't be that she is alive* she thought. She tried to tell Ben, Violet, and Arianna what had happened but again she was at a loss for words. "I think he is putting me on a visitors list," was all she could manage to say coherently. She hadn't thought of this possibility, that her mother was alive. She had believed Violet and Ben when they said Marta had overdosed, and died, in prison. *Maybe they were wrong.*

Marta was in the prison library when a prison officer approached her. She had been thinking of Martina all day.

"Marta, you have a visitor who isn't on your visitors list. You actually don't have a visitors list at all," said a prison officer, "Do you want to have a visitor? The name is Martina Rodriguez. She says she is your daughter."

"Me?" Marta managed to say. She could feel her heartbeat pick up pace. Her mind raced. She thought *Martina! Mi hija can it be true?*

The officer asked her again if she wanted visitors.

"Yes! Yes, please," she said excitedly. She could hardly contain her feelings. She felt like crying but didn't want to alarm the prison officer. She wanted to voice her joy but had no one to listen. She followed the officer to the visiting area.

"Wait here," said the officer, "I'll get your visitor signed in." He left Marta waiting in the visitors area sitting in stunned silence.

"Visitors list? What the fuck," Ben exclaimed, "they must be confused."

Violet began to pace. She couldn't stop moving. Thoughts of Marta filled her mind as they had since the night before when she met Martina. She thought of the many talks she had with her only friend. She thought of the secrets she had shared and the ones that she had held. She watched as the front desk person came into the lobby to approach the group. She stopped pacing.

"Martina Rodriguez? Follow me, you have been added to your mother's visitors list," he said without looking up from his clipboard.

Martina didn't get up to follow. She was stunned and unable to move.

Suddenly Violet cried out, "Marta is alive? She's alive?" She started to sob, her chest heaving, her breath fleeting. "I thought she died, oh god, she is alive? It can't be!"

Ben could see Violet was becoming increasingly upset. He grabbed her into an embrace as he said, "Mom, let Martina go and meet this woman. It's the only way to find out."

The clerk cleared his throat loudly. "Do you want to visit your mother? You can also leave a message," said the desk clerk, showing impatience at what appeared to be family drama.

Martina was able to gather her thoughts quickly. She stood to follow the clerk. She was unable to speak. She nodded at him to go on. He unlocked a door and held it open for her. Martina looked back to make eye contact with Ben just as the heavy door closed loudly.

Ben stood holding Violet as they watched Martina go into the prison. Arianna stepped in close to them to say, "maybe Marta didn't die. We'll find out soon."

CHAPTER THIRTY-SEVEN

Marta was standing when the clerk led Martina into the room. She had been pacing with her eyes on the door. Her mind raced with thoughts. *She must not hate me if she is here! How did she find me? It must be Martina. Mi hija!* She told herself she wasn't going to hug Martina because she knew prison policy on inmates and visitors touching. *I won't run to her! I won't grab her! Please let it be true that she is here.* She stopped pacing when the door opened. She found herself looking down to a height Martina was when she had last seen her. When she raised her eyes she saw what she had been longing to see for so many years. Her daughter's face beamed at her. "Mi hija, Martina," she cried out, "mi hija." She could not find words to express the feelings that reeled thought her mind, through her body. In two swift steps she had Martina in her arms. She squeezed her tightly.

"Step apart, no touching. Step away, inmate," the clerk said loudly. He took a step toward the women. "Visiting will end if that happens again," he said as they took a step apart. He looked at Marta with a stern look and said, "this is your first visitor, don't abuse the privilege."

The women sat in chairs on either side of the table with their faces as close as they dared. They cried together, gazing into each other's eyes. They longed to touch. They held back their hugs but expressed their love with their eyes and fast-beating hearts.

"I have looked for you for so very long," said Martina between sobs, "I never knew what happened to you, Mami, I am so happy to find you."

Marta took a moment to catch her breath. She put a hand over her heart. "I tried to come after you, hija, I tried to find you, too. But I got caught trying because I was looking the wrong way. I lost track of the men who took you in Mexicali. I was arrested and put in here for running with men like them. Oh, Martina, you are here! Mi hija. How did you find me? It has been twenty years since I last saw you! Oh, mi hija!"

"Mami! I am here," cried Martina, " I am here! Only yesterday I didn't know where you were!" She paused as she tried to straighten her thoughts. So much had happened in the last twenty hours. She tried to explain, "my boyfriend's mother, I met her yesterday, she recognized me as your daughter. Violet? She thought you had died here from a drug overdose. But you are alive! Oh, Mami, I missed you so much! I never forgot your face. Your love." She wiped at her eyes, ceaseless tears streamed down her cheeks.

"Violet? A! Mi Violet," cried Marta, "I never wanted her to know about my overdose. I never told her. We used to write to each other daily. One day I didn't get a letter. She didn't write to me again." She was quiet for a moment, staring at Martina. She looked down and said, "she thought I was dead. Why write to a dead woman? But how did she find out? I never told anyone. I guess it was prison gossip for a while. One woman did die that night from the same junk I had. It was fentanyl we smoked, not heroin. I never touched the stuff again."

"She is here with me today," said Martina, "and Ben. And Arianna. Her kids. Oh, mami, you look so beautiful I can't stop looking at your face!" More tears streamed down both their faces. "Do you want to see Violet? She is upset and confused. She has felt terrible guilt for a long time thinking that you were dead because she taught you to use heroin. She still doesn't know what is happening and won't until I leave here. But I can't go! Not until they come and tell me to, okay?" She paused. "I promise to have her write again if they won't let her visit."

Two hours passed quickly. In that time the two women returned in time to the years before Martina was taken. They talked of Sinaloa, of the joyful days they shared, and of the men they had lost. They talked about Mexicali and the time they both spent there, separately. And then time was up. A prison clerk interrupted the women engrossed in conversation, "visiting time is over for today. Two hour limit." He stood waiting for Martina.

Martina said to her mother, "I will be back tomorrow, Mami, I will be back every day until you can come home with me!" She listened to her mother sob loudly as she was led back to the lobby.

Ben had waited in the prison lobby with Violet. He kept his arm around her, giving her a squeeze whenever a sob escaped, she cried the entire time. As time passed, Ben and Violet realized that it must indeed be true that Marta was alive. It seemed like Martina was gone a long time. Ben looked at the clock. *Two hours!* he thought *it must be true that Marta is alive!* Now he understood why they could not find an obituary. They had thought it was because Marta was born in Mexico. Or that she had died in prison with apparently no family to write an obituary for her. Back then the prison wouldn't talk to Violet or Ben about Marta. Local press had published a small article about a prison overdose but they never found more information. They never got details. Violet had started drinking again. She lost her job. She stopped caring about the night runs which had been inspired by Marta. She left Ben and ended up in Santa Cruz.

Ben was relieved to see Martina finally emerge. She rushed to Ben. She put her hands on his cheeks. She pulled his face close to hers then said, "she is alive!" She turned to Violet and Arianna. "Mi mami, my mother, she lives! She did overdose but she *did not die!* Violet, she misses you terribly," she paused to catch her breath, "she thought you found out she had overdosed. She thought you were angry with her for using drugs when you told her not to. Do you want to see her? We need to get you checked in, she put you on her visitors list."

Violet at last found words to express herself. The pent up grief she held for years had seemed to drain out of her in her tears. She began to have strange thoughts. Hopeful thoughts. "I have never been so happy as I am right now," she started, "I will be even more happy to see my only friend, yes! I want to see her more than anything." She felt her body flood with warmth. She beamed a huge smile at Martina. "Can I sign up to go in now? I want to! You guys can leave me here if you need to, then come back for me," said Violet, "I will do whatever it takes."

Martina beamed a smile back at Violet. She linked elbows with her and led her to the reception desk to sign in."We will get you signed in. You'll get two hours. Me, Benny, and Arianna will go get some food. The plan is to bring food back for mami to give to her after you visit," she said, "she is craving tamales!"

The reception clerk handed Violet a clipboard. Violet was reluctant to sign in but only for a moment. She felt creepy about going into the prison even if she wasn't staying but her desire to see Marta overrode her fear. Soon the heavy door was clanging shut behind her. She was in prison again. But this time she was just a visitor. *Oh, Marta!* Violet thought *our years together were my best years, please don't hate me!* The visiting area was familiar to Violet. Ben had come here hundreds of time to see her. She saw Marta in the small room through a window. *Marta, it's you!* She could feel her heart beat faster, she could hear it as she felt heat rise up her neck and face. She fainted. This time Ben wasn't there to catch her. She fell to the ground with a thud just as the door swung open.

"Violet," screamed Marta out, then to the clerk, "do something! Please, my friend fainted, please help me!" She broke the rules again. She scooped Violet's head into her lap. She leaned over her friend.

She called softly, "Violet? Vee, honey, it's Marti! Honey wake up so you can visit me!"

Violet began to wake as a prison officer entered the room. Marta helped Violet to her feet. Violet was realizing what happened. She stared at Marta. She started to apologize, "I'm so sorry! It's nothing really. I do it all the time when I get nervous or excited." She let go of Marta. She pleaded with the prison officer closest to her, "please let me stay!"

Tension in the room heightened. Then the officer left the room without saying anything. The women could feel the tension change as they turned to look at each other, fear turning to wonder. They sat across from each other on either side of the table. Almost simultaneously their tears started. Violet sobbed. She couldn't take her eyes of Marta.

Marta was first to break the silence. "Oh, Vee! I am so glad to see you," she exclaimed, "and you brought mi hija to me!" Her voice caught in her throat. Fresh tears rolled down her face. "I have missed you! I am so sorry for anything I did. I thought you stopped writing to me because you found out I overdosed. It was Melanie who died that night." She was quiet. Her eyes pleaded with Violet to understand.

"I'm glad it was Melanie," started Violet, "I mean, I'm not glad Melanie is dead!" She paused. "I can't believe I am looking at you, is what I mean. I knew someone had died. I never got another letter from you. I thought it was you who died. So I stopped writing. If only I had written just one more time!"

"It was me who should have written again," said Marta quietly, "to tell you what happened. There was fentanyl in the dope we got that night. I survived. I never thought you would think it was me who died. I am so sorry, Violet!" She paused. "How is it that our children found each other? They are the ones responsible for this! They are in love? You look great!" Martina couldn't stop gushing questions and proclamations.

"So do you, Marta, so do you," said Violet, "I lived with you for a decade and never wanted to hug you like I do right now!" She held back the urge. "I do think they are in love, yes. Ben was working at the restaurant where I worked for a while. Martina got a job there, that's how they met. She started going to school in Santa Cruz so they moved up there. I'm not sure of details because I only met her yesterday. It was me who recognized you in your girl. She looks like you. She even has your handwriting."

Marta was thinking there was so much she didn't know about her girl. "Oh, Violet! I talked to her for two hours! But there wasn't time to talk about what her life is like now," said Marta, "or about the future. I told her how I came to be here. She told me how she came to meet you in Santa Cruz. I told her about my life here. How I've finished college these past years. I'm ready for law school. I am trying to get permanent citizenship here in the United States. I go up for parole in August, Vee! I hope to be free!"

It seemed like only minutes later when a prison officer interrupted Violet as she relayed her recovery story. "Visiting time is over, inmate, five minutes left," he said.

"I'll be back tomorrow or as often as they will let me in," said Violet, "I will figure out a way!"

"Tell mi hija how much I love her, Vee, you know I do. I was sure she hated me for not being a stronger mother to her. Tell her for me," said Marta, "you know I love you, too, Vee. I am so happy this has all happened!" More tears streamed down her face as she stood to watch Violet exit the room.

The tamales waiting for her when she got back to her cell were evidence that she wasn't dreaming. She felt like she was floating, as if she were looking down on her life from above. She felt a lightness in her heart that she hadn't felt since before Martina was taken from her. *The universe has smiled on me* she thought *I will smile back.* She fell into a restful sleep, dreaming of Martina's smiling face.

Ben was relieved to see Violet when she came out from visiting Marta. He had never seen her so refreshed, so happy looking. While she was visiting, the rest of them had rented two hotel rooms nearby. They got tamales for Marta. Ben had come back for Violet on his own. He realized when he saw her that he hadn't thought about methadone in hours. *I think I am done with that shit* he thought. But he had to think of Vee. She would need methadone in the morning. He planned to call Dennis at the methadone clinic in the morning to get her set up.

"How you feeling, Vee? It has been a long day," said Ben, "I can't believe this is happening! Are you okay?" He ushered her out the door. "We have rooms nearby. Are you hungry?"

Violet followed Ben to the car. The strange thoughts that she had been having in the prison lobby, hopeful thoughts, seemed to burst open in her mind as she started thinking of all the possibilities. *Marta will be free in August* she thought *I will move here until then, I'll get a job.* She wondered if Ben still made the night runs. She hoped that he did.

Ben didn't press her for answers. They rode in silence for a few minutes. It was the most peaceful time Ben had ever spent with Violet. He was happy to see her without her face pinched into a grimace because she wanted booze or dope.

Violet surprised Ben when she broke the silence by saying, "I don't deserve, you, Ben, I just don't. I was such a shitty mother!" She started to sob anew then drew a breath. She composed herself. "I have something to live for now! Because of you. I don't deserve to be here but am so glad, Benny, thank you. I …" Her voice trailed off. She took a deep breath.

"I know what it's like," started Ben, "I don't deserve Martina."

"Martina! Yes, she is a prize," said Violet, "she is the inspiration of the night runs, the reason we started them, for Martina. For Marta. I am so sorry I left you, Benny! Do you still do the night runs? Does

Martina know about them?" She paused, then,"you can pull in here, I'll grab a burrito."

Ben pulled into a convenience store parking lot. "Are you sure? I'll take you somewhere else if you want," said Ben. He knew she had lived for years off convenience store burritos. Violet was already heading in to the store by the time he finished asking. Once back in the car he said, "the night runs happen legally, I mean openly, now. I guess openly is the wrong word, too. See, I told Martina about them and she connected me to the people who saved her from being trafficked. Now they do the runs. Most likely at night. I think they will save many more people than we did. They are legit."

"Well it seems that because you kept them going, and stayed down here after I left, you have saved us all! If you hadn't met Martina then …"

Ben cut her off mid sentence. "But I did meet her," he said as he turned to smile broadly at Violet. Martina came out to greet them as they arrived at their hotel. Ben felt a rush of warmth toward her as she neared. She went to Violet's side of the car to open the door for her.

Martina was elated about seeing her mother. "I am so happy Violet, thank you so much," she exclaimed, "in my wildest dreams I didn't think I would see her today! I thought I would be seeing her death certificate." She hooked elbows with Violet and led her into the room she would share with Arianna, who was walking to a nearby restaurant. Martina talked nonstop about the gratitude she felt about the strange but exciting turn of events. "Do you need anything?"

Violet, who had in moments eaten her burrito, stretched out on one of the beds. "I need to stay around here until August," answered Violet, "your mom is up for parole in August. I don't want to leave her again." She paused. "This bed is a close second … thing I need."

Martina sat in a chair across the room. She, Ben, and Arianna had made an agreement to not leave Violet on her own in case she felt like getting dope. Or worse, booze. They knew if Vee decided to get blasted again that booze would likely be her first choice. It could be cheap and easy to get. They hadn't found a recovery meeting to attend. They had been distracted by the events at the prison.

Violet was genuinely exhausted. She slipped off her shoes and rolled onto her side. She vaguely noticed when Arianna came in to dismiss Martina. She stirred only when Arianna draped a blanket over her and then it was just long enough to say, "thank you, Ari, I love you honey."

Ben was awake at five the next morning. He laid still in bed next to Martina feeling deep love for her. He was looking forward to talking to Dennis. He was not looking forward to going to the clinic for Violet's methadone. He was thinking of asking Arianna to go with Violet. He felt great. Especially physically. *I swear this is the first morning I can remember not waking up craving dope or needing methadone* he thought *or being scared of getting dope-sick.* He decided to leave a voice mail for Dennis instead of showing up like he used to, things were different now, in just a few short weeks. He had told Martina about Violet's needing methadone but had not mentioned his own recent challenge. He slipped out of bed to step outside to make the call.

Ben was surprised when Dennis answered the phone. "Hey, Ben," he said when he saw Ben's number flashing on his phone, "I was hoping to hear from you. I have an interesting opportunity for you. How are you, man? I haven't talked to you in over a week."

"I'm surprised you are already at work," said Ben, "I was going to leave a message. I'm doing great. I feel great. I need some help though, that's why I'm calling. My mom is here and needs methadone. We got unexpectedly stuck down here."

"How about this … I'll get paperwork together for your mom. She is currently a patient in Santa Cruz, right? Give me a couple hours, I'll call you when she can come to our clinic. It'll probably be around eight," said Dennis, "I have something for you to do in the meantime."

"Okay … I'm listening," said Ben. He could tell Dennis was excited about something.

"My brother-in-law is looking to sell his truck. I think you might want it," said Dennis. "I think you should go look at it. He wants someone to take over payments and operation."

"Operation? What do you mean? I already have a truck. It's paid for, too, all mine. You know that," said Ben, "Besides, I can't make payments. I haven't found a job in Santa Cruz yet."

"Just go look at it. It's at 115 Fonda. Back behind your restaurant. It's in the driveway. You can't miss it," said Dennis, "look for the 'for sale' sign. Just drive by, think about it. I'll talk to you in a couple hours."

Ben went back inside. Martina was still asleep. He slipped into bed next to her. He thought of everything that had happened in the last thirty hours. He wondered how Violet had slept. He wondered if she were awake.

CHAPTER THIRTY-EIGHT

Violet was laying in bed listening to Arianna's even breathing. She had never felt so hopeful. For the first time in a long time she woke up looking forward to her day. She didn't wake up thinking hateful thoughts. It didn't even occur to her that she needed methadone until she was awake for an hour. She thought she heard Ben outside talking to someone. She decided to stay in bed to cherish the warmth that newfound hope was bringing to her. She drifted back to sleep. She slept until Arianna started talking to her. She thought she was dreaming.

"Mom? Are you awake? It's almost eight," said Arianna, "we're going for breakfast ..."

Violet started to dream about omelets. And burritos. Then her stomach rolled. She felt like she was going to puke. *Fuck* she thought *I'm not dreaming*. She jumped up almost knocking Arianna to the floor. She made it to the trash can before vomiting everything in her stomach, which wasn't much.

She turned to look at Arianna. "I'm sorry," she said, "I should call the methadone clinic. I'm going to be sick if I don't get over there. I really want to stop methadone but I am still at sixty milligrams." She rinsed her mouth. She tried to stand but could only sit on the bed clenching her stomach. She lamented, "I want an omelet ... damn I am so hungry!"

"Ben called the methadone clinic already. We can go there now then come back for him. He doesn't want to go there," explained Arianna, "it's all good. Let's go. Martina is going to ride with us."

Violet had no problems getting her methadone. By the time the women got back to the hotel she was feeling much better. Very hungry, but much better. They picked up Ben then headed out for breakfast. The four of them were lost in thought. No one spoke for a long time.

The last two days had been a whirlwind of new, exciting information for all of them. Martina's constant joy was bolstering the group and it was contagious. "I wrote to my school," she explained, "spring break is in three weeks. They are going to let me finish my work early. I plan to do the work from here. I've been looking for a cheap studio to rent for a month. After that, who knows?" She glanced at Ben. They had spent the night talking of the possibilities. Martina planned to do everything she could to get her mom released early.

Violet had laid awake all night thinking of the very same plan. Or something like it. She wanted to be near Marta until she was released. She decided to speak up. "She is due for parole in August. If we can't get her out early, we can wait six months. We can testify at her parole hearing. You can, Martina. I will keep my mouth shut," said Violet, "I want to find a sober house down here until she gets out." Everyone was quiet for a few minutes. "Can I use your phone to call Santa Cruz? I should call," Violet said to Arianna, "I have to call the methadone clinic up there, too." She didn't feel like she was jeopardizing her sobriety. In fact, all this excitement had distracted Violet from thinking of even her body's response to getting her methadone later than usual.

"Let's consider getting a place together," said Martina to Violet, "I mean, you can stay with me if you want to. It will be temporary. August at the latest, right? Then we can bring Mami to Santa Cruz!" Martina looked at Ben. She had made the suggestion before talking with him. She started to backtrack, "… I mean, we should talk about the possibility. Okay?"

Ben finally spoke. "I feel like we should look around to see what we can find! We need a base here until Marta is free," he smiled broadly. His eyes shone with love. "I have a truck to look at that my friend says I should see. How about you guys stay here and do some research, line up some places to see. I'll go look at the truck. It should only take me a few minutes, it's about a mile from here."

"You are awesome, Ben. I love you so much," exclaimed Martina, "we will be right here." She smiled back at him.

Dennis was right. Ben couldn't miss the truck. It sat in a driveway with a 'for sale' sign stuck in a side window. Ben parked to look at it. *Holy shit* he thought *Dennis is genius! But I can't afford this, I'm sure!* It was a panel truck. It looked clean, it was in great shape. Painted on the side of the truck were two words. 'Traveling Tortilla'. He called Dennis from where he sat looking at the truck.

"Man, this is a great idea! But I don't have a job now. I'm broke," said Ben, "I've never owned anything except this old truck I paid cash for."

Dennis had been hoping Ben would call. "Go to the door. Talk to my brother-in-law. His name is Frank. I told him about you," said Dennis, "trust me. Just go talk to him. I have to go but can call you back in a couple hours. Okay?" Silence. "Ben? Trust me."

"Alright. I'll go talk to Frank," said Ben, "I'll call you later." He got out of his truck to walk around the prospect. It was a great looking food truck. As he was checking it out a man came out of the house.

"Hi Ben," he said with a smile, "I'm Frank. Dennis told me you might be stopping by."

Ben shook hands with Frank. "I love the truck. I think it's a great idea. I'm broke, though, I wish that weren't true," said Ben. He had job applications in for work at few restaurants in Santa Cruz. He was talking with two of them. He expected to have work in the next couple days.

"Well, here's the thing," said Frank, "Dennis saved my life. I owe him to the end. Maybe he saved yours, too, I don't know. I do know he wants to help you get your life on track like he did for me." He opened the truck, they went inside. "Dennis inspired me to get this truck almost ten years ago. It's been my purpose since then."

Ben looked around the interior of the truck. He could see that the kitchen was top quality. *It would be a pleasure to cook here* he thought. Everything had a place, utensils attached to the wall magnetically. Stainless steel glistened everywhere.

Frank could see that Ben was impressed. "The steel is thin. It's super light. A lot of people think it would be heavy but it's not," he explained, "this truck has brought a lot of good things to me. But now I have a full time job after finishing college. I am going to teach at the local elementary school … also inspired by Dennis! I will tell that story another time. Thing is, I don't have time for the truck anymore." He paused, running his hand along the steel countertop. "I want someone else, someone like you, to find purpose with this truck like I did. If you are interested, you can make payments. We can start the payments once you are in operation. I'm not desperate is what I'm saying. I was just waiting for the right person to take over the truck. I think it's you."

Ben continued to look around the truck. "I don't know what to say," he started, "I've never been in a food truck before. I love the idea. Dennis is … wow … he is the coolest. I never thought …"

"I haven't operated the truck for almost a year. I miss it but know it's time to pass it on," said Frank, "I'm thinking Santa Cruz is a great place for a food truck. Think about it. If you want it, we can make an agreement. I can give you contacts for stocking the truck, too."

"I'm thinking that, yes! I want it," exclaimed Ben, "this is perfect for me. I will get started with payments soon. I can work nights for a while until the truck is generating. Thank you for the chance! Damn,

I can't believe this! Thank you so much, man, wow." He extended a hand to Frank. The two men shook hands.

"I'll write up an agreement. Can you come back later today? I'll have the truck ready to go," said Frank, "I am excited for you, this feels really good. We can thank Dennis!"

"Sounds great, Frank," said Ben, "thanks again. I can't thank you enough! I'm going to call Dennis now. See you around four? Wow."

"Four it is," said Frank, "I'm glad we met."

Ben called Dennis from his truck intending to leave a message. Dennis answered on the first ring, "I told you so, man, I told you so. But I can't talk now. I'll call you later." Ben was elated. In these last two days he had seen Martina find deeper purpose in life in finding her mother. It seemed he had deeper purpose now, too, beyond the love he had for Martina.

By the time Ben returned to the restaurant an hour later the women had found two prospects for short term rental. Violet had called the house where she had been staying, she was officially absent without permission by their standards. They had informed her to come get her stuff. She had also called the methadone clinic in Santa Cruz to arrange to temporarily get her methadone daily from the clinic near the prison. Arianna was thinking of renting a car to get back to Santa Cruz which is what they were discussing when Ben arrived.

"Here's Ben," said Arianna as Ben approached them, "we were just talking about me driving back to Santa Cruz in a rental car. I have to work tomorrow."

Ben joined them at the table. He kissed Martina lightly. His excitement was palpable, catching. "Tell us! You are holding something back, I can tell," exclaimed Martina, "what happened? Did you like the truck?"

"I did. I think you will, too" he said to Martina. Then to Arianna, "you won't have to rent a car." He winked at her. "Any luck finding a place? I bet there are a few," he said to no one in particular, deflecting their questions.

"I didn't know you could be such a tease," said Violet unexpectedly, catching Ben's excitement. She smiled. "We found a couple places. Now that its March first, there are a lot of vacancies," she said, "one of them is walking distance from here. Let's go there first. Then we can go see Marta."

Ben realized that Violet had also found purpose in the last two days. She had found purpose in Marta's resurrection. Liberation had become the goal. The prospect of Marta's liberation lifted their spirits.

Marta's spirits were also lifted. She was so elated at seeing her daughter again that she thought about almost nothing else. The gratitude she felt toward Violet also filled her mind. She knew Violet to be deeply flawed through no fault of her own so she had not taken it personally when she stopped getting letters. Now she longed to listen to her outrageous stories of survival. She wanted to share with her what life had been like in prison without her. She had spent many hours making plans for when she got out of prison. She had earned an undergraduate degree. She planned to get a law degree. She hoped the degrees could help her gain citizenship- something she desperately wanted. Though she never voiced it she feared they would send her to Mexico when they set her free. Now that she had Martina it was even more important that she stay in the United States.

She had lain awake all night replaying the sight of Martina's smiling face. Hearing her voice was the sweetest symphony. *They say she looks like me* thought Marta *but I was never so beautiful.* By six in the morning she knew sleep was lost for the night. She skipped breakfast to report to her library job. The library had saved her after Violet was gone. She came to the library at first to sit while she wrote to Violet. She became friends with the inmate who worked in the library. When that woman was released from prison, Marta took over her job. She had earned her college degree in the prison library. Now she was going to find a way to get out of the cage while she waited to see her girl again.

After breakfast they headed out walking to see the rentals. They found a cute one bedroom with a huge back porch where Violet could smoke all she wanted. She could relax in privacy. Martina could have the bedroom to set up for studying. They ended up renting the place. Martina signed a month-to-month lease. The plan was for Violet to stay with Martina, who would returning to Santa Cruz in a few days to gather belongings. Arianna and Ben would drive back to Santa Cruz in Ben's new truck because both of them had to work. They were all so busy there wasn't time for ruminating or hateful thoughts. No one thought about booze. Or heroin. Joy was in the air even as sadness at Marta's incarceration dominated their plans.

They left the rental to head for the prison. Martina and Violet went in to visit Marta together while Ben and Adrianna waited in the prison lobby. Ben sat watching the muted television that was displaying college football. Arianna was engrossed in answering work related messages. Soon the four of them were back together discussing what would happen next.

"I have to get back to Santa Cruz," said Arianna, "I missed a lot of work lately. I need to catch up. I want to stay down here but should get going. I really don't mind renting a car to go back on my own …"

Just then Ben pulled up and parked. "This is it," he said as he gestured to the panel truck, "my new truck."

Arianna was stunned to silence. Martina gasped.

"Fucking awesome! I love it," said Violet, "the Traveling Tortilla!"

"I plan to specialize in breakfast burritos," said Ben excitedly. It was the first time he talked about his plans. Sharing them was igniting his passion. "I plan to take a job for a while but this will be my future. Our future," he said to Martina, "Santa Cruz is perfect for this food truck! I will drive it back to Santa Cruz today. Arianna can come with me. You and mom can keep the car here for as long as you need." He stopped talking when he heard Violet sob.

Violet stood looking at Ben with tears running down her cheeks. "Are you okay? I'm sorry …" Ben started.

Violet put a hand on his arm. "You called me mom," she said. She smiled through her tears. She caught her breath long enough to say, "the truck is awesome, Benny."

"I have to come back at four to sign papers. After that it's mine to drive away," explained Ben, "my friend Dennis hooked me up with payments that will start once the truck is generating income." He smiled at Martina.

She smiled back at him. "This is perfect! Your friend is a very good friend," said Martina, "the universe smiles on us! Let's go relax. We can hang out at the apartment until four."

"Your mom used to say something like that," said Violet to Martina, "she used to say 'the universe smiles at me so I will smile back'. I'm guessing she still says that! Especially today … "

By five that evening Ben had signed the agreement with Frank to take over the food truck. The truck started right up. The ride was smooth, the engine easily pulling the weight of the truck. Ben was impressed. So was Arianna, who sat in the small seat that folded out near the driver's seat. Every inch of the truck had been designed for efficiency. Clever storage cupboards that could be accessed inside the truck but stocked from the outside filled the passenger seat space. Gas mileage wasn't great but Ben intended to not drive on the highway much. He had the perfect spot in mind for parking in Santa Cruz. He dropped Arianna off at her place then went home to catch some sleep. He had a job interview the next afternoon at a nearby restaurant that he planned to ace.

Arianna was happy to be at her place yet she suddenly felt lonely, something she rarely did. She was normally alone most of the time.

She preferred it, is what she told herself. Now she hadn't been alone in a couple days. She missed those people- Ben, Violet, and Martina. She decided to text Keith, who had promised not to bug her while she was helping Violet. She sent a short invitation for him to come by. She looked forward to talking to him. He didn't know yet about Marta. He texted her back saying he was ten minutes away. She turned on some music. *I have never felt so good, so happy* she thought *the universe smiles at me.*

Chapter Thirty-Nine

V iolet and Martina walked to a nearby grocery store to stock
their new place. They linked elbows, strolling together. "I feel
like I know you," said Violet, "your mom told me a lot about your
childhood."

"I am still in shock about this whole thing," exclaimed Martina,
"I can't tell you enough how happy I am that you could see her in me.
Mi mami, you know. Ben and I have been dating a couple months
but he didn't mention you much."

Violet laughed softly. "Well that's probably a good thing," she
said, "there isn't much to say about me. The years I spent in prison
with Marta were my best years. She is a kind, loving person. And
not gay! We weren't gay together- not that I'm against gay- just that
me and Marta aren't gay."

When they were back at the apartment Martina called the prison
to find out if she could visit twice in one day. She was informed that
if she comes to the prison on a professional visit, say with a lawyer
or psychologist, then she could return as much as she needed. Then
she called everyone she knew until she found the best immigration
lawyer she could find who had experience with criminal justice. She
tried to help Violet find a recovery meeting but was stopped short
in her efforts. By Violet.

"I'm not going," said Violet politely when Martina was done on
the phone. She had overheard Martina asking about local meetings,
she assumed what kind. "I don't relate to those groups. I'm like
Benny. I tried to fit in. I was doing okay in Santa Cruz but thing is,
I just don't fit." She could tell Martina was surprised by her gaping

mouth. "I'm kicked out of that sober house so I'm not welcome at any of them here. I can recover without meetings is all I'm saying. I don't want you to worry about me, okay? I have to check in with methadone clinic nurses daily. Plus I see a counselor there, too."

Martina had composed herself. She asked, "what do you mean like Benny?"

"Benny kicked dope back in October. Without meetings," said Violet. She didn't realize she was breaking anything. She didn't think about anonymity- something very important to some people in recovery from drug abuse. A lot of times people are ashamed of their seemingly self-abasing lives, they don't want anyone to know what awful people they feel they have become. Until someone comes along to show them that they aren't awful. That was certainly true for Violet. Marta had shown her that she wasn't awful. Yes, she had done some awful things, but she was not awful to her core like she had always thought. "Sometimes people need meetings," Violet explained, "sometimes they find purpose in life that fills in time, takes away craving for dope. Or booze."

As she talked, Violet was realizing that Martina didn't know Ben was recovering from drug abuse. *Oh shit* she thought *its my first day here and I already fucked things up for them.* Martina's mouth was gaping. She was gathering her thoughts, Violet could tell, by the way Martina kept stopping herself from finishing a word.

"Ben … shou …" started Martina, "should I know more about this kind of thing? Ben told me nothing except to try to help you get to recovery meetings."

"I'm going to leave it up to Benny to tell you more, okay? It's not my place to tell you. I'm sorry," said Violet, "I should have kept my fat mouth shut." She stared at her feet, her shoulders slumped in shame.

Martina crouched in front of Violet. "Hey," she said softly, " I love Benny. There is nothing you could say that would change that, okay? I love you, too, you know? You have come to mean so much to me, Violet, in this short time. Now let's make some dinner. What did we say? Taquitos? I'll turn on the oven. How many do you want?"

Over the next few days the two women developed a routine of going to the prison in the morning, searching for a lawyer after lunch, then researching any way they could about early release for Marta. Martina talked to Ben daily. They reminded each other that their situation was temporary. Everyone spent time in the library digging up everything they could find from criminal justice reform to immigration policy.

By the end of the week Martina located a lawyer that would not only work for free but would designate Violet to be an employee. They could enter the prison as much as they wanted under the guise of professional purposes- they were on the case. Violet was able to fill an important role which further bolstered her chances of remaining sober. She loved her badge that read 'attorney assistant'. The attorney they hired believed that because Marta had served more than three quarters of her sentence it was appropriate to ask for early release. Everyone was afraid to express their hope trying to avoid disappointment as the days went by.

Ben stayed busy in Santa Cruz. He started working six evenings a week in a nearby taqueria. In the mornings he stayed busy getting city permits to operate his food truck. He started up contracts with an egg seller, a cheese farmer, and a tortilla maker. He was burning through his savings but didn't worry. He worked constantly. He didn't have time to think of being high. He talked to Martina daily but he had been unable to get away from his job. Martina assured him she missed him but that she understood. She also assured him that Violet was fine. "She has even stopped smoking cigarettes," Martina told Ben, "she says they cost too much." They laughed together.

"I have spring break coming up next week on the twenty-first," said Martina, "I will be finished with school work for a while but have to drive up to Santa Cruz to drop off some stuff at the university."

She paused. In the two weeks since she had discovered her mother alive she had been working to get her released from prison. It looked like she was very close to achieving her goal but she didn't want to tell anyone yet. Not even Ben. Especially not Violet or her mother. She didn't want to get their hopes up. Spring break was a week away. She hoped to have her mom free by the end of spring break. "There's really no need for you to drive down here right now, Benny," she said, "me and Vee will drive up there soon. Either on your next day off or the one after that."

Ben called Arianna to leave a message about Violet's status. He remembered that Arianna often stopped contacting him suddenly. She wouldn't call or text for months. He was a little hurt this time. *Maybe because I'm sober* he thought *I'm thinking too much.*

He turned his attention back to his work. The days ran together. They passed quickly for Ben. He wasn't paying attention to local news anymore. He never really did. He was surprised one day when he got to work to find the door locked. A notice was posted to employees to return home, the restaurant was closed. Confused, Ben walked home. There was a moving truck blocking the street in front of house. It looked like the tenants in the upstairs apartment were loading a moving truck.

"Hey, do you guys need help?" Ben called out.

"Thanks. We got it. This is the last of it," said one of the two men, "we cleaned. We're done. The keys are in the kitchen drawer. Beatrice said to leave them there." The men were wearing blue masks on their faces as if they were afraid of catching something. They seemed to be in a hurry.

"Cool," said Ben. *Weird* he thought *I didn't know they were moving out.* He went into the house intending to call his job. Instead he answered a call from Martina. "Hey," he said, "Marti, are you ok?" It was strange that she call at this time of day. Especially since it was her last day of class before spring break. He knew she had to be in class for most of the day.

"Oh Benny! Have you seen the news? Things are changing fast! I have really good news and ... well, some more good news ... then some bad news," said Martina breathlessly. "There is a virus! The governor just ordered that everyone stay home for at least two weeks until things are figured out. Everything is closing! Restaurants, gyms ... Are you at work?"

"No! I was just getting back from there. I was wondering why they were closed. They never close," said Ben, "I hope that isn't your good news." Ben gave a weak laugh. He started to pace.

Martina burst out with the news, "mi mami will be free today! Because this virus is rampant, the state is trying to reduce the number of people living in groups. It is because we have been petitioning the prison for weeks to let her go early that she is one of the first to be released!" Her excitement thrilled Ben, even after hearing about the threat of a virus.

Ben had never been sick other than dope-sick. He didn't know what to think other than the obvious next thought that he voiced, "so you all will be coming here to Santa Cruz?"

"Yes we will," said Martina, "Vee and I are packed. We are heading to Las Colinas to get mi mami then we will be heading home. To you!"

Ben almost dropped the phone. He had been so busy with other things. He didn't usually watch the news. He had been checking out the truck, making sure the grill worked. He had perfected his recipe. He was ready to roll. He had not expected such news. "Baby thats awesome," he almost shouted, "that's fucking awesome!" He stopped pacing. "The upstairs tenants moved out today, maybe your mom can stay there a while," Ben started, "Violet can, too."

Chapter Forty

Suddenly the world had closed. Ben was beginning to understand the gravity of the changes that were rapidly advancing. He walked up to the local market to stock up on food but a line snaked it's way around the entire store. He listened to bits of conversation as he made his way back home. People seemed to be panicking. Ben was hearing rising anxiety in their voices, "only ten people in the store at once" and "they are out of everything". He made his way back to the house. The landlord, who lived on the third floor with her cats, was loading her car when he got back to the house.

"Hi Ben," she said as Ben approached, "I'm going to head to my son's house in Nevada for a while. I'm usually only here part of the year anyway. I don't know what's going on but with everything closed up it sure doesn't look good." Ben helped her to bring her few remaining bags to her car. "I left my address in the kitchen, you can send the rent," she said, "I will miss the summer here." She sighed loudly. "What can we do?" Ben didn't answer. She loaded her cat carriers into the front seat. She got behind the wheel, gave Ben a quick smile, then drove away.

Ben was stunned. Anxiety began to build as he waited for Martina, Violet, and Marta to arrive. He paced on the sidewalk in front of the house for a while. Then he paced on the porch. He knew he was well stocked with some foods because he had stocked his food truck. The four of them could eat for a month he reasoned. He could feed Arianna, too. He had almost three hundred gallons of water on the truck. He tried to relax. Now more than ever he was glad to not be dependent on methadone. Suddenly he wanted a cigarette. *Fuck!*

Will it never stop? Such a fucking junkie addict he thought. Then he had a second thought … *I am better than this! I can't sit here doing nothing, it will lead me to bad shit.* He got busy unpacking with the goal of having the upstairs apartment ready for his mom and her friend. He wondered how the women were doing on the road.

Violet was beaming. Her cheeks were aching because she had been smiling so wide for three hours. They had picked up Marta at the prison without delay. Violet, Marta, and Martina were making their way to Santa Cruz. The women talked, laughed, and cried. Marta cried the hardest. When she first stepped out of the prison she turned to embrace Martina tightly. She cried so hard she was unable to say anything except for , "ah, mi hija, my girl, I am so sorry. Here you are! I am so sorry! I am so glad. Here you are!"

Martina was doing the driving. "Ah Mamí! I can't believe you are here with me. I am in shock," said Martina, "you should never have been in prison, Mamí, you didn't deserve to lose your freedom."

"Life is so very unfair," cried Marta loudly, "that all of you were taken from me was the first injustice! In the decades that followed I tried to learn what I had done wrong to deserve injustice. This thinking led me to realize that there is no judge. There is no one writing the story to make me, and you, victims in life, or heroes … it is random circumstance that ripped us apart. It is random circumstance that has again brought us together."

"Seems like fate to me," said Violet, "pure fucking fate. I can't believe you are alive, I thought you were dead. I deserved to suffer, to mourn, and now I can't believe our kids are in love! That's fate. There may not be a judge but there's got to be someone writing this story, writing fate … too many prayers answered in one day for it to be anything else."

"Maybe we are all the writers," said Martina, "maybe by our own wishes we make things happen in our lives. I have been wishing to see Mamí again all my life."

"It seems to me that granted wishes are the same thing as answered prayers," said Marta, "both are given." She paused, then asked, "who gives? We may never know! We give our hearts to finding ... the universe finds for us, gives. Or it doesn't. I am so glad the universe gave to us! I used to feel betrayed by god, then I felt victimized by him. I used to say to myself *what did I do? I am a terrible person for all this to happen, for this punishment* until I realized that bad things happen to good people all the time. I am the one who punishes me. It is what we do going forward that keeps us from losing the will to keep going."

"Even something as awful as prison can give," said Violet, "now this virus ... another awful thing that will bring us change, I think. It already has!" They rode in comfortable silence toward unknown adventures.

Ben learned as much as he could about the shelter-in-place order issued by the county while he waited for the women. So many things had changed in a few short months. For the first time Ben's anxiety had a positive edge to it- he felt energized to be helpful. To be ready for anything. He was allowing a burgeoning drive to take care of his family blossom in his mind. He thought of Arianna. He had left a message for her this morning- she had yet to find out that Marta was free. He decided to call her.

"Hi Ben," said Arianna when she answered on the second ring, "I was just getting ready to listen to your message, sorry I missed your call. I was exhausted last night."

Ben could hear a man ask Arianna if she had coffee in the house. She hadn't mentioned anyone to Ben. Suddenly he felt a protective reaction rise. "Who is there with you? I heard a man," said Ben. He immediately regretted his question. He tried to rephrase, "I mean, are you okay? I didn't mean to be an asshole, I'm sorry."

"It's okay. We have a lot to get to know about each other," started Arianna, "you know I am an adult." She laughed, lightening the conversation. "His name is Keith," she explained, "I guess we are dating. He's a local crisis psychiatrist for the county. We met one night here in town when we were both getting ice cream."

"Sounds like a good thing," said Ben, "I'm sorry I jumped. What do you guys think of this virus? Are you working from home? Shit! I forgot to tell you! The reason I called is to tell you that Marta was released from prison this morning. Martina is bringing her and Violet up here. They should be here any time."

"That's awesome, Ben! I heard they might be releasing inmates because of the virus. I didn't even think it might be Marta! That is fucking awesome," exclaimed Arianna. She called out to Keith, "Marta is free! They are all headed to Santa Cruz." She said to Ben, "Do you have room for them to shelter-in-place? My place is tiny."

Ben realized Arianna must really like this guy if he got to hang around her long enough to know her recent life stories. He remembered his sister to be a loner who didn't seem to like men much. "Funny thing is everyone moved out of this place so, yep, I have room. You could come stay here, too, if you need to. Do you guys want to come by tomorrow to see mom? Oh shit, I forgot that we are supposed to stay home. Call her in the morning if you don't hear from her. Or call me." He was quiet. He didn't know what he would do not being able to report to work daily. *I wonder if I can open my truck* he thought. He realized that he had been working a lot to keep his mind off dope. *Martina never needs to know I'm a junkie* thought Ben *because I am not a junkie after all.*

Violet had managed to keep her mind off dope and booze in two ways. First, she stayed on methadone. Second, she kept a routine. Every day between the time that Ben had gone back to Santa Cruz with his food truck and Marta was released from prison, Violet would make her way to the prison to sit in the lobby until she was allowed two hours with Marta. Some days she didn't get to see her. Some days she sat in the lobby for hours knitting or trying to read. *I need glasses* she thought. She loved to read but it gave her a bad headache just to try. She hadn't faced one craving or trigger to use drugs or booze in weeks. It didn't occur to her that Santa Cruz itself might trigger some feelings for her. Maybe feelings to drink or use. *I am so glad that Ben is here* she thought as they rolled off the highway onto Ocean Street.

Violet realized she was seeing Santa Cruz differently this time. She could recall being drunk or stoned at any one of the corners they passed. Oddly, the memories didn't cause Violet to crave oblivion. This time she noticed the beauty of the city. She noticed redwood trees, the backdrop of mountains, the ocean air. As they drove through downtown to make their way to Ben, Violet realized this was a part of town where she had no stories.

Martina parked in front of the house. The food truck sat in the driveway. "This is it," she exclaimed, "let's go in then come back to unload. Ben can help us." She was already out of the car by the time she finished talking. She went around the car to open the two side doors for her mom and Violet. Martina then turned to almost run into the house.

"Hi! We're here," she called out as she went into the house. She could smell something delicious as she entered the kitchen. Ben was taking a pan of enchiladas out of the oven. "We made it with no problems," she said to Ben, then "I saw a line of people around the grocery store! This shelter-in-place thing has people really scared. Oh, Ben! Mi Mamí is here! What a time it has been!" She hugged him tightly.

Marta and Violet came into the kitchen together. Marta scooped Martina into a hug as Ben released her. Ben looked at Violet. She was staring at him, a tear rolled down her cheek. Ben opened his arms wide to Violet, gesturing with his hands and inviting her with his eyes. "Come here," he said, "I am so glad you are here." He wrapped his arms around her to hug her close.

Violet

That evening Violet and Ben walked together to the ocean. They stood where they could see the famous Santa Cruz surfer statue that stood on a cliff. "I always thought that surfer was looking the wrong way because he was not facing the bay. I see now that he is gazing out to sea on the watch for the next wave," said Violet. "Do you know what I mean, Ben?" Violet asked.

"Yes, I do," said Ben quietly, thrilled that she had used his name, "I know what you mean."

www.ingramcontent.com/pod-product-compliance
Lightning Source LLC
Chambersburg PA
CBHW020313260626
47156CB00004B/1207